THE LAST OF THE LAIRDS

JOHN GALT

◇

THE LAST
OF THE LAIRDS

or
The Life and Opinions of
Malachi Mailings Esq. of Auldbiggings

Edited from the original manuscript
by
IAN A. GORDON

1976
SCOTTISH ACADEMIC PRESS
EDINBURGH & LONDON

Published by
Scottish Academic Press Ltd
33 Montgomery Street, Edinburgh EH7 5JX
and distributed by
Chatto & Windus Ltd
40 William IV Street
London W.C.2

First published 1976
SBN 7011 2175 0

Introduction and Notes
© 1976 Ian A. Gordon

Printed in Great Britain by
Western Printing Services Ltd, Bristol

CONTENTS

v

INTRODUCTION[1]

I

The Last of the Lairds was first published in 1826. All subsequent editions (the most recent in 1936) have been reprints of the 1826 volume. They all suffer from one defect: the novel they present is not the novel that Galt had written—which is here printed for the first time. Galt in his day had publishing problems, but I doubt if that master of irony could have anticipated that it would take a century and a half for one of his best novels to achieve its first edition.

There has always been something of a mystery about *The Last of the Lairds*. Galt duly included it in the list of his books he appended to the second volume of his 1833 *Autobiography*, but in that work, though all his other novels are discussed (some in great detail), the *Laird* is utterly ignored; it is as if he were tacitly rejecting if from the canon. In his more expanded *Literary Life* of the following year, he acknowledged authorship, but stated bluntly the novel was not what he had intended: He had been 'induced', he wrote, to make alterations. 'I meant it to belong to that series of fictions of manners of which the *Annals of the Parish* is the beginning . . . but . . . it lost that appearance of truth and nature which is, in my opinion, the great charm of such works'.

Beyond this tight-lipped statement Galt would not go, claiming that he had forgotten the circumstances: 'I have no recollection how this happened, nor what caused me to write it as it is'. Considering his powers of total recall, everywhere evident in the two autobiographical volumes, this failure of memory is suspect. He could, in fact, very well remember how his novel had been altered beyond recognition, but an

---

[1] *Introduction*: The sources for this account are (i) my earlier *John Galt The Life of a Writer*, 1972, which contains a full bibliography and (ii) unpublished letters that were exchanged 1823–6 among Blackwood, Galt and Moir. Blackwood's letters are copied in the Blackwood Letterbooks, Galt's and Moir's to Blackwood in the Blackwood papers—all in the National Library of Scotland. Galt's letters to Moir were published in abbreviated form in Moir's *Memoir* of Galt added to his edition of *Annals of the Parish*, William Blackwood and Sons, 1841. Transcripts of the latter, in the possession of Mrs Mary H. Galt of Toronto, are held in copies by the Public Archives of Canada, Ottawa. To all of these I am indebted.

innate tact, and loyalty to two old friends (one now dead), restrained him. He simply ended his brief note on the novel by promising that 'some day' he 'would supply what is wanted'. That day never arrived; and a travesty of his work has continued to be reprinted.

2

John Galt had just turned forty when he sprang into literary prominence with the serial appearance (1820–21) of *The Ayrshire Legatees* in William Blackwood's recently established *Blackwood's Edinburgh Magazine*. Christopher North, the 'editor', announced to his readers triumphantly that it had 'increased our sale prodigiously'. Blackwood had discovered a new and popular novelist. By the end of 1822 he had published in volume form no fewer than six novels by Galt, including such favourites as *Annals of the Parish*, *The Provost*, and *The Entail*, in which Galt exploited with skill and style the life of the small Scottish town of the late eighteenth century as a microcosm of the great world beyond. The series (which Galt wanted to call 'Tales of the West') brought him public acclaim and serious critical esteem. But Galt, becoming increasingly resentful of his publisher's regular attempts to alter and amend what had been written, removed himself and his novels to another Edinburgh publisher, Oliver and Boyd.

He returned to Blackwood in 1825. He had for some years been living in Inveresk, spending months at a time in London, where he was involved in Canadian affairs. Inveresk was a pleasant village, not far from Edinburgh and his publishers. It suited his childrens' education. And it brought the friendship of the local physician, Dr D. M. Moir, a literary man too and, like Galt, a contributor to *Blackwood's Magazine*. Moir proved a ready literary ally; when Galt was on urgent business in 1824 in London, he attended to the proof-sheets of Galt's two Oliver and Boyd books of that year, the novel *Rothelan* and the *Life of Wolsey*, and in Inveresk Galt freely discussed with him his plans for writing.

Towards the end of the summer of 1825 Galt told Moir of his next novel. 'Mr Galt told me this morning', Moir wrote to Blackwood in August, 'that he is immediately to set about "the last of the Lairds", and we had some conversation whether it would be better to make a novel of it, or a personal narrative . . . if he writes it here I shall endeavour to see the M.S. piecemeal, and advise to the best of my judgment.'

Galt at the time had more on his mind than a novel. His London negotiations were going well. There was every likelihood that he would be appointed to a lucrative public position in Canada and, successful novelist though he had become, he nourished a secret ambition (not uncommon among Scots) to be a proconsul. His career as a novelist could be rounded off, and the series that had begun with *Annals of the Parish* brought to a triumphant finale that would at the same time be both comedy and elegy, a concluding 'Tale of the West', celebrating (as he wrote to Blackwood) 'the actual manner which about 25 years ago did belong to a class of persons and their compeers in Scotland—the west of it—but who are now extinct'. He would write the final act of his Dalmailing saga as a kind of comic *Götterdämmerung*.

This was the plan, conceived in Inveresk in August 1825. He was so sure of himself that he wrote confidently to Blackwood on 11 September 'I think you may announce *The Last of the Lairds* or the life and opinions of Malachi Mailings Esq. of Auldbiggings'. Blackwood, with equal confidence, though not a word of the novel had been committed to paper, promptly advertised the new book in the October issue of the magazine as 'in the press and speedily will be published'. He knew well Galt's 'fecundity' and his speed of creation once he started.

Nothing went according to plan. Concern with his mother's health led to a visit to Greenock . . . and no writing. Galt was unwell himself. 'He looks very ill', Moir wrote to Blackwood on 27 November, 'and I must say I cannot augur well his getting on with the Laird under the circumstances'. In December, came the inevitable summons to London, and he remained there for most of the year, in constant conference with the Colonial Office and the Canada Company. But living a bachelor's life in apartments provided by the Company, he had leisure, and he began, after some false starts, on the actual writing. 'I have been doing a little to the Laird', he wrote Moir on 23 January 1826, 'and hope to be able to send a quantity of it by the next monthly parcel.' He sent the first batch of manuscript to Blackwood on 8 March, and his publisher returned it in proof on 7 April, finding the opening chapters 'most singular and original, and make me weary much for more of them'. Galt was fairly launched, and everybody was happy.

It did not last. As each packet of the *Laird* arrived in Edinburgh, Blackwood became increasingly horrified at what he read. He knew that his author could be 'vulgar'—had not one of his other authors, Susan Ferrier, said 'I can't endure that man's writing, and I'm told the vulgarity of this beats print'? But what he read went beyond that: a 'hero' whose birth was related in obstetrical detail; who after seducing a girl had to be forced into marriage by the Kirk Session; a bawdy-minded 'heroine', who rejoiced in her neighbour's sexual 'daffings'; scenes of drunken riot. He wrote to Galt in dignified remonstration: some of the incidents were 'perhaps a little strong'. Galt made some adjustments on his proofs. But the argument continued. Upwards of thirty letters passed between Edinburgh and London as author and publisher grew angrier with each other. Galt defended his writing against the charge of 'coarseness': 'it is impossible', he wrote, 'to delineate a character in which there is *thought* to be coarseness as well as want of feeling without showing instances of both'—how else can an author secure 'the truth of the metaphysical anatomy of the characters'? Blackwood was unimpressed; and Galt was finally driven to write him a furious letter bitterly attacking his publisher for 'interference', not just in the *Laird* but in *all* his novels. 'Nobody', he continued in this letter of 23 August, 'can help an author with the conception of a character'. He will make no further concessions or changes; the novel is complete—'the *Laird* is finished'.

Blackwood was equally stubborn. Ballantyne, the printer, had printed off the first eighteen chapters. Blackwood sent the printer no more, and told Galt he was reducing the size of the projected edition from 3,000 to 2,000. A month passed. No proofs arrived. Galt was being left to stew in his own juice. On 16 September Blackwood issued an ultimatim: either, Galt should come to Edinburgh to 'recast or omit some portions' or, 'it will be necessary to ask our friend Mr Moir to revise the corrected sheets'. Galt had no time for further argument. His position with the Canada Company had been confirmed, and he was in daily expectation of sailing. He capitulated in a letter of 19 September, promising 'I shall write to Dr Moir by this post'. He hung on, however, a little longer, for nearly a fortnight, hoping that his publisher would relent, resume the printing, and send him proofs. Nothing arrived. On 1 October he sent Moir the final chapters of the manuscript and a letter of general authority. He sailed for Canada a few days later.

3

What Galt did not know was that Moir was already involved. Dr Moir, indeed, was virtually a consultant editor for *Blackwood's Magazine*, reporting in full detail on each monthly issue, and acting as required as reader for submitted manuscripts. The evidence of his (unpublished) letters to Blackwood shows that his views on what was suitable for publication matched exactly those of the publisher—on one occasion he reported that a novel submitted was 'spiritedly written but . . . should have been Bowdlerised'. Against this combination, Galt stood little chance of preserving his novel intact.

Among Moir's letters to Blackwood there is a very full 'reader's report' on the *Laird*. It bears no date, but it is clear that Moir had before him the printed proofs of the early chapters and the manuscript for part of the remainder. He did not have the later chapters. It is, in fact, precisely what Blackwood had available when he decided in late August to suspend printing, and he clearly sent Moir all he had, for an immediate opinion. Moir reported with enthusiasm, tempered with some disapproval—'I return the Laird which I have read thro' with a great deal of pleasure. As far as it goes it will do admirably, and is among his best things.' He goes on to deal with its 'excellencies' and then issues his caveat—'The only set out . . . is the leaven of vulgarity and uncleanness . . . we have still too much in the Laird of "trampling claes with kilted petticoats, bare ancles, and cutty stools".' Blackwood must have read this letter (and its advocacy of a 'pruning hook') with relief.

Galt was unaware of this report. All he knew was that Moir (who had done proof-correction for him before) had been again suggested as an editor to see his manuscript through the press; and that Moir had written him saying that the work still had 'blemishes'. It all sounded very reasonable: what manuscript does not require editorial tidying-up to prepare it for the printer? He sent Moir a long letter on 1 October, defending his novel against Blackwood's criticisms, thanking Moir for what he had offered to do, and concluding 'With regard to those blemishes to which you advert, do with them as you think fit; I give you full liberty to carve and change as you please'.

Armed with this full authority, Moir wrote jubilantly to Blackwood on 5 October that Galt had given him 'ample scope and verge enough' —and proceeded with a job of plastic surgery that has no parallel in literary history. Tone, dialect, language and incidents in the novel were altered beyond recognition. Over thirty passages (varying from a few lines to several pages) were deleted. The gaps were papered over with insertions invented by Moir. One chapter was entirely rewritten. Three chapters (and a new ending) were added. Frequently he (or the printer) misread Galt's script, and words which gave the illusion of 'sense' (but never Galt's sense) appeared in the final print. The novel was published in late 1826. Galt on 1 October had asked Moir to add a preface 'stating under what circumstances the editorship came to you'. Not a word of this appeared. Blackwood did not use the note that Moir provided, and Moir's role of 'editor' was not made public until the appearance of his *Memoir* of Galt in 1841. The full extent of his tampering with the novel has only been ascertainable since 1961, when the manuscript of *The Last of the Lairds* was presented to the National Library of Scotland

Moir's series of unpublished letters to Blackwood between August and November 1826 form a running commentary on each stage of the revision. When it was all over, even Moir had misgivings. 'Notwithstanding all Mr Galt's latitude, however,' he wrote Blackwood in late October 1826, 'I doubt not he will be a little surprised to see his old friend with such a new face.' Galt, in Canada, did not see the book till February of the following year. What surprise he felt at seeing 'his old friend with such a new face' he did not register. He sent Moir a letter of thanks, noting (with characteristic irony) 'various points of minor improvement'. For the rest, his later silence on the *Laird* was all the commentary necessary.

4

Galt, in writing *The Last of the Lairds*, decided the best technique was to create a 'narrator', who plays a full part in the action of the story. The narrator is a bachelor author living in Paisley, with an insatiable appetite for the local gossip of 'the west' and a ready ear for other men's stories. But he is no provincial. He knows London political and art gossip. He is well up, too, in the literary gossip of the day, tossing off lightly references to Scott, Lockhart, Wordsworth, the *Literary Gazette*, the *Edinburgh Review*. He has an addiction for the smart use of French terms, Latin tags, even a little Greek, and slips in easy allusions to authors like Molière and Horace. It is this young sophisticate who first meets Malachi Mailings, the Laird of Auldbiggings, a comic and pathetic relic of an older age, who (on the one occasion when he dresses up) dons the ancient powdered periwig and rusty elegance of his eighteenth-century youth. The old man is sunk in debt and in memories. The novel, in one sense, is the story of the narrator's growing involvement with the old man's affairs and (though he calls the Laird specifically an 'idiot') his deepening sense of the Laird's inner strength and individuality. The shabby and foolish old man is shown in sharp contrast with his creditor, the Nabob, a self-made landowner, returned wealthy from India, whom the Laird (to the joy of the narrator, by now entirely on his side) contrives finally to outwit.

Within this framework Galt sets an intrigue. The narrator's busybody neighbour, the widow Mrs Soorocks, suggests that the two ageing spinsters of Barenbraes, Girzie and Shoosie Minnigaff, have been long waiting for a man 'to speer their price'—and who more suitable than the elderly Laird? The fifty-year-old Shoosie is marked down as the prospective bride, and narrator and Mrs Soorocks form an alliance. His part is to persuade the reluctant Laird (who has set his sights on a young Miss, straight from an Edinburgh boarding-school, rather than the 'reisted auld fricht' that he is offered); hers to persuade the less reluctant sisters. Mrs Soorocks combines the instincts of Pandar with the attitudes of the Wife of Bath—she thinks (and talks) in terms of bridal nights, begetting children, 'daffing', 'ploys', and the 'cutty-stool' (that older Scottish symbol of fornication). 'This vile harridan . . . one loathes her so cordially that we always wish to see her ducked in a horse pond', the shocked Blackwood complained to Galt, unconsciously paying a major tribute to his author's powers of creation. After a series of scenes of riotous comedy among the contendants, the whole party is gathered together in Mrs Soorocks' house, where the resourceful lady fills the Laird with neat rum and when she gets him thoroughly drunk forces him into a Scottish 'marriage by declaration'—and then offers, not only her house, but her bed for her consummation of the marriage.

Next morning, to the consternation of the two intriguers, bride and bridegroom emerge, a picture of connubial 'felicity', united against the world. It is discovered that the 'superiority' (which in effect means the voting rights) of Auldbiggings is not subject to the mortgage on the estate and is a separate asset—which the Laird, in one of the great comic scenes in the novel, auctions ('roups') to the highest bidder, outwitting his rival the Nabob, and retiring to Edinburgh with his two ladies, to live in comfort in Edinburgh's gracious Georgian New Town, in a house with 'a genteel door with pillars and architraves such as befit the porch of a family of rank and pedigree'.

Slotted in to this series of comedy scenes, Galt introduces his ancillary characters, each with a part and a set-piece—the Nabob, with his Indian vocabulary and his Maharajah-like ostentation; Mr Tansie, schoolmaster and session clerk, with his astrological fancies; the Stranger, with his shipwreck tale, who is the agent for the Nabob's downfall; Jock the servant, with his tale of drunken riot in Renfrew;

Dr Loulans the minister, the *deus ex machina* of the *dénouement*; the servant-lass Leezie, who never seems able to keep her clothes on. Even the narrator is given his set-piece, with his witty and very much in character disquisition on the steeples of Glasgow. Major and minor characters, inset stories, and descriptive passages interlock, to form a novel that races to a triumphant conclusion. The pace is fast, the characters (as Blackwood saw, though he did not like what he saw) leap from the page. The numerous dialogues are sustained in dramatic comic scenes, told in racy and vigorous Scots.

Yet the book is not wholly comic. An elegiac tone continually breaks through as when (chapter 31) the Laird bids a rhetorical farewell to his garden and his 'forefather's land'. Galt lingers in loving detail over the five pages he gives to the ancient mansion-house of Auldbiggings; the two pages he gives to the Laird's eighteenth-century costume; the three pages he gives to Mrs Soorocks' old-fashioned dining-room cupboard. Like the Laird, these were all part of a vanishing rural society, where every man was concerned with his neighbour. Galt's irony in the final pages is infallible: the triumphant trio retire to the solid middle-class comfort of Edinburgh. But the two sisters have simply become 'great forenoon visitors'; and 'the poor Laird' (as Galt describes him in the final lines of the novel) is reduced to sitting at home, vacantly day-dreaming and looking at shapes in the fire, stubbornly refusing to sign the legal surrender of Auldbiggings. Galt—in the line he penned before he firmly wrote 'End'—promises him 'trouble for his contumacity'. His world is finished. He is the last of the lairds.

5

Dr Moir, given 'full liberty to carve and change', attacked the novel not with a pruning hook but with an axe. The first eighteen chapters were already in proof, some corrected by Galt. There is no way of ascertaining whether Moir made any further changes in these chapters. He certainly, in his 'reader's report' of August, considered a few necessary—'five minutes could correct all'. I suspect his hand on occasion (e.g.) in the description of the maid Jenny Clatterpans in the first chapter—she is there described as a 'nymphantine being' engaged in 'rural or pastoral drudgery'. Elsewhere in the text, Moir insisted on introducing the term 'pastoral', which is contrary to Galt's whole tone. But there is no evidence either way. Substantially, these chapters are by Galt.

For the remainder of the text, the evidence is complete. Galt's original manuscript, heavily amended and rewritten, remained with the Moir family till 1961, when it was presented to the National Library of Scotland. It is now NLS MS 6522. It consists of 206 pages in Galt's hand. At the foot of the last page he wrote the word 'End'— the *Laird* (as he told Blackwood) was 'finished'.

There is not one page of this manuscript that has not been altered by Moir. His amendments run to a total of several thousand, ranging from continuous re-punctuation to deletions, inserted words or passages, inserted extra (or rewritten) passages on the verso of Galt's sheets, and numerous complete sheets in Moir's handwriting, replacing discarded pages of Galt's text. The most extensive of these extra inserted pages contains the text of the final three chapters (38–40) of the 1826 edition. These chapters—apart from a few salvaged lines—are entirely by Moir.

I do not propose to load this edition with a full tally of Moir's alterations. It is sufficient to give some indication of what he did to the *Laird*. He ruthlessly pruned it of 'vulgarity and uncleanness'. Skirts are decently lowered to conceal bare legs; seemingly blasphemous words like 'the Lord' or 'Hell' or 'Providence' vanish, or are replaced with an innocuous equivalent; references to virgins are coyly rephrased; Mrs Soorocks' bawdy conversation is heavily censored—she is not permitted her natural references to 'bowels' or 'begetting sons and daughters', nor her sly references to the Laird's youthful seduction of a village girl and to the details of Miss Shoosy's alleged youthful affair 'in a glen by appointment' with a schoolmaster. The narrator's meeting with Lizzie in a private room loses it sexual overtones. The pungent language of abuse in the scenes of quarrel is consistently softened.

Several major changes alter the structure of the novel. The climactic chapter 32 is entirely rewritten. Moir wrote to Blackwood on 5 October that it had 'a base tone of morality'. In place of Galt's riotous scene, in which Mrs Soorocks deliberately gets the Laird drunk on pure rum till, inflamed with liquor, the old man makes advances to *her*, and then has to be hastily married, and sent with his bride immediately upstairs to bed, Moir wrote a disinfected version, in which Mrs Soorocks gives him a few glasses of wine, tells a long sentimental parable about nuts in the fireplace, and, when the Laird sings a verse of an old ballad, gets the pair married—and sends them off for their wedding night at the Laird's own mansion at Auldbiggings. Moir was forced to make a series of consequential changes in succeeding chapters, to conceal the fact that he had altered both the location of the wedding night and Mrs Soorock's hearty enjoyment of the situation she had brought about.

Four pages of the manuscript chapter 23 are dropped, and with this omission disappeared Jock's 'set-piece' of drunken riot in Renfrew. 'Stuff about Renfrew', Moir wrote disapprovingly to Blackwood, entirely missing Galt's intention. The sad ironic end of the novel Moir simply ignored. He wrote three new concluding chapters, turther sentimentalising the whole work, in which he married off Jock to the maidservant Jenny. In spite of a free use of Scots in Moir's dialogue, the tone is recognisably not that of Galt, who would never have described the Laird's rough and ready handyman as a 'valet' or 'a veritable picture of Adonis—the beau-ideal of a lover'.

Moir's alterations did not cease at this pastoralising and sentimentalising and removal of vulgarity and uncleanness. He misunderstood the function and character of Galt's narrator. The smart sophisticate (who provides an up-to-date point of reference which distances the Laird and his vanishing society) is reduced by Moir to a mere narrator who happens to be in the story. Much of his West of Scotland gossip is axed, his 'steeples of Glasgow' set-piece is discarded, and large tracts of his 'literary' gossip (which establishes him in the setting of the 1820's) are entirely jettisoned. The Nabob, recognising the nature of the narrator, calls him (chapter 29) 'the only man of any *nous* that I'm acquainted with in the county'. Moir altered this to the pallid 'the only man of any sense in the county'. When one adds Moir's thoroughgoing rendering of Galt's Ayrshire/Renfrewshire dialect into the Lothian variety (altering both words and spellings) and over thirty instances where he simply misread the script, one can hardly blame Galt for virtually disowning the novel. The changeling of 1826 had—in his own words—lost the 'appearance of truth and nature'.

6

Other nineteenth-century novelists had to yield to pressures from publishers. But even when they gave in, they retained the major authority over what finally appeared in print. For a novel to be taken out of its author's hands, dismantled, rewritten, and reassembled, and still published under his name must be unique. The reconstruction goes beyond anything that Galt would ever have accepted; he was likely, in the end, to have yielded, grudgingly, to Blackwood, and removed a minimum of 'vulgarities'. He had made concessions before, and he wanted to see his novel published.

But Moir's reconstruction went beyond disinfection. It altered the theme of the novel. Moir rewrote it simply as a Scots comedy, in a romantic pastoral framework. Galt's novel is a comedy; but it is set in a framework of the rural and commercial west of Scotland; where (even from busybodies) neighbourliness was expected, where Lairds could be simple and still respected; where some admiration could also be tendered to self-made business-men like the Nabob; where the 'truth and nature' (even if it were not 'genteel') could be spoken aloud; and where all the community could unite against Mr Loopy, the lawyer (or 'writer'), who menaced their individualistic way of life. It was not for nothing that Galt, when his Laird has finally surrendered to metropolitan respectability, has him set up a brass plate, like 'advocates and writers to the signet'. The collocation is part of Galt's overall irony.

Edinburgh in the early nineteenth century had its literary Establishment. It was ruled by university trained 'advocates and writers to the signet'—Jeffrey, Scott, Susan Ferrier (daughter of a writer to the signet), Christopher North, Lockhart set the tone and the acceptable standards. It was just possible for an outsider to gain admission to this brilliant circle. James Hogg was admitted, as a kind of rural and untrained genius. But his price of admission was serial appearances in *Noctes Ambrosianae* in *Blackwood's Magazine* in the role of court jester—'the Shepherd', the rural comic. His prose and poetry were published, but never in his own day given the serious critical attention they deserve.

Galt was a tougher problem to assimilate. This 'Greenock Burgher' (as Carlyle called him), who had produced a series of brilliant—and popular—successes, who moved with freedom in London political and society circles, met the Edinburgh lawyer Establishment on his own terms of easy, unselfconscious, equality. When, some years later, Lockhart (offering him the commission for a new book) wrote that he would do it well because he 'had the Education and the habits of a merchant', Galt passed over the condescending implications. It was simply a fact. He *did* have only a 'merchant's' grammar school education; he *was* a merchant; he *did* 'belong to Glasgow', and the commercial west. But he was also the author of that series of Tales of the West, *Annals of the Parish*, *The Provost*, *The Entail*. 'I know of no equal in our literature', Coleridge had noted on one of his novels.

Blackwood, an astute publisher, sensitive to the cultural assumptions of the capital city, saw the dangers. Galt came from the other side of Scotland—where the natives were friendly, but inescapably 'vulgar'. He had rapidly become a literary property of some value; but he needed careful watching. Hence the continual 'interference': during the years he was publishing Galt, Blackwood's letters alternated between delighted cries of 'Capital!' and proposals, which mounted on occasion to commands, to 'omit'. So long as Galt was dependant on Blackwood for part of his income, he could not afford to do other than adjust to his publisher's 'Edinburgh' tastes. By 1826, when the 'habits of a merchant' had brought him public office at £1,000 a year, he could insist, in his final Tale of the West, that his text be left untouched.

He could also afford, on his final page, the luxury of having the last word, neatly deflating the legal Establishment in one unobtrusive and slyly ironical phrase. Galt has the Laird set up a brass plate on his door, an action which he affects not to understand. 'That advocates and writers to the signet should *like other tradesmen* have recourse to such brazen devices to make themselves notorious and bring custom seems not unreasonable . . .' he notes with wry humour. The italics are mine, not Galt's. He had no need to underline the implications. Moir saw the irony clearly, and firmly deleted the phrase 'like other tradesmen'. It has been here restored—a century and a half after it was written—along with the 'stuff about Renfrew', and Mrs Soorocks' vulgarities, and Galt's litany of praise on the eighteenth-century skyline of Glasgow, and the rest of Galt's original novel.

John Galt would have appreciated another irony. This edition has been prepared, and these lines written, in a fine Georgian house in Edinburgh, with 'a genteel door with pillars and architraves'. Its long-vanished 'family of rank and pedigree' has been supplanted by a small community of scholars.

Institute for Advanced Studies in the Humanities,   I.A.G.
University of Edinburgh.
March 1975

NOTE ON THE TEXT

This edition is intended to present *what Galt expected to see in print* in the edition of 1826. An editor faces two separate problems:

(1) *Chapters 1–18*: Galt saw at least the earliest chapters of these in proof and had already made some adjustments to meet Blackwood's criticism before Moir took over. I suspect some Moir interventions, but only one is capable of demonstration: in the manuscript Galt invariably wrote forms like 'hersel'. Moir corrected these in the manuscript, equally invariably, to 'hersell'. Since 'hersell' is the spelling printed in 1826 chapters 1–18, it must have originated with Moir. I have restored Galt's spelling. Apart from this, the 1826 edition of these chapters has been accepted, as substantially the work of Galt.

(2) *Chapters 19–37*: the remaining chapters present a quite different problem. They form the original manuscript—not a fair copy—sent by Galt to Edinburgh in 'portions' as completed, heavily corrected by Moir and interleaved with his additions. If Galt's intentions are to be honoured, editorial control is called for. Merely offering a faithful, 'diplomatic', transcript of this massively corrected manuscript would result in an unreadable monstrosity—and ensure a continued and unwarranted emphasis on what Galt did *not* write. In this edition, therefore, Moir's deletions, over-writings, amendments and additions (his script and the colour of his ink being distinctive) have been silently peeled off, and the original Galt text restored. (Some samples of Moir's changes, however, can be found in the explanatory notes.)

What is left still requires sympathetic editing: Galt did *not* expect his printers to reproduce his manuscripts *literatim*. He used frequent contractions (e.g. wou'd; shou'd; bro't; tho't; tho'; Edin^r; w^h; Coy; genr^l; gov^t; gen^t) which he expected his printers to expand. He wrote many Scots dialect forms (e.g. o; wi; needfu) without the 'conventional' apostrophe, but he accepted in his proofs his printer's convention of: o'; wi'; needfu'. In Scots participial forms, however, he wrote, and expected in print, a spelling without apostrophe (e.g. getten; gambollan; meddlin). Names in the manuscript (e.g. Girzy; nabob; Mailins; Domine; Auldbiggins; Barrenbraes and its variants) do not correspond with his final decision on these forms in the proofed

xix

chapters (though Galt has carefully corrected throughout 'Susy' to 'Shoosie'). Variant spellings of some words occur (e.g. pilaster/pillaster, both on the same manuscript page). Occasionally, when he deleted, he did not quite complete his correction; and on a very few occasions he made an inadvertent slip (e.g. 'say' for 'said'). His final intentions, however, are never in doubt.

His punctuation (for which there is considerable corroborative evidence in his letters and the manuscripts of *Ringan Gilhaize* and *The Howdie*) was self-consistent as he wrote it, but he did not expect to see it reproduced in his proof-sheets. In writing, he made much use of a short dash [–], leaving it to the printer to express this as an m-rule, a full point, a comma, or even when appropriate an exclamation or a question mark (where he *required* an m-rule in print, he wrote it in the manuscript in the form |—|). Ends of sentences, followed in the next line by a speech in quotation marks, have in the manuscript sometimes no punctuation, sometimes a full point, sometimes a short dash. In the proofed sheets these are represented by [,–] or [–], less frequently [,], [.–], [:–]. In the present edition, the editorial method has been to follow this 'house style', which Galt accepted in the proofed chapters.

What this edition now offers is what Galt had hoped to get from Moir, a clean, uncluttered, and readable novel, in which (apart from the tidying up of minor inconsistencies) his substantive text is left intact but the accidentals of punctuation brought into conformity with Ballantyne's practice and Galt's clear intentions, for which proofed chapters and manuscript provide firm evidence.

THE LAST OF THE LAIRDS

CHAPTER I

The Mailings have long occupied a distinguished place in the laws and
annals of Scotland. That they were of Celtic origin many learned
antiquaries shrewdly suspect, nor are we disposed to controvert the
opinion; although it must be allowed they have never been without
a taint of Saxon blood in their veins, being from time immemorial
regarded as of intimate propinquity with the Pedigrees, whose
eminent merits and great actions are so worthily celebrated in the
chronicles of venerable virginity.

In what part of the country they first struck their inextricable
roots would now be hard to tell; but the forefathers of Malachi had,
from unrecorded epochs, flourished in the barony of Killochen, a
fertile and pleasant tract of Renfrewshire, and it is meet that we should
describe their habitation.

The mansion-house of Auldbiggings was a multiform aggregate of
corners, and gables, and chimneys. In one respect it resembled the
master-piece of Inigo Jones—Heriot's Work[1]—at Athens—no two
windows were alike, and several of them, from the first enactment of
the duty on light, had been closed up, save where here and there a
peering hole with a single pane equivocated with the statute and the
tax-gatherer. The pête-stones, or by whatever name the scalar ornaments of the gables may be known,—those seeming stairs, collinear
with the roof, peculiar to our national architecture, were frequented
by numerous flocks of pigeons. The invention, indeed, of that species
of ornament, is a fine monumental trait of the hospitality of our
ancestors, who, while they were themselves revelling in the hall, after
their Border joys of speed and spoil, thus kindly provided convenient
places, where their doves, when returning home heavy and over-fed,

[1] *Heriot's Work*: the xviith century Heriot's Hospital, in the style of Inigo Jones,
in Edinburgh ('the Athens of the North').

I

with foraging on their neighbours' corn-fields, might repose, and fatten for spit or pie, in unmolested equanimity.

Appended to the mansion, but somewhat of lower and ruder structure, was a desultory mass of shapeless buildings—the stable, sty, barn, and byre, with all the appurtenances properly thereunto belonging, such as peat-stack, dung-hill, and coal-heap, with a bivouacry of invalided utensils, such as bottomless boyns, headless barrels, and brushes maimed of their handles—to say nothing of the body of the cat which the undealt-with packman's cur worried on Saturday se'enight. At the far end was the court-house, in which, when the day happened to be wet, the poultry were accustomed to murmur their sullen and envious whiggery against the same weather which made their friends the ducks as garrulous with enjoyment at the middenhole, as Tories in the pools of corruption. But so it is with all of this world; the good or evil of whatsoever comes to pass, lieth in the sense by which the accident affects us.

The garden was suitable to the offices and the mansion. It was surrounded, but not inclosed, by an undressed hedge, which in more than fifty places offered tempting admission to the cows. The luxuriant grass walks were never mowed but just before haytime, and every stock of kail and cabbage stood in its garmentry of curled blades, like a new-made Glasgow bailie's wife on the first Sunday after Michaelmas,[2] dressed for the kirk in the many-plies of all her flounces. Clumps of apple-ringgie, daisies and Dutch-admirals, marigolds and nonsopretties, jonquils and gillyflowers, with here and there a peony, a bunch of gardeners-garters, a sunflower or an orange-lily, mingled their elegant perfumes and delicate flourishes along the borders. The fruit-trees were of old renown; none grew sweeter pears; and if the apples were not in co-rival estimation with the palate, they were yet no less celebrated for the rural beauty of their red cheeks. It is true, that the cherries were dukes, but the plumbs were magnumbonums.

Where the walks met, stood a gnomenless dial; opposite to which, in a honey-suckle bower, a white-painted seat invited the Laird's visitors of a sentimental turn to read Hervey's Meditations in a Flower-garden;[3] and there, in the still moonlight nights, in the nightingale-

[2] *the first Sunday after Michaelmas*: newly elected bailies took office at Michaelmas. See *The Provost* (O.U.P. ed), p. xiii.

[3] *Hervey's Meditations*: James Hervey's *Meditations among the Tombs* (which included 'Reflection on a Flower Garden') pub. 1746 and still being reprinted in the 1820's.

singing season of southern climes, you might overhear one of the servant lasses keckling with her sweetheart. But it is time to approach the house, and make our way towards the innates.

On approaching the door, and applying your hand to the knocker, you catch a broken key hanging by a string from the lion's mouth. The ring was wrenched away at the time of the auld laird's burial by Sparkinhawse, the drowthy portioner, of Drycraigs, when he was coming out from the dirgie, to try if he could find the road to his own home; but, nevertheless, by the key, or your knuckle, you make a noise, which, after being repeated some three or four times, causes the door to open, when either one of the lasses looks from behind it, and says, "What's your wull and pleasure?" or Jock, the Laird's man, comes forth, and leaning his shoulder against the door-cheek, looks in your face till you have propounded your interrogation. On the present occasion it is Jenny Clatterpans, the kitchen-lass, and, as usual, snodless, snoodless, and shodless, who answers to the summons.

Jenny was not altogether just such an amiable and nymphantine being as the moral master of Lights and Shadows[4] has discovered, glowing and gleaming in the poetical regions of Scottish life; but a substantial armful of those virtues and graces, which, in the shape of well-fleshed, clear-skinned, sonsy, and hardy queans, may be seen, with their legs bared above the knee, trampling in washing-tubs, at the open burnside, or haply, with the handle of an old spade, pursuing forth the kail-yard a marauding cow, or engaged in some of those other vocations of rural or pastoral drudgery, which are equally natural and prosaical. In truth, Jenny had more of a thorough-going havrelism about her, than of that fond and fine otherism, so interesting in the heroines of romance. She was neither particular in her attire, nor methodical in her work, and her words were unculled—in short, she was a wench likely to be brought to book without much blushing. But we forgot our duty, and have not yet answered to her "wull and pleasure," though she has opened the door, and has dropped behind her the hearthbrush she happened to have in her hand, when our summons was sounded.

Having inquired for the Laird, Jenny replies,

"Deed, sir, he's no right."

"Ay, Jenny, I'm sorry for that—what ails him?"

"Ails! I canna say mickle's the matter wi' him, poor bodie, but he's

---

[4] *the moral master of* Lights and Shadows: David Wilkie, whom Galt admired and corresponded with, frequenting his exhibitions. Wilkie painted scenes from Ramsay's *The Gentle Shepherd* in 1823 and 1824, which are referred to here.

dwining, and he's no ill either—trowth, ony ha'd o' health he has, is aye at meal-time, and yet he puts a' in an ill skin."

"Is he confined to his room, Jenny?"

"Room, sir! neither a doctor nor a doze o' physic would keep him intil his room."

"Indeed!—Then he must be greatly altered, Jenny; for he was rather always of a sedentary turn."

"That's a' ye ken about him, he's a busy man."

"Busy, Jenny!"

"Ay, sir, dreadful!—He's putting out a book—Loke, sir, if he's no putting out a book! O that wearyfu' jaunt to Embro' to see the King![5] It has skail't the daunert wits o' the master—the like o' you and the minister may put out books, but surely the 'stated gentry hae come to a low pass indeed, when they would file their fingers wi' ony sic black art!"

"And what is this book about, Jenny?"

"Na, that's a question amang divines, sir; ye may speer, and I may say yea or nay, but what will't make you the wiser?"

"True, Jenny, I'll never dispute that; but is Mr Mailings not visible?"

"Veesible, sir!"

"May I not see him?"

"What for should ye no see him? At this precious moment of God's time, ye may see him writing his book through the key-hole."

"Through the key-hole, Jenny!—no possible? I never heard of a man writing a book through a key-hole."

"Weel, weel, sir, no to summer and winter on idioticals, or sic like matters o' fact—the Laird told me, that he would na be at hame to a living soul in the king's three kingdoms; 'cause he was inditing his book;—the which I thought was—I'll no just say it was a lee; but if it wasna a lee, it was surely very like it; and therefore, sir, though the master said it was an innocent deplomatical, I hae a notion that it was cousin, and sib to the first-born of Satan, the whilk is Untruth."

This colloquy with Jenny greatly disturbed our wonted philosophical composure. The Laird! Malachi Mailings, writing a book, was a marvel most indigestible; for although he had become of late years somewhat addicted to reading, particularly of the Newspapers, and

[5] *to Embro' to see the King*: George IV visited Edinburgh in 1822. Galt wrote a 'Glasgow' sketch of the occasion, *The Gathering of the West*, for *Blackwood's Magazine*. Galt is unobtrusively signalling that he is writing a 'contemporary' novel.

the Edinburgh Review, which he borrowed from me, about a month after publication, the idea of the inspiring mantle dropping down about his shoulders, surprised me as with the amazement of a new creation, and under the excitement of the moment, pushing Jenny aside, I hastened to his parlour.

CHAPTER II

On entering the Laird's apartment, I was struck with several changes, additions, and improvements, in the appearance of the room, the consequence of his visit to Edinburgh. For the old map of Europe, which from the days of his grandsire had hung over the mantle-piece, and which time had tarnished into a brown and yellow illegibility, a new one of the two hemispheres was exhibited, with a portrait of the King on the side, and of the Duke of Wellington on the other. The most conspicuous object, however, was a handsome leather covered library chair, in which he was sitting at a table with books and papers and the other implements of writing before him, like an Edinburgh advocate warsling with the law.

He was apparelled in a dressing-gown, which had evidently been economically made out of two of his deceased lady's flagrant chintz gowns of dissimilar patterns. His head was adorned with a blue velvet cap, wadded and padded not only to supersede the use of his wig, but even to be warm enough to cause a germination of fancies, if ideas could be raised by anything like the compost in which gardeners force exotics.

As I entered he pushed up his spectacles upon his forehead, and raising his eyes from the paper on which he was writing, threw himself back in the chair, and looked not altogether quite satisfied at being so interrupted.

After the interchange of a few preliminary strictures on the weather on both sides, I began to inquire what he thought of the King, and how he had been pleased with his jaunt to Edinburgh.

"For the King," replied the Laird, " I never looked for a particular civility at his hands, though I have been a Justice of the Peace for the shire more than fifteen years, and was moreover of great service to his crown and dignity, as one of the officers of the first crop of volunteers.— But yon's a pleasant place, yon toun of Embro'; and the literawty are just real curiosities, and a' philosophers, the whole tot of them. I had an e'e in my neck when I was among them; and maybe some of them shall hear tell o't before long."—And he glanced his eyes significantly towards the papers before him.

6

"Indeed, Laird! and which of them have you seen?" said I, desirous of hearing his opinion of persons so self-celebrated; but instead of heeding my question, he continued—

"It's my persuassion, however, that there's a state o' matters yonder in great need of a reformation. But it's my intent and purpose to show the consequence of making men of family functy—offeeshy."[1]

"What, Laird?—making men of family—what?"

"Cutting them off by sic legalities as writers to the signet, and advocates, and critics, frae the power of begetting a posterity."

The Laird was in this a little beyond my depth, and I could only rejoin somewhat simply, "And how is it, Laird, you intend to make out all that?"

"Am I no writing my biography—my own life—wherein the grievance will be made most manifest?"

"Your life, Laird! What can there be in your life to record? The holly-bush before the door has, I should think, had almost as many adventures."

He was plainly piqued at my remark; but he replied, chuckling with the consciousness of being witty,—

"No man in his senses would ever expect to see an ignoramus bush, far less a doddered holly-bush, take up a pen to write a book—Branches are not hands—No, no—no, no."

To an observation at once so pertinent and unanswerable, I could only say, in a subdued tone, that I had no doubt his Memoirs would be highly instructive and interesting.

"It's to be a standard work," was his calm and modestly expressed reply; "and the like o't has been long wanted; for if a stop is not soon put to the growth and increases of the conspiracy that I have discovered, there's no telling what our gentry will be brought to."

"Conspiracy, Laird—what conspiracy?—and discovered by you! I should as soon have expected to hear you had discovered the longitude or the philosopher's stone, as anything of the sort?"

"And is't no the proven fact, that, what with the government at the one end with the taxes, and the labourous folk at the other with their wages, the incomes of our 'stated gentry is just like a candle lighted at both ends?"

"I see, I see, Laird, you have been among the Political Economists—who have neither honour for the rich, nor charity for the poor."

---

[1] *functy—offeeshy: defunctus officii.*

For the space of a minute or so he looked at me eagerly and suspiciously, and then raising himself into an erect posture, said emphatically,

"No man stands in need of a reason to convince him of the animosity of a rhinoceros—do you admit that?"

"For the sake of argument," said I, "the proposition may be allowed."

"Na," said he, falling back in his chair, and spreading out his arms at the same time in the attitude of an astonishment in marble,—"If ye deny a first principle, it is of no use to pursue the argument."

That the Laird had indeed been among the Athenian philosophers, could no longer be doubted; and that he had in consequence suffered a material change in the habits of his mind, was equally evident. Before the visit to Edinburgh, he was seemingly the easiest of mankind—more like a creature made of wool than of clay; such, indeed, was the sleepy quietude of his nature, that except when stirred by some compulsion of business, or obligation, nothing seemed capable of molesting his tranquillity. But when molested—rare as were such occasions—he was testy, snappish, and self-willed; and the little spurts of temper in which he then indulged, betrayed the spirit of controversy which was slumbering within him, and which, in the vicissitudes of things, it was not improbable events might occur to rouse and call forth. I was, therefore, much less surprised at his propugnacity than at the course his opinions had taken; and becoming more solicitous to see what he had written, than to continue the controversy, I said—

"But in what manner, Laird, have you shown the existence of this alleged conspiracy between the government and the people, to overthrow the ancient gentry of his Majesty's hereditary kingdom?"

"Is na there the changes in the value of money? I can assure you that I have well considered this portion of the bullion question."

"I should like," said I, with all possible gravity, "to hear your opinion of the bullion question[2]—of course, you examine the causes that affect the circulating medium and originate the agricultural distress?"

"The circulating curse—it's as clear a tax of five per cent on our income, as the five and ten deevelry of the war."

"But, no doubt, you have exposed it properly, and in its true colours—will you have the goodness to read what you have said upon the subject?—for it is a subject which comes home to the business and

[2] *opinion of the bullion question*: Galt himself (under a nom-de-plume 'Bandana') wrote serious articles on both currency and agricultural problems. See Gordon, *op. cit.*

bosoms of us all. Five per cent! really, Laird, you surprise me—I never imagined it was so much."

"No man can maintain that it's one farthing less—for, since the coming out of the sovereigns, and the crying down of the old honest coin of the realm, both in the price of horse and horn-cattle, a mulct of a full shilling in the pound has been inflicted on the whole agricultural interest."

"And where does that shilling go to, Laird?"

"Where? but to the bottomless pit, the pouch o' government that they call the sinking fund; and is that no a depreciation?"

"Not to interrupt you, Laird," said I, "but how does the change in the money affect your income?"

"How! I'll show you how—is na small coin the evidence of cheap labour; and when labour is cheap, has not a man of rental the mair to hain for lying money? But the sight o' a farthing now-a-days is good for sair een; it's no to be met wi', but now and then in the shape of a blot in a town grocer's 'count, made out by his prentice in the first quarter of the school-laddie's time. It was a black day for Scotland that saw the Union signed, for on that day the pound sterling came in among our natural coin, and, like Moses' rod, swallow't up at ae gawpe, plack, bodle, mark, and bawbie, by the which mony a blithe ranting roaring rental of langsyne has dwinet and dwinlet into the hungry residue of a wadset."

"But, Laird, without calling in question the correctness of your historical observation, I am at some loss to understand how it happened you have been moved to write your life?"

He made no immediate reply, but, leaning forward with a particularly knowing look, he said, in a half whisper,—

"I'll tell you a secret—it's to pay off one of my heritable bonds. That silly auld havering creature, Balwhidder o' Dalmailing, got a thousand pounds sterling, doun on Blackwood's counter, in red gold, for his clishmaclavers; and Provost Pawkie's[3] widow has had twice the dooble o't, they say, for the Provost's life. Now, if a minister got sae muckle for his life, and a provost twice the dooble for his, I'm thinking a 'stated gentleman should surely get a brave penny for the like wark."

[3] *Balwhidder . . . Pawkie*: a typical Galt 'cross-reference'—to the *Annals* and *The Provost*. The £1000 from Blackwood is comic exaggeration. Galt received sixty guineas for the *Annals*, and a hundred guineas for *The Provost* (see Gordon, *op. cit.*).

9

"I will not dispute your logic, Laird; but where are the materials for your life to be found?"

"Here and there," he exclaimed in exultation, striking, at the same time, his breast and forehead; adding, "No man, unless he writes from his own brains and his own bosim, need put pen to paper."

I assented to the justness of the observation; and, after ingratiating myself as well as I could into his confidence, he, in the end, invited me to stay dinner, and promised, as an indemnity for my consenting, that he would entertain me "with a feast of reason and a flow of saul"—a temptation too strong, and too exquisite, as served up by him, to be resisted.

CHAPTER III

The Laird's work consisted of about half-a-dozen small copy books, such as schoolboys are in the practice of using, two or three of them with marble covers; on one I observed a parrot, and on another the ruins of Palmyra. The penmanship was not very legible; it was narrow, crampt, and dotty, and the orthography made me pause at the first sentence.

"Ye're troubled wi' my hand o' write," said he, "and deed I must own it's no a schoolmaister's, but wi' a thought o' pains ye'll soon be able to read it."

"I think, Laird, I could make my way with the writing, but the spelling is not for a man in haste."

"Ye may weel say that—no man can spell wi' Johnny Sellblethers the town-bookseller's pens—the bodie had ne'er a christian-like ane in his aught; and I can assure you, that an ill pen is baith a crabbit and a fashious implement—I now speak from experience; and I hae had words wi' him concerning his pens—but the creature has no a mouthfu o' sense—he's a thing that has nae mair sense nor that bottle—that bottle did I say?—he has nae mair sense nor that fender."

Upon some farther inspection of the manuscript, I saw, as the Laird had justly remarked, that by and by, with some pains, I should be able to make my way through it, in spite of the penmanship, even too of the orthography, but the matter was more difficult to manage than either. It was not a continued and methodical narrative, but consisted of detached notes and memoranda, somewhat like Lord Byron's unpublished Biographical Dictionary;[1] instead, however, of relating to things and accidents which had befallen himself, they were entirely made up of reflections on the price of grain and cattle—denunciations against wages and taxes, ill-paid rents, and all the other evils which agricultural distress is heir to, with here and there an incidental note, such as "my mother died this year, and her burial cost me a power of

---

[1] *Byron's unpublished Biographical Dictionary*: the narrator—and Galt—showing off their 'inside' knowledge of the literary information of the day. Galt had known Byron, travelled with him in the Mediterranean, and wrote a *Life of Byron* later (1830).

money—the coffin was more than five pounds, but it was very hand-some;" or, "obligated to roup out John Lownlan's widow—a clamorous woman that." Whether these were in the first or second of his books, I do not exactly recollect; but I could not help remarking, that although the world would justly appreciate the value of his information, I was yet apprehensive the critics would expect some account of his family before he entered on the matter of his own life and opinions. His reason for having omitted it was most satisfactory.

"It would hae been a right down wastrie o' time and paper; and the need o' writing about my progenitors is not an indispensable. Has na our family been a family o' note—that's an ocular fact in history—frae afore the ragman's roll? But if ye think the laws o' the Republic o' Letters call for an account at my hands, I'll no be weighed in the balance and found wanting."

"To be frank and friendly with you, Laird, the laws of the Republic of Letters certainly do require that your book should begin with some account of the family before you were born, and it should likewise tell us something of your mother's family. It was not, I believe, of the same degree as the Mailings?"

"It's no an easy task," replied the Laird, with a sigh, "to write a history book that will please everybody; but as to my mother, she was come o' pedigree blood, though, it may be said, no just the degree o' our family's."

"Who was she?" said I.

"Her father," resumed the Laird, "was Custocks of Kailyards, an ancient and as weel kent a race as ony within the four quarters o' the realm; she was a co-heiress, and her name was Barbara—Moss o' Peats was married intil her uterine sister, Martha, the other co-heiress o' Kailyards: and they had issue, a son, Ramplor Moss, begotten of her body, meaning the body o' aunty Marthy; and he, being a captain in the king's army, gamblet his property wi' riotous living in foreign lands, till it came to be sold by a decreet o' Court: and so through him there was an end o' that branch o' my mother's family—"

"All this, Laird, said I, "is most important and interesting—And so your father married one of the co-heiresses o' Kailyards—and what then?"

"And what then!—am not I the fruit and issue o' that marriage, in the male line?—But, poor man, he wasna sparet to beget a better."

"That," replied I, "is much to be regretted, greatly, indeed; but I always heard he died early, and in very melancholy circumstances."

"As to his dying early, I'll no say it's a' truth, for he was weel stricken in the fifties before his espousal o' my mother; but his latter end was an event to be held in remembrance; oh, sir, it was a momento mori."

"Then you have neglected," said I, "by not describing it in your book, an occasion on which you might have given the world a fine impressive moral lesson."

"I am very sorry to hae been sae neglectfu', if ye think sae," replied the Laird.

"Indeed you have been much to blame; and, considering your talents, I must say you have hidden your candle under a bushel, Laird.—How did your father happen to die?"

"It's a heavy tale; but it came to pass after this manner: ye see he was ane of the Langsyne Club, that some threescore Yules bygane had its howf in a public in the town, keepit by a wife that was by name Luckie Gawsie—and he was a man (meaning my father) o' a pleasantrie in company, as I have often heard the late Sparkinhawse o' Drycraigs tell; mony a sooh and sappy night they had wi' ane anither: there was na a blither bike o' drowthy neibours in a' the shire; Quaigh o' Plunkcorkie was the preses, and Luggie o' Dramkeg the croupier. But mirth and melancholy are the twins o' mortality—walking hand in hand, to and fro', roaring like lions seeking whom they may devour—heh, sirs, that night they visited the public o' Luckie Gawse—weel may I recollect what Sparkinhawse told me; it was wi' the tear in his e'e, for he was a warmhearted bodie. We had been squeezing the sides o' the gardevin, and neither o' us were then fasting, but baith jocose, the whilk, as he said, put him in mind o' the auld langsyne. 'Laird,' quo' he—we were sitting in Luckie Gawsie's back room, wi' her tappit hen o' claret wine on the table, according to the use and wont o' the club, and Luggie o' Dramkeg was singing the Gaberloonie like a nightingale —oh, he was a deacon at a pawky sang—I use his ain words," said the Laird.—

"And what happened?"

"What happened! Drycraigs, in the way of a peradventure, some short time after the sang, gied a glimpse out o'er the table at my father and seeing something no canny in his glower, said to the preses, 'Plunkcorkie,' said he, 'I'm thinking Auldbiggings is looking unco gash.' 'Gash!' quo' Plunkcorkie, 'nae wonder, he's been dead this half hour; his e'en flew up and his lip fell down just as Dramkeg was singing the verse about the courting at the fire-side; and was I to spoil a gude sang for the likes o' him? so when it was done, through an accidence of

13

memory, I forgot to tell you o' the poplexy.—But,' continued Plunk-corkie, as Drycraigs told me, 'now that it's noticed, we, for a decency, must get the corpse ta'en hame to its ain house.' Whereupon they all raise frae their seats, said Drycraigs.—Was na that a moving sight? and they filled lippies, and in solemn silence drank their auld frien' for the last time; and Quaigh o' Plunkcorkie, the preses, held a glass to my father's mouth, but he couldna taste, which was a sure sign he was a dead man; whereupon they all fell to the greeting with the hearts o' men, mourning in affliction."

I exerted myself to the utmost to sympathize with the Laird during this affecting description of the langsyne nights of claret in tappit hens, and my endeavours were of necessity redoubled by his moral reflections on the occasion.

"But," said he, "as one door steeks another opens, and my father's death brought me into the world mair than two moons afore the common course of nature; for ye see, when my mother, through the mist o' a grey March morning, heard a sound coming towards the house, and lookit out at her window, she discern't the three fou lairds bringing her dead gudeman hame—Drycraigs and Dramkeg were harling the body through the mire by the oxsters, his head dangling o'er his breast like an ill-sewed-on button—Plunkcorkie, the preses o' the club, was following in a sorrowfu' condition, carrying my father's wig and his hat, and one of his boots that had come off, no man could tell how, as they were hauling the corpse along the road; and Drycraigs told me that poor man, Plunkcorkie, was so demented wi' grief, that when he came into the house he had the shank o' the very glass in his hand he had held to his old frien's lips, which, you must allow, was a very touching thing."

"And when they brought home the Laird, what was done?"

"Done! muckle was done—does na everybody ken I'm a seven-month's bairn,[2] the which is the cause of my weakliness, and has been o' the greatest detriment to me a' my days; because had I no been sae defective wi' infirmity, I might hae been walking the Parliament House o' Edinburgh, wi' a blue shaloon pock to haud fees—but a want is no a fault."

"Very true, Laird," said I; "what you say is a most sagacious remark —but if by reason of any innate weakliness of faculty you have been

<hr>

[2] *a seven-months bairn*: this guarded reference represents a revision by Galt. Some of the original bluntness can be seen in Blackwood's letter of 7 April 1826, where he objects to 'whamling the young one onto the world'.

kept from the bar, the world may have no cause to rue the loss of you as a lawyer, since we are so likely to profit by you as an author."

"No, man," was his emphatic answer—"no, man—I was going to make an observe in the way of philosophy, but let that pass, and do something for the good o' the house."

I had by this time sipped unconsciously the entire contents of my toddy tumbler, and accordingly, upon the Laird's suggestion, I began to replenish.

CHAPTER IV

After the account which Malachi had given of his birth and parentage, I was curious to see what he had said of his education; but on lifting and opening the first volume, (for he dignified his books with that title,) I found nothing whatever recorded respecting it, nor of anything which had befallen him till he reached his eighteenth year.

"Dear me, Laird," said I, "how is this? You have omitted what is even more important than the account of your family—all the happy days of your childhood."

"Happy days! that's a' ye ken o' them. Oh, if ye but knew what I suffered in the tender years of my childhood! I was persecuted like a martyr—the blains o' Dominie Skelp's tawse ye may yet discern by an inspection—a' the week there was nothing for me but read, read, read your lesson—write, write, write your copy—add, subtract, multiply, and divide; and on the Sabbath day, when man and beast and spinning-wheel got leave to rest, I was buffetted by Satan ten times waur in the shape o' the Psalms o' David—The deevil hae his will o' them, mony a time thought I, that begat the Question-book."

"But, Laird, pains are pleasant in the recollection, and I should have expected, from the manner in which you of course passed your youth, that there would have been a vernal freshness in the description, such a dewy blossoming in the memory of your sports and recreations, as would have moved the world to reveries of innocence and delight."

"Poo, poo! what is't to be a slave, a nigger slave, but to be flogged on the back wi' a whip?—well do I know a tenderer part than the back, and a whip has but ae scourage, our schoolmaister's tawse had seven—neither intemperance nor old age hae in gout or rheumatic an agony to compare wi' a weel-laid-on whack o' the tawse on a part that for manners shall be nameless."

"Well, Laird, though there is some truth in what you say, yet I never should have thought you were likely to have required any excessive degree of admonition *a posteriori*."

"But I was hated by the master—he had a pleasure and satisfaction in gripping me by the coat-neck and shaking me wi' a gurl, because I had no instinct for learning. It's my opinion, had I been a justice of the peace at that time, I would hae prosecuted him to the utmost rigour of the law. Do you know, that once in his tantrams he flew on me like a mad dog, and nippit my twa lugs till he left the stedt o' his fingers as plainly upon them as the mark o' Peter's finger and thumb can be seen on the haddock's back. There was na a day I did na get a pawmy but ane, and on it I got twa, the whilk was ca'd in derision a double morning."

"He appears to have been indeed a most irascible dominie; but all was no doubt made up to you, when the blessed hours of play and sunshine came round—buoyant and bounding with your school-fellows—"

"Haud your hand! nane o' your parleyvooing, ye loon that ye are," exclaimed the Laird, half slyly half earnestly, "for the laddies at our school werena like ither laddies—the thought o' the usage they gied me gars me grind my teeth to this day. The master infectit them wi' his hatred against me, and they never divaul't wi' their torments—sure am I, if there be a deevil that's called Legion, that deevil was the hundred and thirteen laddies at Dominie Skelp's school—for though many in number, they were but ane in nature. Now just think o' what they did —they ance liftit me o'er the minister's dyke and gart me steal his apples!"

"But you were rewarded with a share of the spoil?"

"Ay, yes—I was rewardit—that's nae lee—but how? tell me that?— They made me gie them my hatfu', and when they got it, they a' set up a shout and a cry o' a thief in the yard, which brought out Gilbert the minister's man like a raging bear. He was a contemptuous wretch."

"What did he do to you?"

"Do! he laughed me to scorn wi' a gaffaw, and said he thought I had na spunk for sic a spree—and then out came Mrs Glebanteinds the minister's wife, knocking her nieves at me as if I had been an unright-eous malefactor, till I was sae terrify't that I terrify't them wi' my cries o' dread. It has been said, indeed, I ne'er got the better o' that fright; and I hae some cause to think no without reason, for I grue wi' the thought o' an apple to this day, like Adam and Eve, when they had begotten their sons and daughters. But I had my satisfaction o' that finger o' scorn, Gilbert, though it was mair than fifteen years after."

Well as I was aware of the Laird's disposition to treasure and cherish resentment, this confession of satisfaction at enjoying revenge so many years after the school-boy prank, made me say in a tone very different from that in which I usually addressed him,—

17

"Is it possible that a man could harbour anger so long?" My indignation was, however, soon bridled, for I presently recollected to whom I was speaking: his answer was characteristic.

"Had ye felt my provocation, ye would hae been angry at him a' your days, though ye had lived to the age of Methusalem—and yet I was na very austere either."

"What did you to him?"

"I'll tell you, if ye'll thole and listen like a man o' jurisprudence. Ye see, it came to pass that the minister, being weel stricken in years, stretched out his legs on the bed of sickness and departed this life; whereupon his wife, Mrs Glebantiends, being sequestrated from the stipend, left the manse and went to live in the town on Sir Hairy's Fond,★ which is, as you know, a grand provision for the like o' her. Thus it came to pass, that auld Gilbert was ordained to earn his bread by the sweat of his brow, which is the portion of man that is born of a woman, and his lot was to howk ditches. When he had laboured at that some dozen years or the like, after the death of his master, he was afflicted wi' an income, and no being able to handle spade or pick, he was constrained to beggary; and so it happened that on the very first morning that he took up the meal-pock for eikrie o' life, as the folk called it, I was standing at the yett looking to see wha might be going to the town, and wha coming frae't, when, lo and behold! I saw an auld beggar-man, wi' a grey head and a cleaner pock than usual, and it was toom—ye see it was first morning at the trade—hirpling wi' a stilt towards the avenue; and so hirpling, when he saw me he stoppit, and swither't, and turned round, and was blate to come, the which made me wonder; but belyve, he took off his bonnet and cam to me wi't in his hand, wi' his bald head bare; and when I was marvelling wha this new-set-up beggar could be, (for I had no thought o' Gilbert,) he said, 'Laird, will ye hansel my pock?'—for he was aye a jocose body,—'Will ye hansel my pock, for auld langsyne, Laird?'—'For auld langsyne!' quo' I, 'a hansel in the jougs would better serve you than an almous—gae awa wi' you, ye fause loon! an ye come within the bounds o' Auld-biggings, I'll set the dog on you, for what ye did to me in the manse garden—that's the auld langsyne I keep in memento.'"

"And did he knock you down with his crutch?"

"Na, na, he durstna do that—but I trow he was dauntit, for he turn't

★ The Laird would seem to have forgotten that the "Widows' Fund" was not, at the time of which he was speaking, under the able management of the Rev. Sir Harry Moncrieff. [Author's note]

on his heel and put on his bonnet wi' a splurt like a Highlandman in a pet, and powled himsel awa wi' his stilt.

"But," continued the Laird after a pause, during which he looked somewhat doubtfully at me—"but I see ye think I didna do right," adding, "I'm no, however, so hard-hearted as I let wot—for when I saw that I had made an impression, I ran after him and touched him on the shoulder, and putting my hand in my pouch, I gave him a whole penny —twa new bawbees, gude weight, for it was then the days o' the tumbling Tams."[1]

"And what said he?"

"Ye'll aiblins think he was full o' thanksgiving—nae sic thing, but as proud as when he was the minister's man—he took the penny—twa beautiful bawbees it was, and he looked at them, and what do you think he said?—'I'm a beggar noo, and I oughtna to refuse God's charity!' so, withouten a bethank, he hobbled on his way, leaving me standing in the middle of the road wi' my finger in my mouth."

There was something in this story, which at the moment damped my curiosity, and, notwithstanding the Laird's earnest entreaties to prolong my visit, made me rise abruptly: a little more hastily, too, than was quite consistent with good manners, I bade him for that afternoon farewell. But as I walked homeward, I reflected on the singular circumstance of such a being attempting a history of himself, and soon settled it to my own contentment, that if his book was not likely to furnish many materials for amusement, there was yet enough in his recollections and observations worthy of being a little further sifted; accordingly, although I had left Auldbiggings half resolved never again to pass the threshold, it so happened that before I reached home, my determination was formed to visit him again on the following day.

[1] *tumbling Tams*: heavy copper coinage of George III.

CHAPTER V

I have a notion that the auto-biography of an idiot might not only be interesting, but prove an acquisition of no inconsiderable value to the most philosophical thinkers; and it seemed to me, upon reflection, that the Laird's undertaking was less preposterous than I had at first imagined. It was possible that although always regarded by the neighbours as a mere ruminating animal, he might yet, in the course of his time, have observed, in the passing current of things, something worthy of notice which had escaped the attention of men reputed wiser. This idea changed in some degree the estimation I had formed of his labour; I could not, indeed, refrain from thinking even of himself with feelings of augmented consideration.

In this speculative frame of mind I took my hat and stick next day, and walked saunteringly across the fields towards Auldbiggings, keeping a path which trended towards the house at some distance from the high-road, in order that I might not be disturbed in my reveries by any accidental encounter with those sort of friends who are ever socially disposed to inflict their company upon you, especially when you most desire to walk alone.

This path winded over the Whinny Knowes, an untenanted and unrentable portion of the Laird's domain, famed from time immemorial among the school-boys of the town for nests and brambleberries, and for which they, as regularly as the equinoxial gales, waged a vernal and autumnal war with Jock the Laird's man. For his master, by some peculiar and squire-like interpretation of the spirit and principles of the game laws, claimed and asserted a right of property over them, as sacred and lawful as that which he possessed to his own dove-cot, or the fruit of his garden. Accordingly, as soon as the gowans began to open the silvery lids of their golden eyes in the spring, Jock was posted among the blooming furze and broom, particularly on the Saturday's blessed afternoon, to herd the nests. And in like manner, and as periodically as the same play-hallowed day of the week returned, as soon as the celebrated ruddy apples began to blush on the boughs, he was again sent thither to defend the berries, nor were the oranges of the Hesperides guarded of old by a more indomitable griffon.

It happened on the occasion of which I am speaking, that the warder had taken post for the first or second time for the season to watch the nests—I am not sure if the day, however, was a Saturday, but if it was not, the weather was so bland and bright that it ought to have been. Jock was sitting in a niche of golden broom, and, inspirited by the influence of the birds and blossoms around him, was gaily whistling, it might be for the want of thought, or from the enjoyment of happiness, as he tapered a fishing-rod with an old table-knife of the true Margaret Nicholson edge and pattern.[1] On seeing me approaching, he rose, leaving his task and implement on the grass, and in a style I had never remarked in him before, he raised his hand to his hat, and held it there till I requested him to use no new ceremony. I said, however, to myself, this is another effect of the King's visit; but as Jock did not accompany the Laird on the occasion to Athens, I became a little pryish to ascertain whether this debonair touching of the hat was derived from the special tuition of his master, or had been acquired from some compeer's authority. Before I had time, however, to ask any question, Jock inquired if I was for "The Place," as the house of Auldbiggings was commonly called by the servants and villagers.

"Ye'll fin' the Laird," said he, "a busy man."

"Indeed—and what is he doing?"

"Doing? what should he be doing, but sitting on his ain louping-on stane, glowing frae him?"

"And call ye that being busy, John?"

"And is't no sae? Is na idleset the wark o' a gentleman—and what more would ye hae him to be doing in that way? what could he do more?"

"Then he has given up writing his book, has he?"

"He maun think o' what to put in't—King David made his Psalms in the watches of the night."

"'Tis my opinion, John," said I, "that the Laird might do worse than consult you on the subject, considering how long and how well you have been acquainted with himself and all his family."

"I'm thinking," replied Jock, casting his eyes on the ground, "he would come but little speed without the help and counsel o' somebody, living sic a lonely life as he has done; till he gaed to the King's coming hame, it could na be said in a sense that he had cast an ee on the world."

[1] *Margaret Nicholson edge and pattern*: i.e. 'murderous'. Margt. Nicholson in 1786 attempted to stab George III.

"But your experience in that way, John, has been great; and if he consults his own renown, he will take your advice in every sentence." I had in this my mind's eye on Moliere's Old Woman[2].

"I'll no deny that I hae had a finger in the pie already; but I was telling him yestreen, after ye went away, when he gied me an account of your applauses, that I thought the book would be better if he would saw it here and there wi' twa three bonny kittle words out o' the dictioner. If it has a fault, (and what has na?) it's a want o' gentility."

That Jock had long been viceroy over the Laird, was well known to the whole parish; but that he was so deep in his literary counsels, and so participant in his lucubrations, I had not suspected. I felt, therefore, that to indulge curiosity further, by leading him on to the unconscious disclosure of his master's secrets, would be as little consonant to gentility, as the want of kittle words in the Memoirs. Accordingly, partly to appease my own compunctions, and partly to soothe him into an oblivion of the impertinence of which I had been so guilty, I complimented him on his long and faithful attachment to the Laird, and on the confidence which he enjoyed, and which he merited.

"And he weel deserves to be weel servit," was the answer. "Is na he come o' a parentage o' pedigree, and born wi' a silver spoon in his mouth to an heritage o' parks and pastures, woods and waters, and a' the other commodities that mak blood gentle?"

Hitherto I had known little more of Jock than by sight; but I discovered by this accidental conversation that he was worthy of all the celebrity he enjoyed among the neighbours for the sagacity of his remarks, and the singularity of his sayings, many of the latter having acquired the currency of proverbs; but whether owing to the value of the bullion, or to the peculiarities of the mintage, might perhaps admit of some controversy. It was clear, however, that Jock was worthy of his master; nor in the sequel will it be questioned, that the Laird deserved such a man. But as it is both fit and expedient that the courteous reader should also become a little more acquainted with Jock, it may be as well to mention a few particulars of his personal history and character, while the scene of my own role in the drama is changing from the Whinny Knowes to the parlour of Auldbiggings.

Jock, or John Dabbler, as he ought to be called, when we quit the free vernacular of our colloquial pen, and indite with the recondite dignity of history, was the son of one of the Laird's cotters. For some four or

[2] *Molière's Old Woman*: Madame Pernelle in *Tartuffe*.

five years after his birth, it was the unshaken opinion of his mother that he was born to distinction, inasmuch as he had, according to her account of him, always showed a greater inclination to eat than to work; but increase of years, which expanded his capacity for the former, brought no compensating alacrity for the latter; and in consequence, as he would neither learn a town-trade, nor help his father in the labour of dykes and ditches, she obtained for him, about the age of seven, a sort of ashypet office in the Laird's kitchen, where, in course of time, he acquired a grey duffle coat with a red collar, and was regarded as the helper and successor of an old man, who had spent his whole life in the honourable vocation of flunkie to three generations of the Auld-biggings.

At the era of which we are treating, Jock, though far advanced into the wane of manhood, still retained the familiar callant abbreviation of his baptismal epithet, and still as devoutly believed, as on the first day when he entered the house, that the whole earth contained but two men worthy of worship—the King and the Laird—but to which the prime honour and the firstlings of homage were due, he had never determined to his own satisfaction. The leaning certainly, however, was in favour of the Laird; for, never having seen the King, he justly remarked, when sometimes drawn into controversy on the subject, that far-off fowls had fair feathers—thereby intimating, that upon a nearer inspection, and closer comparison, the difference would be found less between them than in the alleged disparity of the pomp and circumstance of their respective conditions.

Besides this personal opinion of the superiority of his master, Jock had as strong a feeling of property in everything belonging to the Laird as the Laird had himself, and probably considered himself as much an integral portion of the estate as the time-honoured holly-bush on the green, of which I have already spoken. But in this feeling there was none of that persuasion of a community of goods, which is some-times discovered among the domestics of the best-regulated families. On the contrary, Jock was as faithful to his menial trusts as the key or the mastiff; as true as the one, and not less vigilant than the other. It was owing to the impulse of this fidelity that our conversation on the Whinny Knowes was so suddenly interrupted, and the leisure afforded for the digression. For, just as I was on the point of sifting his opinion as to the constituents of gentle blood, he happened to discover a piquet of the school-boys advancing towards the Knowes, and abruptly darted from me to challenge their intrusion.

CHAPTER VI

I did not find the Laird, as Jock said I should, sitting busy with idleness on the louping-on stone at his gate, but in the parlour, and with the insignia of authorship arranged before him, installed in the library chair so particularly before described.

After the customary interchanges of visitation inquiries, he reverted to the subject of our yesterday's conversation.

"I hae been," said he, "a thought ravelled in mind wi' what ye were saying concerning the specialities o' my father and mother's kith and kin; but the book ye would hae me to make, is no like what I mean to do—mine's to be a book o' soleedity, showing forth the wastrie of heritages by reason o' the ingrowth o' trade and taxes."

I was grieved to find the old gentleman really so much of a political economist; but as to have disputed with him would have served no purpose, I only replied—

"No doubt, Laird, any book you write will be well worthy of attention; and if it does not suit the plan of your present work to enter into those domestic details and circumstances of householdry, which none can describe better, perhaps you may favour the world with something of that sort hereafter."

"Ye're no without a nerve o' discernment—I can see that," was his self-complacent answer; "and I'll no say what's in the egg-bed o' my brain—but no to keckle ower soon, I hae been thinking a' this morning's meditation, that if I get a satisfactory solacium for the turn in hand, I may be able belyve to pay off another o' the bonds, and so, by a graduality, clear the estate and die wi' a free income."

When he first told me that his motive in undertaking to write his life was to pay off one of the mortgages, the idea was too ludicrous to leave any serious impression; but this repetition of it made me suspect the debt lay more heavily upon him than I was aware of. I knew, indeed, that from the death of his wife, his affairs had been ill managed, and that for many years the residue of his rental—that which remained after paying the interest on the heritable bonds, was scarcely sufficient for his thriftless expenditure; but that he felt anything like the acrual pinchings of pecuniary difficulty, had never occurred to me. I did not, however, then choose to ask him any direct question on the subject; but it was impossible not to pity the helplessness and infirmity of the poor old man, who could imagine that from any resource so ineffectual as his pen, the means might be obtained to abate the pressure of embarrassment; nevertheless, I said to him, half jocularly,—

"But what can it signify to you, Laird, to die with a clear income, unless you intend to marry again, and mean to provide for a young family, seeing that at present you have no descendent, nor even an heir within the fifth degree of cousinship?"

He looked at me steadily askance for about the space of a minute, and then said with an accent in which there was a slight inflexion of sadness,—

"Ye're no acquaint wi' Hugh Caption, the writer?"

"I have heard of him; but I hope you have more sense, Laird, than to go to law?"

"So think I mysel," was his answer, expressed somewhat sedately; "but it's no the case wi' everybody."

"How, Laird!" cried I, startled by the import of the observation, and really feeling for him more anxiety than I affected; "blameless in walk and conversation as you have always been, is it possible that you can have fallen into the snares of Caption?"

"He's but the claw o' the case," replied the Laird, adding, with a half-suppressed sigh, as it were in soliloquy, "and it's a claw that needs parin': an eagle's talons may tear the flesh frae the bone, but his grasping grip's enough to rive the seven senses out o' the soul."

"I am grieved to hear you say so. How did you happen to fall into his clutches? By whom is he employed?"

"Stop, stop," interrupted the Laird; "the mair haste the waur speed —bridle the unicorn o' your impatience, and I'll tell you all the outs and ins o't. Ye see, when Mr Rupees the Nawbub came hame frae Indy, and bought the Arunthrough property frae the Glaikies, who, like sae mony ithers o' the right stock o' legitimate gentry,[1] hae been smothered out o' sight by the weed and nettle overgrowths o' merchandise and cotton-weavry, he would fain hae bought Auldbiggings likewise, and sent that gett o' the de'il and the law, Caption, to make me an offer; but I was neither a prodigal son nor an Esau, to sell my

---

[1] *gentry . . . smothered . . . by . . . merchandise and cotton-weavry*: the late eighteenth-century expansion of trade with America and the West Indies and the growth of manufacture led to new wealth in the west of Scotland, which was able to buy out many of the old estates.

patrimony for a mess o' pottage, so I gied him a flea in his lug, and bade him tell the Nawbob to chew the cud o' the sin o' covetousness, the whilk is disappointment."

"And from that I suppose, Laird, you and Mr Rupees quarrelled?".

"Oh no, it was the beginning to a great cordiality o' friendship, for he came o'er here the next day, and made a decent apology, inviting me in the civillest manner, to dine wi' him, and was most enterteening about hoo they hunt elephants wi' tygers instead o' hounds; telling me, among ither news, o' the braw thing he did to a great Mogul, that was a Pishawa in Hydrobab, and had a Durbah. In short, we came to an understanding, and ae night, when we were sitting by ourselves, drinking a bottle o' his best Madæra wine, that was eleven years in wood in Bengal before he bought it, and sixteen in the bottle after; he said that he had some spare money, which he would be glad to lend on easy terms, for seven years, or even a langer period, begging, if I should hear of ony gentleman in want, to gie him an inkling."

It was not difficult to discern from this the machination of the Nabob's friendship for the innocent Laird, and I shook my head.

"Deed," said Malachi, "ye may weel shake your head, for his wine was a flee, and his money a hook, that I was a silly saumon to swallow. But he won upon me, so I told him o' the wadsets on Auldbiggings, and of the twa heritable bonds[2] o' the doers[3] for the young leddies o' Hainings, the which might be called up in a day's notice, and thus it came to pass, frae less to mair, that I covenanted to take as meikle o' his siller as would pay off that precarious obligation, the thought of which was like guilt to my night's rest."

"And having so allured you to take his money," said I, "he now vexes you for repayment?"

"Na, he does far waur. He has gotten, the gude kens how, the rights to the other wadsets, and put them intil the Nebuchadnezzar-like talons o' Caption, who has sent me word, that if the debt's no redeemed afore Whitsunday, he's instructed to proceed; and he's, I needna tell you, a sinner that skips, when he says the Lord's prayer, 'forgie our debts as we forgie our debtors'; so ye see there is a neddcessity for me to do something—and books being in request, I could think o' naething easier than making ane to help me in the coming stress, money being scarce to borrow, and land ill to sell."

[2] *heritable bonds*: (Scots law) bonds for sum of money, secured against convey-ance of land.
[3] *doers*: trustees.

By this disclosure, it was evident that the poor Laird's circumstances were much worse than I had conjectured; for upon inquiring the amount of the mortgages, I was grieved to find it almost equal to the reputed value of his whole estate, depreciated as the value of land was at that time. I thought, however, if the character of the transaction was properly represented to the Nabob, that the apprehension of public odium might induce him, if not to forego the prosecution entirely of so harsh a suit, to mitigate the pressure of it by some indulgence as to time, especially as, from the date of his arrival in the neighbourhood, he had cultivated popularity, and not by the least ostentatious means. Accordingly, I offered to call on Dr Lounlans, the minister of the parish, to beg his mediation in the business; but on mentioning his name, a change came over the complexion of the Laird, and a slight convulsive shudder of repugnance vibrated through his whole frame. He made no answer, but looked at me suspiciously askance; and then taking off his purple velvet cap, rubbed his bald head with his hand, and fetched a deep breath, which terminated in something like a sigh.

"You do not seem," said I, "to approve of my suggestion. But a man of Dr Lounlans's personal character, with the great ascendency which his eloquence gives him over the minds of all who approach him, is, in such an affair as yours, Laird, the most likely to prove an effective advocate."

"When that Neezam o' the Carnatic, Rupees, offered me his money, he shook me by the hand, wi' meikle flattering confidentiality," replied the Laird, after a pause of about the space of a minute; "but the thought o' his covetous deceitfulness is neither sae sour nor sae bitter, as to think I would come under an obligation to the like o' Dominie Lounlans."

The energy with which this was uttered, had more in it of alarm than of contempt. The tone was at variance with the language, and the look was expressive of aversion rather than of dread. It was evident, indeed, that some skinless feeling had been touched; and that something had occurred in the previous history of the Laird, regarding the amiable and eloquent preacher, of which I had not heard. In that moment my eye happened to glance towards one of the biographical copy-books on the table, and I suddenly recollected the note respecting the widow Lounlans, whom the Laird had been obliged to roup out of the farm, and whose clamour on the occasion he had so emphatically recorded.

"Is Dr Lounlans," said I, "any relation to that widow, who gave you so much trouble long ago?"

"Isna he her son? and didna he set himself in revenge against me to get the kirk? If he hadna been stirred up, and egget on by a malice prepense, would he ever hae daur't to show his face in this parish, far less in our poopit, driven out o't as his mother and the rest o' them were, black wi' disgrace in my debt, that wasna pay't for ten years, though to be sure when it was pay't she alloo't interest on the interest; but that was only out o' a pridefu' spite to humble me, 'cause o' my justice; for there was no need o' sic payment, as I would hae been content wi' the single interest. But it's what we're to expec frae the upsetting o' the lower orders. It was the machinations o' thae very Lounlans that first opened my een to the conspiracy that's working the downfall and overthrow of sae mony birthrights o' our national gentry. But if ye kent the original cause of their hatred to me, ye would be none surprised to see me sae grue at the thought of being behadin to ane o' them."

"Why, I think that's pretty well explained by what you have just told me. It was to be expected they would bear a resentful remembrance of the manner in which you drove them from the parish."

"They went of their own free wull," exclaimed the Laird, eagerly, as if to defend himself from a reproach—"Had my rent been paid, I wouldna hae molested them, and they might have staid in the parish for me, when I got them off the farm—but the woman had a hatred o' me lang afore a' that."

"And for what reason?"

"For no reason at a' but the very want o't; for when she was young she was a bonnie lassie, wi' blithe e'en, and cheeks like a Flander-baby[4]; and I would hae made her leddy of Auldbiggings—But I hae written a' the particulars about it here; the which ye may read, while I step to the Whinny Knowes, to see what Jock's doing; and when ye're done ye can follow me."

As soon as the Laird left the room, I accordingly began to read; but I had not proceeded many sentences when I was tempted, of course by the Evil one, to copy the chapter verbatim. Whether, in doing so, I have been guilty of any breach of faith, the critic may determine for himself, while the compositor is setting the extract.

[4] *Flanders baby*: wooden doll (imported from the Low Countries)

CHAPTER VII

The Laird began the record of his eighteenth year in these words:—

"There livt at this time, on ye fermsted of Broomlans, a pirson that was a woman, by calling a widow; and she and her husband, when he was in this lyf, had atween them, Annie Daisie, a dochter; very fair she was to look upon, cumly withal, and of a feeleeceety o' nature.

"This pretty Annie Daisie, I kno not hoo, found favor in my eyes, and I maid no scruppel of going to the kirk every Sabbatha day to see her, though Mr Glebantiends was, to a certentye, a vera maksleepie preecher. When I fore-gathered with her by accidence, I was all in a confewshon; and when I would hae spoken to her wi kindly words, I coud but look in her cleer een and neigher like Willie Gouk, the haivrel laddie; the whutch maid her jeer me as if I had a want, and been daft likewyse; so that seeing I cam no speed in coorting for myself, I thocht o' telling my mother, but that was a kittle job—howsoever, I took heart, and said

"'Mother—'

"'Well, son,' she made answer, 'what woud ye?'

"'I'm going to be marriet,' quo' I.

"'Marriet!' cried she, spredding oot her arms wi' a consternayshun—'And wha's the bride?'

"I didna like just to gie her an even-down answer, but said I thought myselph old enough for a helpmeat to my table, whutch caused her to respond with a laff; whereupon I told her I was thinking of Annie Daisie.

"'Ye'll shoorly ne'er marry the like o' her—she's only a gairner's dochter.'

"But I thocht of Adam and Eve, and said, 'We're a' come of a gairner.' The whuch to heer, caused her presentlye to wax vera wroth with me; and she stampit with her foot, and called me a blot on ye skutshon o' Auldbiggings; then she sat doon, and began to reflek with herself; and after a season, she spoke rawshonel about the connexion, saying she had a wife in her mind for me, far more to the purpose than sitch a cawsey danser as Annie Daisie.

"But I couldna bide to hear Annie Daisie mislikent, and yet I was fear't to commit the sin of disobedience, for my mother had no mercy when she thocht I rebell't against her othority; so I sat down, and was in treebolayshon, and then I speert with a flutter of affliction, who it was that she had will't to be my wyfe.

"'Miss Betty Græme,' said she, 'if she can be persuaded to tak sic a headowit.'

"Now, this Miss Betty Græme was the tocherless sixth dochter o' a broken Glasgow Provost, and made her leeving by seamstress-wark and floowring lawn; but she was come of gentle blood, and was herself a gentle creature, though no sae blithe as bonnie Annie Daisie; and for that, I told my mother I would never take her, though it should be the death o' me. Accordingly I ran out of the hoos, and took to the hills, and wistna where I was, till I found myself at the door of the Broomlands, with Annie Daisie before me, singing like a laverock as she watered the yarn of her ain spinning on the green. On seeing me, however, she stoppit, and cried, 'Gude keep us a', Laird, what's frighten'd you to flee hither?'

"But I was desp'rate, and I ran till her, and fell on my knees, in a lover-like fashon; but, wha would hae thocht it? she dang me over on my back, and as I lay on the ground she watered me with her wateringcan, and was like to dee with laffing: the which sign and manifestation of hatred on her part quencht the low o' love on mine; and I raise and went hame, drookit and dripping as I was, and told my mother I would be an obedient and dutiful son. Soon after this, Annie Daisie was marriet to John Lounlans; and there was a fulsome fraising about them when they were kirkit, as the cumliest cupple in the parish. It was castor-oil to hear't; and I was determin't to be up-sides with them, for the way she had had jiltit me.

"In the meanwhile my mother, that never, when she had a turn in hand, alloo't the grass to grow in her path, invited Miss Betty Græme to stay a week with us; the which, as her father's family were in a straitened circumstance, she was glad to accep; and being come, and her mother with her, I could discern a confabling atween the twa auld leddies—Mrs Græme shaking the head of scroopolosity, and my mother laying doon the law and the gospel—all denoting a matter-o'-money plot for me and Miss Betty. At last it came to pass, on the morning of the third day, that Miss Betty did not rise to take her breakfast with us, but was indisposed; and when she came to her dinner, her een were blear't and begrutten. After dinner, however, my mother that day put down, what wasna common with her housewifery, a bottle o' port in a decanter, instead o' the gardevin for toddy, and made Miss Betty drink a glass to mak her better, and me to drink three, saying, 'Faint heart never won fair leddy.' Upon the whilk hint I took another myself, and drank a toast, for better acquaintance with Miss Betty. Then the twa matrons raise to leave the room, and Miss Betty was rising too; but her mother laid her hand upon her shoother, and said, 'It's our lot, my dear, and we maun bear with it.' Thus it came to pass, that me and Miss Betty were left by ourselves in a very comical situation.

"There was silence for a space of time between us; at last she drew a deep sigh, and I responded, to the best of my ability, with another. Then she took out her pocket napkin, and began to wipe her eyes. This is something like serious coorting, thocht I to myself, for sighs and tears are the food of love; but I was na yet just ready to weep; hoosever, I likewise took out my pocket napkin, and made a sign o' sympathy by blowing my nose, and then I said—

"'Miss Betty Græme, how would ye like to be Leddy of Auld-biggings under my mother?'

"'Oh, heavens!' cried she, in a voice that gart me a' dinle—and she burst into a passion of tears; the whilk to see so affectit me that I couldna help greeting too—the sight whereof made her rise and walk the room like a dementit bedlamite.

"I was terrifyt, for her agitation wasna like the raptures I expectit; but I rose from my seat, and going round to the other side of the table where she was pacing the floor, I follow't her, and pulling her by the skirt, said, in a gallant way, to raise her spirits—'Miss Betty Græme, will ye sit down on my knee?'—I'll ne'er forget the look she gied for answer—but it raised my courage, and I said, 'E'en's ye like, Meg Dorts'[1]—and with a flourish on my heel, I left her to tune her pipes alane. This did the business, as I thocht; for though I saw her no more that night, yet the next morning she came to breakfast a subdued woman, and my mother, before the week was out, began to make preparations for the wedding.

"But, lo and behold!—one afternoon, as Miss Betty and me were taking a walk at her own requeesht on the high road, by came a whusky with a young man in it, that had been a penny-clerk to her father, and before you could say, hey cockilorum, she was up in the gig, and down at his side, and aff and away like the dust in a whirlwind.

"I was very angry to be sae jiltit a second time, but it wasna with an

[1] 'E'en's ye like, Meg Dorts': 'just as you please, haughty Meg'. Adapted from a line in Ramsay's *The Gentle Shepherd*.

anger like the anger I suffert for what I met with at the hands of Annie Daisie. It was a real pawshon. I ran hame like a clap o' thunder, and raged and rampaged till Mrs Græme was out of the house, bag and baggage. My mother thought I was gane wud, and stood and lookt at me, and didna daur to say nay to my commands. Whereas, the thocht o' the usage I had gottin frae Annie Daisie bred a heart-sickness o' humiliation, and I surely think that if she had not carried her scorn o' me sae far, as to prefer a bare farmer lad like John Lownlans, I wad hae sank into a decline, and sought the grave with a broken heart. But her marrying him roosed my corruption, and was as souring to the milk of my nature. I could hae forgiven her the watering; and had she gotten a gentleman of family, I would not have been overly miscontented; but to think, after the offer she had from a man of my degree, that she should take up with a tiller of the ground, a hewer of wood, and a drawer of water, was gall and wormwood. Truly, it was nothing less than a kithing of the evil spirit of the democraws that sae withered the green bay-trees of the world, when I was made a captain in the volunteers, by order of the Lord-Lieutenant, 'cause, as his Lordship said, of my stake in the country. But guilt and sin never thrive, and she had her punishment."

Thus far had I proceeded with the extract, when I heard the Laird's foot on the stair. I knew it by the sound of his stick on the steps, by which it was accompanied, and it made me hastily, and, I must confess, not without something like the trepidation which is supposed to attend the commission of a larceny, fold up the paper, and hide it in my pocket, which I had scarcely done and composed myself into a studious attitude, with the manuscript in my hand, when the old gentleman entered the room.

CHAPTER VIII

When the Laird had resumed his place in the library chair, I saw by his manner, and particularly by the peculiar askance look he gave me, and which was only habitual to him while under the influence of jealousy or of apprehension, that something had occurred, during his visit to the Whinny Knowes, to ruffle his wonted equanimity; but as he evidently made an effort to conceal his perturbation, I abstained from saying anything which might lead him to suppose I observed it: on the contrary, I remarked, with reference to the treatment he had received in his courtships, that he certainly had suffered much from the cruel hands of womankind.

He again looked askance at me, and smiled for a moment, with a countenance as pleased and simple in its expression as the naif relaxation of sorrow on the features of a child, when indemnified with an apple or a toy for some heart-felt affliction; he then said:—

"But in those days, I was better able to bear a' that and meikle mair, than within that volume of the book it written is of me, as in the words of King David, I may say, speaking specially of that volume beneath the cuff of your sleive; for now I'm auld, and a wee blast o' a blighting wind snools the pride o' the doddered tree. What would ye think? There was Caption, and Mr Angle the landsurveyor, wi' brazen wheels within wheels, and the Nawbub, (Belzebub's ower gude a name for him,) directing ane of his flunkies to run here wi' the chain, and there wi' the mark. They were measuring my lands—the lands o' my fore-fathers!"

"Not possible," said I, unaffectedly participating in the feelings of the helpless and dispirited old man. "If no better sentiment existed among them, some deference to public decorum might have restrained Rupees till the mortgages were regularly foreclosed, or at least till he had your permission."

"For the possibility of the trespass," replied the Laird, "I'll no undertake to argue; but for the fact, that has been proven a truth by deed o' payment."

"Payment! to what do you allude?"

"I'll tell you. You see, when I beheld them around the brazen racks

33

and torments of valuation, I stood still, marvelling if I wasna dreaming the vision o' Ezekiel the prophet, and Jock seeing me in that trance, came running in a splore o' wonder, crying, 'Odsake, Laird, if John Angle, the surveyor, hasna a loadstone watch[1] in his curiosity, that tells the airts o' the wind!' "

The Laird's eyes at this crisis of his narrative kindled, and he became agitated with indignation. "My corruption rose," said he, "and stamping wi' my foot, I said to Jock, 'How durst you let the Boar into our vineyard? The bairns o' the town would tak but eggs, and birds, and blackberries, but Rupees and his rajahs are come to rob us o' home and ha'.' Whereupon Jock, he's as true's a dog, before the shape o' my breath was melted in the air, ran to them, and wi' the butt o' a fishing-rod he had in his hand, smashed at ae blow a' their wheels o' evil prophecy into shivers, and told Caption, that it he didna leave our land, he would mak sowther o' his harns to mend them. Then there arose a sough and sound o' war, and rumours o' war, which caused me to walk towards them in my dignified capacity as one of his Majesty's Justices of the Peace, and I debarred them in the King's name, and with his royal authority, from trespassing on my ground; trampling the rising corn, doing detriment wi' their hooves to the herbage, and transgressing the bounds o' dyke and fence, to say nothing of yetts and ditches, taking John Angle to be a witness against Rupees, and lodging instruments o' protest, in the shape of a shilling, in the hands of Caption himsel, 'cause he's a notary public."

"And did he take them?" said I, not less surprised than astonished at such unwonted spirit and decision on the part of the Laird.

"Tak them! he durstna refuse; for I told him, if he did, his refusal was a thing that would make the fifteen Lords o' Embro[2] redden on their benches."

"What then happened?"

"It would have done your heart good to see what happened. There was Rupees slinking and sidling awa' wi' his tail atween his legs, and John Angle, wi' a rueful countenance, gathering up the catastrophes of his oglet."[3]

"But what did Caption do?"

"He's the seventh son of Satan, and, of course, has by birth and instinct mair skill in deevilry than his father. He stood looking at me

[1] *loadstone watch*: pocket magnetic compass.
[2] *fifteen Lords o' Embro*: fifteen Lords of Session (judges) at Edinburgh.
[3] *oglet*: Jock's attempt at 'theodolite' (through which one 'ogles').

wi' a girn that was nothing short o' a smile o' destruction, and then he said: 'Laird,' quo' he, and ye wouldna hae thought that honey could hae melted in his mouth, 'I'll say nothing of this here, but—' and wi' that he walked away. Noo, what could he mean wi' that 'but'?—I'm frightened for that but—But's an oraculous word frae the lips o' the law."

I could not but sympathize with the poor Laird's apprehensions. The character of Caption allowed of no doubt as to the persecution which would ensue, and it was not uncharitable to think that his malicious machinations would be supported by his rich and unprincipled client. Under these feelings and that impression, I again said: "You must indeed permit me to beg the mediation of Dr Lounlans. If any man can avert the trouble and vexation to which you are so unhappily exposed, he alone of all the parish—"

"Do you see that picture of the King on the wall?" replied the old man. "Bid it come out frae ahint the glass, and go to the Manse, and drink a glass o' wine wi' Dr Lounlans, and I'll be there when it does that, and beseech the Doctor to supplicate for me."

"Really, Mr Mailings, you surprise me. Forty years might have quenched the anger you felt against his mother for rejecting your suit, the proffer of your love."

"O! I was willing to forgie her for that—I had forgien her, and had amaist forgotten't; but when her gudeman dee't, and I was constrained by course o' law to roup her out o' the farm, I'll never forgie what she did then—no, no, never. She stir't the country like a wasp's byke about me—I durstna mudge on the King's highway without meeting revile and molestation. It's no to be told what I suffer't. The cripple bodie, auld Gilbert, that was the minister's man, wadna tak an amous ae day frae me—he ne'er get the offer o' another—'cause, as he said, surely I was needfu' o't mysel. Heard ye ever sic impiddance? and a' this for acting according to law, as if to do sae were a sin!"

There was enough in this statement to convince me that the conduct of the Laird towards the widow and her children had not been exactly in unison with public opinion, and I replied, "that certainly, although to act according to law never ought to be regarded as a sin, yet times and occasions will sometimes arise when it may be thought a shame—as, for instance, Laird, the treatment you are now suffering from Rupees."

"But there's an unco difference atween the like o' me and Mrs Lounlans," was his answer; the force of which derived considerable emphasis from his pettish and mortified accent. He added, however, in a lowlier tone—"Rupees might hae a decency for a neighbour that he was sae blithe to mess and mell wi', either in his ain house or here."

This egotism would perhaps have moved other feelings than it did, had it been said at another time, and not so immediately in comparison with his own harsh treatment of her, on whom he had been so willing to bestow his undiminished fortune; but to have reminded him of any similarity in the aspect of their respective impoverished circumstances, while he was sitting in the defencelessness of age, and with such evidence of effectless endeavour to avert inevitable ruin lying on his table, would have required the extenuation of some apology for myself. Guilt in fetters hath claims on Charity which Justice dare not forbid.

The reluctance of the old man to allow the mediation of Dr Lounlans, was plainly to be ascribed to any sentiment but contrition. The paleness which overspread his countenance when I first suggested the expedient, showed that his feelings had a deeper source than pride, and were mingled with recollections which awakened the associations of sensual repugnance, as well as those of moral antipathy. My curiosity, in consequence, became excited to hear something more of the history of Dr Lounlans's family; and as I was still desirous, notwithstanding the Laird's determination to the contrary, to procure the Doctor's good offices to mitigate the severity of the Nabob's proceedings, I resolved to call at the Manse on my way home, partly to represent the unhappy state of the old man, and partly, if chance favoured, to obtain some further account of transactions so manifestly bitter in the remembrance. Accordingly, after a few general observations, chiefly of an admonitory cast, as to the caution requisite to be adopted in dealing with his adversaries, I bade the Laird good afternoon, with a promise to return next day.

CHAPTER IX

After leaving the house, and having proceeded about half-way down the avenue towards the gate, which opened upon the highway, I paused and looked back with a much greater disposition to indulge in an amicable sentimental vein, than I had ever thought it possible for the mortgage-mouldered gables of Auldbiggings to have awakened. But in that same moment I was roused from the reverie into which I was falling, by the pattering of footsteps nimbly approaching from the gate. I knew those footsteps by the sound of haste which was in them, and, could I have escaped unnoticed, I would have eschewed the evil of the owner's presence. I was grieved, indeed, to think that the Laird's impending fate had already become so publicly known as to call forth the afflicting commiseration of Mrs Soorocks, whose sole business and vocation in life consisted in visiting those among her neighbours who were suffering either under misfortune or anxiety, and feelingly, as she herself called it, "sympatheesing with their dispensation." But as it was impossible to retire without being observed, I went forward with a quickened pace, in order that I might not be detained by her. In this, however, I failed; for although I affected to be in quite as much haste as herself, and on more urgent business, she laid her hand upon my arm, and entreated me to tell her all the particulars, and if it was true that Mr Rupees had been knocked down by the Laird; sedately, and with a sympathetic voice, asserting her perfect conviction that the rumours in respect to that must be unworthy of credit.

"But," said she, "when the waur has come to the warst, Auldbiggings has only to step o'er the way to the house of Barenbraes, and make choice of one of the sisters for his livelihood. Poor leddies, they hae lang waited for a man to speer their price; and in his state of the perils of poverty, he needna be nice, and neither o' them has any cause to be dorty."

Now it happened that the maiden sisters of Barenbraes, Miss Shoosie and Miss Girzie Minnigaff, had long been the peculiar objects of Mrs Soorocks' neighbourly anxieties, and the source of her great interest in their fate and fortunes requires that some account should be given of their family and peculiar condition.

37

In the days of their youth they had never been celebrated for any beauty. Miss Shoosie was at this time only in her fiftieth year, but so mulcted of the few graces which niggard nature had so stingily bestowed, that she was seemingly already an aged creature. Her sister looked no younger, even although, as Mrs Soorocks often said, she had two years less of sin and misery to answer for.

Originally there had been three sisters; but the eldest, during the life of their father, made what he called an imprudent marriage, at which he was irreconcilably indignant, because it did not suit the state of his means to give his daughter any dowry, an expedient not singular on similar occasions. Captain Chandos, the husband, an English officer of family and good prospects, was on his part no less offended at being so undervalued, and in disgust carried his bride into Warwickshire, declaring his determination never to hold any communication or intercourse with her relations. Thus it happened, when the old gentleman died, that the two spinsters succeeded to the house and heritage,—of course there was no money; but the estate was entailed, and Mrs Chandos, as the first born, was the heiress. Her sisters, however, never deemed it expedient to make any inquiry respecting her; at the same time, they held and gathered as if they hourly expected she would revisit them as an avenger. This apprehension was accepted by their consciences for the enjoyment they derived from the indulgence of their natural avarice.

When they had been some four or five years in possession, a rumour reached the neighbourhood that Captain Chandos had succeeded to the title and estates of his uncle, a baronet; and Mrs Soorocks being one of the first who chanced to hear the news, with all the christian eagerness for which she was so justly celebrated, lost no time in hastening to congratulate the sisters on the accession of dignity, which had come to their family by that marriage, which they with their father had so expediently reviled.

After relating what she had heard, she added, in her most soothing manner: "The only thing, Miss Shoosie—the only thing that I'm grieved for, is the thought of what will become of you and Miss Girzie in your auld days."

"Auld days!" exclaimed Miss Girzie.

"Deed, Miss Girzie," resumed the sympathizing visitor, "it's a vera melancholious thing; for, as ye are baith never likely to be married, it will come to pass in the course of nature, that ye'll belyve be at a time o' life when ye can neither work nor want; and no doubt Sir Rupert

38

and his Leddy will call on you to count and reckon with them for every farthing ye hae gotten o' theirs. Nothing less can be expected from their hands, after the way they were driven, in a sense, from home and hall, by your father—I hope it wasna true, though the fact has been so said, that ye were art and part in that unpardonable iniquity and crying sin against family affection. But for all that, as the English are well known to be a people of a turn o' mind for generosity, I would be none surprised to hear that the Baronet intends to be merciful —surely, indeed, he'll never be so extortionate as to make you pay merchant's interest at the rate of five per cent, when it is well known ye have been getting no more than four from the bank; and as for the wadset o' your heritable bond on the lands of Auldbiggings, there will be room to show you great leniency, for I am creditably informed that if the estate were brought to sale the morn, it wouldna pay thirteen shillings and four pence in the pound."

But notwithstanding these prophetic anticipations, the spinsters were not molested. It could not, however, be altogether said they were allowed unquestioned possession, for Mrs Soorocks never saw them, either at church or in her visitations, without obliging them to endure the kindest inquiries concerning Sir Rupert and Lady Chandos.

One morning she called on them at rather an unusual early hour with a newspaper in her hand, and a condoling spirit, most amiably expressive in the sad composure of a countenance evidently dressed for an occasion of great solemnity.

"I'm in a fear, leddies," said she, "that the papers hae gotten doleful news this day for you—Heh, sirs! but life is a most uncertain possession, and so is all wordly substance. But maybe it's no just so dreadful as is herein set forth; but if it should be the worst, you and Miss Girzie, Miss Shoosie, are no destitute of a religious support; and it never could be said that the Baronet was a kind brother, though, for that matter, it must be alloo't no love was lost between you; nevertheless, decency will cause you to make an outlay for mournings, and considering the use ye have had of his money, ye oughtna grudge it."

"And what's this Job's comforting ye hae brought us the day?" said Miss Girzie, somewhat tartly; but Mrs Soorocks, without answering her pungent interrogation, gave the newspaper to Miss Shoosie, saying—

"Ye'll find the accidence in the second claw of the third page; see if ye think it's your gude-brother that has broken his neck."

She then addressed Miss Girzie.

"And if it should be your gude-brother, Miss Girzie, really ye have much cause for thanksgiving, for the papers say he has left a power of money, over and forbye his great estates; and all goes to his only surviving child and daughter, Clara,' ceps a jointure of three thousand pounds to his disconsolate leddy—My word, your sister has had her ain luck in this world! Little did either o' you think, in the days o' your worthy father's austerity, that a three thousand jointure would blithen her widowhood. But I doubt, Miss Girzie, ye'll no can expec her to domicile with the like of you, now when she's come to such a kingdom."

Miss Shoosie having in the meantime read the paragraph, handed the paper to her sister, as she said—

"Really, sister, it's very like the death of a baronet; but I see no legality that he was our sister's."

"What ye observe," interposed Mrs Soorocks, "is no without sense, Miss Shoosie; and surely, if ye're treated by Lady Chandos just with a contempt, it's no to be thought that ye'll put more hypocrisy on your backs than ye hae in your bosoms. But, leddies, leddies, I see a jeopardie gathering over you. Miss Claurissie, your niece, she'll have doers; and though her mother, and her father, that the Lord has taken to himsel, scornt to molest you in this poor heritage o' Barenbraes, the doers will be constrained by law to do their duty as executioners—depend upon't, they will demand a restoration to the uttermost farthing. Maybe, and it's no unpossible, the doers may have heard of your narrow contracted ways, and may think the money cannot be in closer hands; but for all that, be none surprised if they come upon you like a judgment. But even should they no disturb you, as maybe Sir Rupert may in his will have so ordered it, to show how little he regarded the beggarly inheritance of your family, ye yet daurna wile away ae plack, the which is a sore misfortune, for I doubt not, considering how light the beggar's pock returns from your gates, that both o' you have a kind intention to give the parish a mortification. But come what may, put oil in your lamps, and be awake and ready, for it will fare ill with you if ye are found not only helpless old maids, but foolish virgins, when the shouts of the bridegroom are heard—I mean, when your niece comes to be married; for it's very probable that she'll be the prey o' a spendthrift; and if such is the Lord's pleasure, think what will become of you then!"

Such for many years had been the circumstances and situation of the maiden sisters of Barenbraes: still they were unmolested by any inquiry from England, and still, as often as the various vocations of her neighbourliness permitted, they were as kindly reminded by Mrs Soorocks of the audit to which they were liable to be so suddenly summoned. Her idea, however, of counselling the Laird to pay his addresses to one of them, as an expedient to avert the consequences of his impending misfortunes, was not without a sufficient show of plausibility, although it might really seem to be only calculated to furnish herself with additional causes for the afflicting sympathy she took in their destinies, and to augment the pungency of her condolence.

At this period more than thirty years had elapsed since the elopement of Lady Chandos, and still no intimation had been received, in any shape or form, tending to verify the predictions of Mrs Soorocks; it was therefore not altogether improbable, that the martyrs of her anxiety might be permitted the quiet enjoyment of their possessions, at least so it appeared to me at the time; and accordingly, having wished her all manner of success in her undertaking, I pursued my own course towards the Manse, while she posted on to Auldbiggings.

CHAPTER X

Dr Lounlans was one of those modern ornaments of the Scottish Church, by whom her dignity, as shown in the conduct and intelligence of her ministers, is maintained as venerable in public opinion, as it was even when the covenanted nation, for the sake of their apostolic bravery and excellence, broke the iron arm both of the Roman and of the Episcopal Pharaoh.[1] He was still a young man, being only in his thirty-third year; but patient study, and the gift of a discerning spirit, had enriched him with a wisdom almost equal in value to the precepts and knowledge of experience.

In his person, he affected somewhat more of attention to appearance than is commonly observable in the habits of country pastors, the effect of having had the good fortune to spend several years as a tutor in a noble family, distinguished for their strict observance of those courtesies and etiquettes which characterised the aristocracy of the past age. His great superiority, however, consisted chiefly in the power of his eloquence, and the serene and graceful benignity of his manners, in which the calmness of philosophy and the meekness of piety were happily blended with the self-possession of worldly affability.

He had at this time been only eighteen months in the parish, and although the Manse, under his superintendance, had received many embellishments, yet traces of the ruder taste of his predecessor were still evident in the house, the offices, and the garden. Mr Firlot's belonged indeed to another age and generation—he was one of those theological worthies who divided their sermons into fifteen heads, and planted in the same flower-bed cauliflowers and carnations. The pulpit became paralytic under his emphatic logomachies; and docks and nettles grew as rankly in all his borders, as epithets unpleasant to ears polite flourished in the mazes of his doxology. The docks and nettles, under the auspices of his more refined successor, had now given place to roses and lilies. The pulpit was repaired, and the desk thereof beautified with a new covering; the weedy pathway to the Manse door was trimmed into a gravelled sweep edged with box, and alternate

[1] *broke . . . the Roman and . . . the Episcopal Pharoah*: the reference is to the stand of the Scottish church at the times of the Reformation and the Covenant.

tassels of red and white daisies, interspersed with flowers of rarer name and richer blossom, adorned the bed within.

On entering the house, I was shown into the parlour, and obliged to wait some time before the reverend young Doctor made his appearance.

I have always thought that the sitting-room of a gentleman afforded no equivocal index to his character, and certainly the parlour of Dr Lounlans tended to confirm me in this notion. It was in all respects well-ordered—everything was suitable, but a degree of taste pervaded alike the distribution and the style of the furniture, producing something like fashionable elegance on the whole, notwithstanding the general Presbyterian simplicity of the details.

I observed some indication of preparation for a journey—a portmanteau with the key in the lock stood on one of the chairs, and near it on another, lay several articles of apparel, with a pocket Bible in two volumes, very handsomely bound in purple morocco, and apparently quite new; indeed the paper, in which it would seem the volumes had been wrapped, lay on the floor.

When the Doctor came into the room, I could not but apologize for having intruded upon him; for although dressed with his habitual neatness, his complexion was flushed, and he had evidently been interrupted in some exertion of strength and labour.

"I am on the eve of going for some time from home," said he; "and the fatigue of packing obliged me to strip to the work."

Curiosity is the sin which most easily besets me, and this intimation of a journey, a journey, too, for which such packing and preparation were requisite, produced the natural consequence.

"You are, then, to be absent for some considerable time?" replied I.

"About three weeks, not longer."

"You do not, I hope, go soon?"

"This evening, that I may be in time for the earliest steam-boats from Greenock, in order to overtake the mail at Glasgow, in which I have secured a place."

"But you might as well stop till the morning, for the Edinburgh mail will be gone before you can possibly arrive at Glasgow by the steam-boats."

"It is the London mail in which my place is secured."

"You surprise me—No one has heard of your intention of going to London."

The Doctor smiled, and replied, a little, as I felt it, drily—he doubtless intended that it should be so felt,—

43

"Nor am I going so far as London;" he then added with his accustomed ease, "My journey is to Warwickshire, and I only take the mail to Carlisle."

To Warwickshire, thought I: What can he have to do in Warwickshire? It is very extraordinary that a Minister of the Kirk of Scotland should be going to Warwickshire. In a word, I was constrained to reply—

"I hope your journey, Doctor, is to bring home the only piece of furniture the Manse seems to want?"

He blushed a little and said, "You are not far wrong; the object of my journey is indeed to bring home a wife; but whether she will become a fixture in this house, is not yet determined."

"I regret to hear you say so: I had hoped you were among us for life.—I have not heard of your call. Is it to Glasgow or Edinburgh? Dr Chalmers is removed to St Andrews,[2] and a new church is building in Edinburgh."

"If there be any call in my removal from this parish, I fear it may not be ascribed to the wonted inspiration which governs, as it is said, the translations of my brethren."

My curiosity was repressed by the cold propriety with which this was accentuated, and bethinking that the object of my visit was not to pry into the movements of the Doctor, but to procure his mediation with the Nabob, in behalf of our defenceless neighbour, the Laird—I accordingly said,—

"Dr Lounlans, I ask your pardon for the liberty I have taken; but in truth there is reason to lament your absence at this particular time, for your assistance is much wanted in a case that requires a charitable heart and a persuasive tongue, both of which you eminently possess: Mr Mailings has fallen into some difficulties with Mr Rupees."

"I have heard," replied the Doctor, "something of it; he has incurred debts to him, and to a large amount."

"Even so; and the Nabob, as he is called, threatens to foreclose the mortgage."

"In what way can I serve the old man?"

This was said with a peculiar look, as if there was a movement of some reluctant feeling awakened in his memory.

[2] *Dr Chalmers is removed to St Andrews*: Thos. Chalmers (1780–1847), minister of the Tron Church at Glasgow till 1823, when he became Professor of Moral Philosophy at St. Andrews. One of the narrator's many specific indications of a 'contemporary' setting.

"By representing to Mr Rupees," said I, "the harshness of the proceedings in which he has embarked, and in what manner the effects will injure his own reputation amongst us. Without giving the poor Laird the slightest notice of his intentions, he is already surveying and valuing the estate."

"Indeed, indeed," replied the Doctor, "that is severe; almost as much so, to one so old and helpless, as it is to turn the widow and the fatherless out of doors. I am grieved to hear of Mr Mailings' misfortune, but my business does not admit of postponement. Did he request you to ask my interference?"

"I will be plain: he did not. I have heard something of the reason of his reluctance, but I am assured, from your character, that you will delight in returning good for evil."

"I cannot pay his debts," said the Doctor, after a short pause, "and Mr Rupees is not a man who will be persuaded to relent from his purpose by any other than the golden argument."

"Could you, however, try? He has but of late come among us, and is evidently ambitious of influence; you might represent to him the aversion which such indecent haste must universally provoke. He may yield to shame what he would refuse to virtue."

"Does the matter so press, that it may not stand over till my return?"

"So special a question, Doctor, I cannot answer; I am not acquainted with the actual state of the poor old gentleman's circumstances. It is only notorious that he is in the power of his creditors, and that the Nabob shows no disposition to mitigate the severity which the law perhaps enables him to inflict."

The Doctor appeared to be somewhat embarrassed; he looked upon the floor; he felt if his neckcloth was in proper order; he bit his left thumb, and gathered his brows into a knot, which indicated the predominancy of the earthy portion of his nature in the oscillations of his religion, his reason, and his heart.

I looked at him steadily,—but his eye was downcast, not shunning the inquisition of mine, but with that sort of fixedness which the outward organ assumes when the spirit looks inward. For some short space of time, it might be as long as it would take one to count a dozen, he remained thoughtful and austere. He then began to move his foot gently, and he glanced his eye aside towards me. There was sternness in the first glance, in the second the lustre of manly generosity, which in the third was dimmed with a christian's tear, and he covered his face with his hands, as he said with emotion,—"How true hath been

45

my mother's prophecy! The cruel, selfish, arrogant man, whose all of worth lay in the earth and turf of his inheritance, has—I forget myself, no; he has not yet supplicated the help of those in whose beggary he so exulted."

After a brief pause, and having wiped his eyes and forehead, he turned round to me and said, with a lighter tone,—

"I will postpone my journey for another day, and take a pledge in doing so from good fortune to provide me with a seat in the next mail. But I fear you overrate my influence with Mr Rupees—nevertheless, the task is one which I feel may not be omitted, and I will do my best endeavour to persuade him to pursue a course of mercy. There have been things, sir, which make this duty one hard to be undertaken; but, thank God, the sense of what my character as a minister of the Gospel requires, is livelier in motive, than the resentful remembrance of early affliction."

It was accordingly agreed that he should visit Mr Rupees in the morning, and I soon after took my leave.

CHAPTER XI

After quitting the Manse, I returned towards the path by which I had crossed the fields in the morning. This course led me to pass the gate of Auldbiggings, on approaching which, I observed Jock sitting on one of the globes, which, some time during the last century, had surmounted the pillars of the gateway. He was busily employed in feeding a young hawk, which he held compressed between his left arm and his bosom.

At first I resolved to go by without speaking, my thoughts being engrossed with the retribution to which Dr Lounlans had alluded, but Jock himself, forgetful entirely of the ceremony which he endeavoured to practise when I met him on the Whinny Knowes, without rising or even suspending his occupation, looked askance from under the brim of his hat, and bade me come to him. There was something in this over affectation of negligence which convinced me he was sitting at the gate not altogether at that time by accident, and I had indeed some reason to suspect that he had placed himself there on purpose to intercept me on my return home; for presently he began to sift me with a curious sinister subtlety peculiar to himself.

"This is fine weather for a sober dauner," said he, as I went up to him. "And whare will ye walk in a path o' mair pleasantness, than the road atween your house and the Place; no that I would misliken the way to the Manse, now and then, especially in the fall of the year, when the yellow leaf tells of our latter end, and the wind howls in the tree, like a burgher minister hallylooying about salvation."

"Upon my word, John, you spiritualize a walk to the Manse as ingeniously as the Doctor himself could do."

"Ah, isna Dr Lounlans a capital preacher?—isna he a great gun?[1] He's the very Mons Meg o' the presbytery."

"And yet, John, I understand that the Laird has no particular esteem for the Doctor."

"Gentlemen are nae great judges o' preaching," said Jock; "it wouldna hae been fair o' Providence to hae allowt them both the

---

[1] *a great gun . . . the very Mons Meg*: Mons Meg, a large cannon in Edinburgh Castle.

blessings o' religion and the good things o' this world; and so the Laird being a true gentleman, by birth and breeding, is by course o' nature no a crowder o' kirks."

"But I should have expected that such a faithful servant as you are, John, would have been of the same way of thinking as your master."

"In temporalities, in temporalities—I'm a passive obedient; but in the controversy with the auld tyrant that is called Diabolus, a name which the weighty Doctor Drystoor says may be rendered into English by the word Belzebub, my soul is as a Cameronian,[2] free upon the mountains, crying Ha, ha, to the armed men. But, sir, though I will allow that Dr Lounlans is in the poopit a bright and shining light, yet I hae my doots whether the mere man o' his nature hath undergone a right regeneration."

"Indeed! You do not call his piety in question?"

"No; but I dislike his pride. He has noo been the placed minister and present incumbent of our parish mair than a year and a half, and he has never paid his respeks at Auldbiggings. I'm sure if I were the Laird, I would ne'er do him the homage o' entering his kirk door—no, not even on a king's fast."

"John, there must be some reason for an exception so singular to the usual pastoral attentions which Dr Lounlans pays to all his parishioners. I have heard something o' the cause."

"Nae doot of that, for I see you are frae the Manse, and I'se warrant was treated there baith wi' toddy and jocosity, on account of our peradventure wi' John Angle's keeking wheels. It would be mother's milk to the Doctor—weel kens he, that there's no a claw the fifteen lords can put forth, the whilk Caption will leave unhandled to rive the flesh frae the Laird's banes. I'm speaking o' the Doctor in his capacity o' a mere man."

"Then, John, let me tell you, you are very much mistaken. Dr Lounlans feels for the situation of your master as a gentleman and a Christian ought to do."

"As a Christian—as a Christian he may—But will he pacify the Nabob?"

It was plain from this incidental expression, that the cunning creature had been informed by his master of the object of my visit to the Manse, and that notwithstanding the repugnance shown by the old gentleman

<hr />

[2] *Cameronian*: James Cameron (d. 1680), covenanter and field preacher—hence 'free upon the mountains'. Galt uses 'Cameronian' and 'covenanter' interchangeably.

at the idea of being obliged to the Doctor, he was yet anxious to obtain his mediation. It may be in supposing such meanness I do him wrong, but that his servant had no scruples on the subject, was quite manifest; for in reply to my assurances that the Doctor was not only distressed by what had taken place, but had undertaken to interpose with Mr Rupees to avert litigation, and to suspend this annoying survey of the estate, which I the more particularly explained, in order that it might be reported to the Laird, he said—

"It would hae been an unco thing had he refus't it, for he has baith the spiritual motives of Christian duty and the carnal spite of upstart pride to egg him on;—but whether it be the minister or the mere man that leads captive captivity—I'll sing wi' thankfulness,

> Behold how good[3] a thing it is,
> And how becoming well,
> Together such as children are,
> In unity to dwell."

"But, John," said I, "what is the true cause of the animosity between the Laird and the Doctor? I cannot think that the rouping out of Mrs Lounlans, though a very harsh proceeding, could have occasioned feelings of such deep and durable resentment. There must have been some other cause."

"Cause, cause—there was nae cause at a'—If courting a young widow by lawful means be a cause, that was the cause—Ye see, the short and the lang o't is this, as no young gentleman's education can be properly finished till he has broken in on the ten commandments, the Laird, after the burial of John Lounlans, threw a sheep's e'e at the bonnie widow, as she was called, and thought to win her love by course o' law, for her gudeman died deep in his debt. But whereas is an ill-farr'd beginning to a billydoo—so ye see, Mrs Lounlans, instead o' being won to amorous delights by multiplepoinding,[4] grew demented, and taking the doctor minister, who was then a three-year auld bairn and orphan by the hand, she stood in the kirk-stile—the better day the better deed—it was on a Sabbath—and there she made sic a preaching and paternoster about a defenceless widow and fatherless babies, that when our Laird was seen coming to the kirk, soberly and decently, linking wi' his leddy mother, the weans in the crowd set up a shout—

[3] *Behold how good* . . . : No. 133 *Scottish Metrical Psalms.*

[4] *multiplepoinding*: (Scots law) court action which requires several claimants to unite. But here used simply as 'legal jargon'.

and he was torn frae her side, and harlt through mire and midden dub, to the great profanation of the Lord's-day, and the imminent danger of his precious life. For mair than a month he was thought beyont the power o' a graduwa, and his leddy mother, before the year was done, diet o' the tympathy or a broken heart. But how the Doctor should hate our Laird for that hobbleshaw, I ne'er could understand, for the Laird was the ill-used man."

Before I had time to make any comment on this affair, we were joined by the indefatigable Mrs Soorocks, returning from the Place. She did not appear, by the aspect of her countenance, to have been so successful in her voluntary mission as I had been in mine; but I could nevertheless discover, that she had not altogether failed, and that she had something to tell; for immediately on coming up, she took me by the arm and was leading me away, when she happened to observe the work in which Jock was employed.

"Goodness me!" she exclaimed, pausing and looking back at him, "no wonder poor feckless Auldbiggings is brought to a morsel—sic servants as he has! As I hae my een, the wasterfu' creature's feeding the bird wi' minched collops—worms are ower gude for't—and he's cramming them down its throat wi' his finger! For shame, ye cruel ne'erdoweel—ye'll choke the puir beast."

What answer Mrs Soorocks got for her meddling, it may not be fitting to place upon immortal record; but she observed, when she had recovered her complexion and countenance, as we were moving away, that Jock was a real curiosity, "He's just what Solomon would hae been wi' a want, for his proverbs and parables are most extraordinar!"

CHAPTER XII

Mrs Soorocks' road homeward lying aside from the path across the fields, I was obliged in civility to accompany her along the highway, and to forego my intention of taking the more sequestered course, not that she probably would have scrupled to have gone with me in any direction I might have proposed, but the public road was the shortest way to her residence. When the tasks of politeness are not agreeable, it is judicious to abridge their duration—a philosophical maxim worthy of particular attention, whenever you undertake to see an afflicting old lady safely home.

When we had passed some twenty paces or so from the entrance to the avenue of Auldbiggings, my companion began to repeat the result of her mission, by complaining of the familiarity with which the Laird allowed himself to be treated by his man.

"When I went into the room, there was the two," said she, "holding a controversy about your mediation wi' Dr Lounlans, and Jock was argle bargling wi' his master, like one having authority over him, the which to see and to hear was, to say the least o't, a most seditious example to the natural audacity of servants. It's true, that when Jock saw me he drew in his horns, for the creature's no without a sense o' discretion in its ain way, and left the chamber; but it's plain to me that yon is an ill-rulit household, and were it no a case of needcessity and mercy, I dinna think I ought to hae the conscience to advise the leddies o' Barenbraes to hae onything to say till't."

"Then you have made some progress with the Laird?"

"I hae made an incession, but no to a great length; for what do you think is the auld fool's objection? He's in a doot if either o' the leddies be likely to bring him a posterity."

"A very grave and serious objection indeed; considering the motive by which you have been so kindly actuated, it could not but surprise you."

"Surprise! na, I was confounded, and said to him, 'Mr Mailings,' quo' I, 'my purpose o' marriage for you, at your time o' life, and in your straitened circumstances, ought to hae something more rational in view than the thoughts of a posterity. But Miss Shoosie's no past

51

the power o' a miracle even in that respeck; for Sarah ye ken was fourscore before she had wee Isaac, and the twa-and-fifty mystery o' the Douglas Cause,[1] should teach you to hae some faith in the ability of Miss Girzie, who, to my certain knowledge, was only out of her forties last Januar, for I saw their genealogy in their big Bible. It was lying on the table when I called at Barenbraes on Sabbath, and neither o' the leddies being in the room, I just happened to observe that twa leaves at the beginning were pinned thegither, nae doot to hide some few o' the family secrets. Gude forgie me, I couldna but tak out the prin, and you may depend upon it, that Miss Girzie was just nine-and-forty last Januar. But I couldna advise him to hae onything to say to Miss Girzie, and so I told him."

"What do you mean? I have never heard of aught to her prejudice—I have always indeed understood that she was the most amiable of the two."

"Nae great sang in her praise: but amiable here or amiable there, is no a thing to be thocht o', for it's no a marriage o' felicity that we're to speed, but a prudent marriage; and would it no be the height o' imprudence for a man to lay hands on the wally draig when he has it in his power to catch a better bird?"

"I do not exactly understand you, Mrs Soorocks, for if there is any superiority possessed by the one sister over the other, you allow that Miss Girzie has it."

"I alloo of no such thing—and were the Laird to marry her, what's to prevent some other needfu' gentleman (and when were they plentier?) frae making up to Miss Shoosie—she is the old sister, ye forget that—wouldna deil-be-lickit be the portion o' the younger couple?—No, no, if Auldbiggings is to marry any o' them, it shall be Miss Shoosie. It would be a tempting o' Providence if he did otherwise."

"But, my dear madam, are you not proceeding a little too fast, in thus disposing of the leddies without consulting them—should you not ascertain how far either of them may be inclined to encourage the Laird's addresses?"

"What can it signify to consult them, if it be ordained that the marriage is to take place? But if I hadna seen the auld idiot so set upon a posterity, it was my intent and purpose to have gone ower to Baren-

[1] *Douglas Cause*: xviiith century lawsuit between Archibald Douglas (first Baron Douglas) and the Duke of Hamilton, settled 1769 by House of Lords on appeal from the court of session.

braes the morn's morning, and given Miss Shoosie an inkling of what was in store for her. But the matter's no ripe enough yet for that."

"The growth, however, has been abundantly rapid; and I am sure, Mrs Soorocks, whatever may be the upshot, that the whole business hitherto does equal credit to your zeal and intrepidity."

"It is our duty," replied the worthy lady, seriously, "to help ane anither in this howling wilderness; and noo may I speer what speed ye hae come wi' Doctor Lounlans? for Auldbiggings told me that he had debarred you from going near him, the which, of course, could only serve to make you the mair in earnest wi' the wark. I'm shure a debarring would hae done so to me, though ye're no maybe the fittest person that might hae undertaken it. But weakly agents aften thrive in the management of great affairs, and if ye hae succeeded with the Doctor, I hope ye'll be sensible of the help that must have been with you—not that your task was either a hard or a heavy ane, for the Doctor is a past ordinar young man—but there's a way of conciliation very requisite on such occasions. Howsomever, no doot ye did your best—and I hope the Doctor has consented to pacify the Nabob."

"Whether he may be able to succeed, is perhaps doubtful," said I.

"And if he should fail," cried the lady, interrupting me; "I'll then try what I can do mysel; in the meantime, it's a comfort to think he has promised, for really the circumstance o' poor Auldbiggings requires a helping hand;—weel indeed may I call him poor, for it's my opinion he hasna ae bawbee left to rub upon anither."

"But the promise," said I, "was given under circumstances which makes it doubly valuable. You are probably aware, though I had not heard of it before, that the Doctor is on the eve of marriage?"

"Going to be married, and none of his parish ever to have heard a word about it! I think it's a very clandestine-like thing o' him—and whare is he going, and wha's he to marry? She canna be a woman o' a solid principle, to be woo'd and won, as it were, under the clouds o' the night."

"The Doctor and the lady, madam, I am persuaded, have been long acquainted."

"I dinna doot that, and intimately too," replied Mrs Soorocks, insinuatingly. "But whatna corner o' the earth is he bringing her frae? We'll a' be scrupulous about her till we ken what she is."

"I do not question the prudence of the parish in that respect; but if I understand him right, she resides in Warwickshire."

"In Warwickshire!—that's a heathenish part o' England. And so

53

Madam o' the Manse to be, is an Englishwoman, and of course o' a light morality, especially for a minister's wife.—She'll be a calamity to the neighbourhood, for it will be seen that she'll bring English servant lasses among us to make apple-pies and wash the door-steps on the Lord's-day, as I am creditably told a' the English do. But did ye say Warwickshire? Lady Chandos and her dochter, the heiress by right o' Barenbraes—they live in Warwickshire; oughtna we to get her sisters, the leddies, to open a correspondence wi' her concerning the minister's prelatical[2] bride—for she canna be otherwise than o' the delusion o' the English liturgy and prelacy; and if neither o' them will write, I'll write mysel, for it's a duty incumbent on us all to search into the hiddenness of this ministerial mystery. Warwickshire! I canna away wi't —the very sound o't flew through the open o' my head like a vapour— weel indeed may I say that it's a mystery, for noo when I think o't, the vera first time that Doctor Lounlans drank his tea wi' me—it was the afternoon o' the third day after his placing—he speer't in a most particular manner about the leddies of Barenbraes, and how it came to pass that they keepit no intercourse by correspondence wi' Lady Chandos. But is't no wonderfu' that I never thought, then nor since syne, o' speering at him about what he ken't o' her leddyship?—surely I hae been bewitched, and mine eyes blinded with glamour, for I sat listening to him like an innocent lamb hearkening to the shepherd's whistle. But I hae always thought there was a providence in that marriage of Lady Chandos, for she was an excellent and sweet lassie, and now it has come to pass that she may be a mean to guard her native land, and her heritage too, against the consequence of the manifest indiscretion o' Dr Lounlans' never-to-be-heard-tell-o' connexion."

During the harangue, I endeavoured several times to arrest the progress of the good lady's suspicion and the growth of her conviction, that the Doctor's marriage must be in some way derogatory to his character and pestilent to his parish, but it was all in vain; my arguments only rivetted her opinion more and more, until wearied with the controversy I bade her adieu, ungallantly leaving her to find the path to Barenbraes alone, whither she determined forthwith to proceed, "before it might be too late."

[2] *prelatical*: i.e. Anglican in religion.

CHAPTER XIII

Although I did not expect to see Dr Lounlans until after his interview with the Nabob, nor was under any apprehension of a visitatian from Mrs Soorocks, and had predetermined not to call on the Laird without being able to carry with me some consolatory tidings, I yet rose an hour earlier than usual next morning, and felt very much as those feel who have many purposes to perform.

This particular activity was ingeniously accounted for by Mr Tansie, the parish schoolmaster, who in passing by happened to observe me at breakfast an hour before my accustomed time; and the parlour window being open that I might enjoy the fragrance of the sweetbriar which grows beneath it, he came forward and complimented me on the good health which such solacious participation in the influences of the season, as he called it, assuredly indicated.

The worthy dominie was generally known among us as the philo, a title bestowed on him by one of his own pupils, and which, not inaptly, described about as much of the philosophical character as he really possessed.—I was no stranger to his peculiar notions, for we have often had many arguments together, and in reply to his observation on the source of my enjoyment of a spring morning, I said, after telling him something of what was impending over the Laird, "But whether the impulses of activity by which I am so unwontedly stirred, arise from any benevolent desire to lighten the misfortunes of the old gentleman, or come from the spirit of the vernal season, it would not be easy to determine."

"Not at all," said he, "they are emanations of the same genial power, which prompteth unvocable as well as intelligent nature to bloom and rejoice in the spring. It were easier indeed to explain the motives of the breast, by considering the signs of the zodiac under which each propelleth action, than by the help and means of metaphysical philosophy.—Are not all things around us luxuriating in the blandishments of the spring? the buds are expanding, the trees are holding out their blossomy hands to welcome the coming on of abundance, juvenility is leaping forth with a bound and a cheer—and there is gladness and singing, and the sound of a great joy throughout the whole earth; universal nature overflows with kindness, and therefore the heart of man is melted to charity and love. The germinative influences of Taurus and Gemini are now mingled, and good deeds and pleasant doings among men have their seasonable signs in the green fields, the musical bowers, and the promises of the rising corn."

"You explain to me, Mr Tansie, what I never before rightly understood; namely, why primroses and public dinners come into season together, and how it happened that lamb and eleemosynary subscriptions at the same time adorn the tavern altars of charity; but now I see how it is, they are all the progeny of the same solar instincts."

"Can you doubt it? why in summer are we less active?—Do not the feelings of the heart then like the brooks run low and small?—no fruit tempteth the hand to gather—the heat is too great for hard labour, and the bosom wills to no action; while we lighten the burden of our own raiment, who, beneath the dazzle of a burning noon, would think for merciful pity of clothing the nude and those who are needful of drapery?"

"But how does it come to pass in autumn, Mr Tansie, when Nature may be said to stand invitingly by the way side, holding out her apron filled with all manner of good things, that man is then of a churlish humour, and delights in the destruction of innocent life?"

"It is indeed," replied the dominie, "a marvellous contrariety: but the sign of the scrupulous balance is a token of the disposition of the genius of the season—were we not moved by its avaricious influence, should we so toil to fill the garnels of gregarious winter?"

"Then, according to your doctrine, Mr Tansie, it must be fortunate for the Laird that his rupture with the Nabob has not happened under the aspect of Libra, and there may be some chance at this genial season of Dr Lounlans succeeding in his mediation?"

"Therein, sir, you but show how slightly you have examined the abysms of that true astrology. Though the time serves, and all humane sympathies are at present disposed to cherish and to give confidence, yet are there things on which the sweet influences of the spring shed bale and woe, for the energy which it awakeneth on the doddard and the old, is as a vigour put forth in age and infirmity, causing weakness while it seemeth to strengthen. Mr Mailings is of those whose berth and office have become as it were rubbish in the highway of events. The day of the removal cannot be afar off—"

In this crisis of our conversation, and while Mr Tansie was thus expounding his philosophy, leaning over the sweetbriar with his arms resting on the sill of the window, on which he had spread his handkerchief to save the sleeves of his coat, I saw Mrs Soorocks coming across the fields. That some special cause had moved her to be abroad so early admitted of no doubt,—but whether her visit should relate to the minister's marriage, or to the misfortunes of our neighbour, it gave me pleasure at the moment, for the imagination of the ingenious dominie was mounted in its cloudy car, and so mending its speed, that I began to feel a growing inclination to follow in the misty voyage, notwithstanding my long-determined resolution never to engage in any sort of ratiocination in the forenoon,—a space of the day, however well calculated for special pleading, particularly unsuitable for theoretical disquisition, as every lawyer and legislator must have often remarked.

On hearing the indefatigable lady's steps, the dominie rose from his inclined position, and gathering up his handkerchief from the sill of the window, replaced it in his pocket; but she had more serious business in hand than afforded time for any sort of talk with him. She came straight up to the door, and announced herself by knock and ring, without appearing to notice him, though he stood with his hat off, and was ready to do her all proper homage.

While the servant admitted her, the dominie turned round again to the window, and said to me, before there was time to show her into the parlour,—

"She hath had an incubus;" and placing his hat somewhat tartly—doubtless displeased that she should have passed him unnoticed—he immediately retired, evidently piqued at being so slightly considered, forgetting entirely the immeasurable difference of rank between the relict of a laird of a house with a single lum, herself the co-heiress of, what Gilbert Stuart[1] calls, the harvest of half a sheaf, and a modest and learned man, on whose originality and worth the world's negligence had allowed a few cobwebs—the reveries of solitary rumination—to hang with impunity—more to the dishonour of those who observed them, than to the deterioration of the material with which they were connected. I saw the good man's mortification, and, although almost as eager to hear what the lady had to tell as she herself was evidently anxious to communicate, I started abruptly from my chair, and, going hastily to the door, cried out, "Show Mrs Soorocks into the library, and I shall be with her immediately."

[1] *Gilbert Stuart*: xviiith century (d. 1786) historian and writer for periodicals.

"No ceremony wi' me—I'm no a ceremonious woman, as you may well know," was the answer I received, and, in the same moment, brushing past the servant at the door, she came into the room, and, looking me steadily in the face for the space of some four or five seconds, portentously shook her head, and, unrequested, walking to an elbow-chair, seated herself in it emphatically, with a sigh.

I have never felt much alarm from any demonstration of that inordinate dread which Mrs Soorocks, and her numerous kith and kin in the general world, and in our particular environs and vicinity, are in the habit of displaying, on occasions which do not at all concern themselves; but the threefold case of anxiety created by the Laird's misfortunes, the minister's marriage, and the intended co-operation with Providence to raise up a husband for one of the spinsters of Barenbraes, presented a claim to attention which I could not but at once both admit and acknowledge, by inquiring, in the most sympathetic manner, what had happened to discompose her?

CHAPTER XIV

When Mrs Soorocks had fanned herself with her handkerchief, and had some four or five times during the operation puffed her breath with a sough somewhat between the sound of a blast and a sigh, she looked for her pocket-hole, replaced the handkerchief in its proper depositary, then stroking down her petticoat, and settling herself into order, thus began:

"It's a great misfortune to be of a Christian nature, for it makes us sharers in a' the ills that befall our frien's. I'm sure, for my part, had I broken Mr Rupees' head with my own nieve, and crushed Angle the land-surveyor's commodity in the hollow of my hand, I could not hae suffert more anxiety than I do in the way o' sympathy at this present time, on account o' the enormities of the law, which Caption, the ettercap, is mustering, like an host for battle, against our poor auld doited and defenceless neighbour. But a' that is nothing to the vexation I'm obliged to endure frae the contumacity o' yon twa wizzent and gaizent penure pigs o' Barenbraes."

"You have perhaps yourself, madam, to blame a little for that; you need not, I should think, meddle quite so much in their concerns."

"But I cannot help it—it's my duty. I find myself as it were constrained by a sense of grace to do what I do. Far, indeed, it is frae my heart and inclination to scald my lips in other folks' kail,—and why should I? Is there any homage frae the warld as my reward? Let your own hearts answer that. And as for gratitude frae those I sae toil to serve, the huff o' Miss Shoosie Minnigaff is a vera gracious speciment.'

From the tenor of these observations, and particularly from the manner in which they were uttered, I began to divine that the worthy lady had not been altogether so successful in her matrimonial project with the maiden sisters as she had been with Auldbiggings, and I expressed my regret accordingly.

"Deed," replied she, "ye were ne'er farther wrang in your life, great as your errors both in precept and in practise may hae been. But no to mind an ill-speaking world on that head, what would ye think I hae gotten for my pains frae the twa, Hunger and Starvation, as I canna but call them?"

"It is impossible for me to imagine—they are strange creatures; I should be none surprised if they were unreasonable in their expectations as to the jointure which Auldbiggings may be able to afford; poor man, I fear he has nothing in his power."

"Guess again, and, if ye hope to succeed, guess an impossibility."

"Pin money."

"Pin snuffy! They too hae their doubts if the Laird will connive at a right way o' education for their children! Did ye ever hear the like o' that? And wha do you think the objection first came frae? Miss Shoosie —auld Miss Shoosie; the sight o' her wi' a child in her arms would be like a hang-necket heron wi' a lamb in it's neb, or a Kitty Langlegs dan'ling a bumbee;—the thing's an utter incapability o' nature, and so I said to her."

"That explains her ingratitude. I certainly, my dear Mrs Soorocks, cannot approve of throwing cold water on her hopes of a posterity, especially as the only objection which the Laird made to the ladies, was an apprehension of disappointment in that respect."

"Sir, the thing is no to be dooted; but I should tell you her speech o' folly on the occasion. 'To be sure, sister,' said she, speaking to Miss Girzie, when I had broken the ice, 'Mr Mailings is a man o' family; and though in his younger years he did marry below his degree, yet noo that his wife is dead, she can never be a blot in a second marriage. But then he's a most stiff-neckit man in the way of opinion, and I doot, if ever him and me were married, that we would agree about the way o' bringing up our children; for if I were to hae a dochter,' quo' she, 'and wha knows if ever I shall'—I could thole this no longer," exclaimed Mrs Soorocks, "and so, as plainly as I was pleasant, I said, 'Everybody kens weel aneugh, Miss Shoosie, that ye'll never hae a dochter.' And what think you got I for telling her the true even-doun fact?"

"Probably whatever she had in her hand."

"O, ye're a saterical man!—to judicate that leddies would be flinging housholdry at ane anither's heads! But she did far waur. I never beheld such a phantasie. She rose from her chair, her een like as they would hae kindled candles, though her mouth was as mim as a May puddock, and crossing her fingers daintily on her busk, she made me a ceremonious curtsey, like a maid of honour dancing a minaway wi' the lord-chancellor, and said, 'Mrs Soorocks, I thank you.' I was so provoked by her solemnity, that I could na but make an observe on't, saying, 'Hech, sirs, Miss Shoosie, it must be a great while since ye were at a practeesing, for really ye're very stiff in the joints. I hae lang kent ye were auld, but I didna think you were sae aged. I canna, therefore, be surprised at your loss o' temper; for when folks lose their teeth, we needna look for meikle temper amang them; the which causes me to understand what Mr Mailings meant when he said, that between defects and infirmities ye were a woman past bearing. But, Miss Shoosie, no to exasperate you beyond what is needful in the way o' chastisement, ye'll just sit doun in your chair and compose yoursel, for ye'll no mak your plack a bawbee in striving wi' me in satericals, the more especially as, by what I hae seen o' your dispositions this day, I canna marvel at your being rejected o' men—na, but rue wi' a contrite spirit that I should ever hae been so far left to mysel, as to even sic a weak veshel to a gentleman of good account—as they say in the babes in the wood—like that most excellent man, Mr Mailings, who, if he were to lift the like o' you wi' a pair o' tangs, ye might account yourself honoured; and yet I was proposing him for a purpose o' marriage! But, Miss Shoosie, I'll be merciful, and treat you wi' the compashion that is due to a sinful creature'—and then I kittled her curiosity concerning the minister's marriage wi' a leddy in Warwickshire; so ye see she's no a match for me, as I could make her know, feel, and understand, but for the restraining hand o' grace that is upon me."

"On the topic of Dr Lounlans' marriage, Mrs Soorocks,—how did you handle that?"

"Weel may ye speer, and the gude forgie me if I wasna tempted to dunkle the side o' truth—for I said, Leddies, what I hae been saying about the sheep's ee that the Laird would be casting at you, is a matter for deep consideration. Be nane surprist if ye hear o' very extraordinar news frae Warwickshire. I'll no venture to guess what's coming out o' that country; but I hae had a dream and a vision of a fair lady dressed in bridal attire—look you to what blood's in her veins."

"How, Mrs Soorocks! did you say that the Doctor is going to marry their niece?"

"I said nae sic a thing,—and I request that ye'll cleck no scandal wi' me;—but, knowing what I do know, and that's what you yoursel taught me, could I omit a seasonable opportunity for touching them on the part of soreness, in the way of letting them know that riches make to themselves wings and flee away to the uttermost ends of the earth? 'Be none astounded,' said I, 'leddies, if ye look forth some morning from your casements, and behold all your hainings and gatherings, your pinchings, your priggings, your counts and reckonings, fleeing away to Warwickshire, like ravens and crows, and other fowls o' uncanny feather, or maybe the avenger, in the shape of a sound young minister of the Gospel o' peace, coming to herry you out o' house and home.' "

"But, my good madam, how can you reconcile all these inuendoes with that strict regard to truth which you so very properly on most occasions profess?—These unhappy ladies cannot but imagine that Dr Lounlans is going to marry their niece, a circumstance which you have not had from me the slightest reason to imagine."

"Is't a thing impossible?" cried Mrs Soorocks; "answer me that; and if it's no impossible, why may it not be? I'm sure Providence couldna gie a finer moral lesson than by making it come to pass."

"Am I to understand, then, from all this, that there is no great likelihood of Mr Mailings being extricated from his difficulties by marriage with either of the sisters?"

"It's no yet to be looked upon as a case o' desperation, for, handlet wi' discretion, I think the weakness on both sides concerning the education o' their posterity—really the very words would provoke a saint—but, as I was saying, if we can overcome that weakness, a change may be brought about."

"But, my dear madam, is there no other among our friends and neighbours whom you might propose to the Laird? Considering the precarious situation of the ladies of Barenbraes, there is some risk, you know, of his condition being made much worse, should a demand for restitution come upon them. I have been much struck, Mrs Soorocks, with the kind interest which you take in the old gentleman's affairs, might I suggest—"

"Would ye even me to him?" cried the lady, raising her hands and throwing herself back in her chair; "and do you think that I would ever submit to be a sacrifice on the altar o' poverty for a peace-offering to the creditors of Auldbiggings—No: gude be thankit, and my marriage articles, I'm no just sae forlorn. It's vera true that, in the way of neighbourliness, I hae a great regard for Mr Mailings, and that the twa innocent auld damsels are far-off connexions of mine, with whom I hae lived on the best o' terms; but regard's no affection, and connexions are neither flesh nor blood; moreover, there's an unco odds atween doing a service and becoming a slave, as the blithe days that I spent with my dear deceased husband have well instructed me to know; I own we had our differences like other happy couples—for Mr Soorocks had a particular temper—but knowing what I know, it would be a temptation indeed that would bribe me to ware my widowhood on another man, especially one of an ineffectual character, like the helpless bodie that's sae driven to the wall."

At this crisis of our conversation we were interrupted by one of the Nabob's servants, with a note, requesting, in the most urgent manner, to see me. However ill-timed, as Mrs Soorocks said it was, I was yet glad at the message, and indeed feigned more alacrity than I felt in obeying it, and in wishing her good morning.

CHAPTER XV

It was a sunny and a hot, rather than a sultry day, when I approached Nawaubpore, the newly-erected mansion of the Nabob—around which, everything displayed the wealth and taste of the owner.

The lodges at the gate were built in the style of pagodas. It was intended that they should represent the grand Taj or Targe of Agra; but some of those defects inherent in all copies, made them, in many respects, essentially different from their model; the minarets performing the functions of chimneys, and the cupolas those of dove-cots: the gate itself was a closer imitation of the Fakeir-gate of Delhi.

The avenue from this gorgeous Durwaja consisted of two rows of newly-transplanted lime-trees, shorn of their tops and branches, each bound with straw ropes, and propp'd by three-fork'd sticks, to keep them in a perpendicular position, until their truncated roots, as the botanists express it, should have again fastened themselves in the earth. In the park, groups of trees were placed similarly circumstanced, protected from the inroads of the cattle by palisades of split Scotch fir, connected by new rough-sawn rafters of the same material. In the distance, notwithstanding the metamorphoses which the moss had undergone, I recognized my old acquaintances,—the venerable ash-trees, which had surrounded and overshadowed the ancestral cottage of the Burrah Sahib, now serving as a skreen to a riding-house, framed of timber, and tinted with a mixture of tar and ochre into a mullaga-tawny complexion.

The court of offices occupied the fore-ground between the Hippodrome and the Burrah ghur. They were in the purest style of classic architecture. Whether the plan was suggested to the Nabob by that delicate discrimination, and that exquisite feeling of propriety in art, for which Mr Threeper of Athens, his legal adviser, is so justly celebrated, or was procured for him by his maternal relative, a prosperous gentleman, Archibald Thrum, Esq. of Yarns, and manufacturer in Glasgow, from the Palladio of the northern Venice,[1] I have never been able satisfactorily to ascertain; but the pile was worthy alike of this

[1] *northern Venice*: Galt uses this term of Glasgow (with its river and shipping) to match the common use of 'Athens' for Edinburgh.

Venice, and of that Athens, for in looking in at the gate, a copy of the triumphal Arch of Constantine, you beheld the cows tied to Corinthian pillars, looking out of Venetian windows.

The Burrah ghur, or mansion of the Burrah Sahib, was a splendid compilation of whatever has been deemed elegant in antique, curious in Gothic, or gorgeous in Oriental architecture. It was a volume of Elegant Extracts, a bouquet of the art as rich and various as those hospitable hecatombs of the cities on the banks of Clutha, amidst which, according to the veracious descriptions of Dr Peter Morris of Aberystwith,[2] the haggis and blancmange are seen shuddering at each other. There a young artist might have nourished his genius with a greater variety of styles and combinations than the grand tour, with an excursion to Greece and Stamboul, could have supplied. Instead of a knocker or bell, a gong of the Celestial Empire hung in a niche within the verandah, at the sound of which, the folding doors

—"self open'd,
On golden hinges turning."[3]—

On entering the vestibule, a Kidmutgar, who was squatted on his hams in a corner on a mat, rose to receive me; he placed his palms together, touching his forehead three times with his thumbs, bowed to the ground, and then standing upright, pronounced in a voice of homage, "Salaam Sahib."

He was habited in a kind of shirt of blue cloth, with long open sleeves, and bound round the loins with a blue and yellow rope. On his head he wore a turban shaped like a puddock-stool, and trimmed with yellow cloth and gold lace. His wide silk drawers hung down to the ground, and his slippers, embroidered with silver, looked up in the toes, like other vain things in the pride of splendour.

I inquired for his master, and with a second saluation as solemn as the first, he replied, "Hah Sahib," and showed me into a room, one entire end of which was occupied with a picture representing a tiger hunt, in the fore-ground of which, seated on the back of an elephant, I discovered a juvenile likeness of Mr Rupees, and in the back-ground an enormous tiger almost as big as a Kilkenny cat, was returning into the

[2] *Dr Peter Morris of Aberystwith*: the allusion is to J. G. Lockhart's *Peter's Letters to his Kinsfolk*, which Blackwood published in 1819.
[3] *"golden hinges turning"*: *Paradise Lost*, vii, 205. Galt's quotations are always from memory and usually differ from the original.

jungle with a delicate and dandyish officer of the governor's guard in his mouth.

When I had some time admired this historical limning, another Oriental conducted me to the library door, where, taking off his slippers, he ushered me into the presence of the Burrah Sahib. The room was darkened according to the Indian dhustoor, and from the upper-end, by the bubbling of a hookah, I was apprized that there the revelation was to take place.

On approaching the shrine I beheld the Vishnu of Nawaubpore, garmented in a jacket, waistcoat, and trowsers, of white muslin, with nankeen shoes—his head was bald to the crown, but the most was made of what little grey hair remained on his temples by combing it out; that which covered the back of his head was tied in a long slender tapering tail. He lolled in an elbow-chair, his feet supported on the back of another, before which stood his Punkah wallah, cooling his lower regions with a gigantic palm-leaf fan, while the Hookah-burdhar was trimming the seerpoos in the rear.

On hearing me announced, the Nabob started to his feet, and shook me in the most cordial manner by the hand—thanked me for my alacrity in attending his summons, and 'before tiffin,' proposed to conduct me in person through his ghur, modestly intimating that he did not expect me altogether to approve of the prodigality of his tradesmen, at the same time insinuating that, for himself, he was a man of plain habits, and particularly fond of old-fashioned simplicity.

CHAPTER XVI

Having perambulated the magnificent intricacies and chambers of Nawaubpore, praising, of course, to the utmost, all I saw, for which may God forgive me—but this is an age much addicted to hypocrisy, and the purest minds are necessarily tainted by the spirit of the times.

Carving and gilding everywhere appeared in such profusion that no room was left for taste. The furniture was numerous, cumbrous, and excessive, and interspersed with it, above, below, and all around, lay a miscellaneous assemblage of splendid nicknackery, like those relics and remnants of curiosities which remain in the hands of an auctioneer after he has disposed of whatever is valuable or really curious in the executor-ordered sale of a virtuoso's collection. Pictures by such artists as Zoffani[1] covered the walls, purchased, however, at Tulloh's saleroom in Calcutta, at a price which, if told to Mr Peele, would make him chuckle at the bargain he got of the Chapeau Paille[2]—Derbyshire spar vases, plaster busts, French clocks, interestingly ornamental, but deranged in their horal faculties; Dresden china swains and shepherdesses; models, by Hindoo artists, of gates and pagodas; two verd antique pillars on casters in the dining-room, atoned for supporting nothing, by being hollow, and containing within post-cænobitical utensils;[3] feather fans, Pekin Mandarins, Flemish brooms, musical snuff-boxes, large china jars, japanned cabinets, spacious mirrors, and icicled lustres—all so disposed as to produce the utmost quantum of confusion, with the least possible contribution to comfort.

Tiffin was served in the breakfast-room. It consisted of cold meats, hot curries, mullagatawney soup, kabobs, pillaws, and a fowl fried with onions to a cinder, bearing the brave name of country captain;

[1] *Zoffani*: The narrator (and Galt) makes a further display of up-to-date information. Johann Zoffany (d. 1810) was elected R.A. in 1769. He painted mainly in England, but spent some years in India—where the Nabob bought his works . . . at a price. See following note.

[2] *Mr Peele . . . Chapeau Paille*: this famous painting by Rubens cost Sir Robert Peele 3500 guineas. It is now (retitled) in the National Gallery (no. 852). Peele bought it in 1824.

[3] *post-cænobitical utensils*: i.e. chamber-pots. Moir seems to have missed this arch 'vulgarity'.

67

ale (Hodson's of course), claret, genuine from the vaults of Carbonelle, and the far-named Madeira, so fatal to the poor Laird, and which, according to his account, had been sixteen years in wood in the bay of Bengal.

Our conversation in the meantime was various and desultory, so much so that I began to wonder for what purpose my presence had been so urgently requested at Nawaubpore, and for what object I was treated with such distinguished consideration, till I happened to fill myself a glass of Madeira, while partaking of the currie.

"My good friend," said the Nabob, in a tone of alarm, placing his hand on my arm to restrain me, "do you mean to make a suttee of yourself? but I need not be surprised at you doing such a thing, for I have seen a candidate for the Direction, and a successful one too, do the very same thing—Need we wonder at the blunders in the government of India, when we meet with such ignorance of Indian affairs among the ghuddahs of Leadenhall-street?[4] The Paugul was a Cockney banker—do you know he was so absurd as to ask me across the table—it was in the London Tavern—his Majesty's ministers were present—whether the Coolies carried the Dhoolies, or the Dhoolies the Coolies! One of the ministers looked significantly at me, and said that he believed it was a doubtful question; but another, who sat next me, whispered, that if, like the Court of Directors, they got on in any way, it mattered little which was beast and which burden. By the by, it was on the same occasion that the pious member of the Durbah stated, and to me too, the singular progress and great fruits which had blessed the labours of the Missionaries in the East. 'D—n the blessing,' said I—I begged his lordship's pardon for the damn—'they have only taught a dozen or too parish soors to eat beef, and drink as much rum as they can steal.'—'That, however,' said another minister, whom I observed particularly attentive to my remark, 'that, however, is a step in the progress of wants'; and he added, 'having once acquired a desire for beef and rum, their industry will thence be stimulated to obtain these luxuries, and a superior morality will be gradually evolved by the consequent cultivation of industry.'—'The stealing of which you speak, is something like the turbidness of fermentation, a natural and necessary stage in the process of refinement, which will produce wine or vinegar, as the case

[4] *the ghuddahs of Leadenhall Street*: the silly asses of the East India Company. East India House was in Leadenhall Street. 'ghuddah' is one of the many Indian terms used by the Nabob (gādhā—'ass'). Galt shows considerable familiarity with the 'Indianisms' of nabobs. See the *Glossary*.

may be,' replied I; upon which another of them interposed mildly, saying,—'I am quite sure that by the late reduction of the duty on wine, a reduction in the consumption of ardent spirits must supervene, and that the change will be salutary to the best interests of our Indian population.' "

By this time the Nabob had bestowed so much of his tediousness upon me, that I here attempted to break the thread of his discourse; but although I did so with all my wonted address, he was on a subject congenial to the Indian temperament—the sayings and doings of great men—and he would not be interrupted, for without noticing my impatience, which he ought to have done, he continued—

"There was another Peshwa, who had particular views of his own, for what he called the amelioration of Indian society; the principle of his plan was by a transfusion of a portion of the redundant piety of the United Kingdom into what he called the arterial ramifications of Oriental mythology—"

At this crisis one of the servants entered with the customary salaam, and said something in his own language to the Burrah Sahib, who answered him abruptly—"Hemera bhot bhot salaam do doosera kummera recdo bolo;" and turning to me, he added, "Padre Lounlans sent a chit this morning, to say he would call on me about the affairs of that d—d sirdar Paugul the Laird, and I wish to consult you before seeing him. The murderous old decoit and his Junglewallah of a servant, while I was only ascertaining whether or not he had cheated me in the extent of his estate, on which I, like a fool, have advanced twice as much money as I dare say it is worth, charged upon me like a brace of Mahrattas, and with a lump of a lattee smashed my surveyor's theodolite. Mr Caption, my vakeel, is ready to take his oath before a magistrate, (if he has not done it already,) that they were guilty of assault and battery; against the laws of this and every other well-governed realm; inasmuch as, on the 19th of the present month of June, or on some day or night of that month, or on some day or night of the month May preceding, or of July following, they did, with malice aforethought, thump, beat, batter, bruise, smash, break, and otherwise inflict grievous bodily injury on one theodolite—But not to waste our time now on the law of the case, I have no doubt that the Padre is sent to negotiate a treaty. Now, do you think that where a Rajah has an undisputable right to a Zemendary, and the Kilhdar resists his authority in the persons of his army and artillery, (I mean Caption, Angle, and his theodolite,) the Rajah ought not to tuck him up, as was done at Faluari in the business of the Deccan?—By the by, the delay in the payment of the Deccan prize-money is too bad; had my friend old Frank suspected such proceedings, he would have made a drumhead division of the loot. I remember when I was attached to the Residency at Rumbledroog, about thirty years ago, that a detachment under the command of my friend Jack Smith, stormed a hill fort where be found considerable treasure; so he told the paymaster to make out a scale, and all the coined money was first divided, and then the bullion and jewels were weighed and measured out. Jack got two quarts of rings, which were picked off by the drum-boys from the toes of the ladies of the Zenana in the glorious moment of victory; but the d—d lootwallah of a paymaster slyly cribbed a large diamond, which immediately touched him I suppose with the liver complaint, for he soon after gave in his resignation on that pretext, and sailed for Europe. On reaching London, he went immediately into Parliament, and has ever since been presiding at missionary meetings and Bible societies, and be d—d to him!"

At this pause I interposed and reminded the Nabob that Dr Lounlans was waiting.

"True, true," said he, "I had forgotten him; but old stories, and anything like fraud or oppression, make me forget myself, and neglect my own affairs. Had it not been for the warmth and generosity of my feelings in that way when I was at—devil take it, I am at it again— let us go at once and hear what the Padre has got to say."

CHAPTER XVII

The Nabob bustled on before me to the room where Dr Lounlans was waiting, and, leaving me to follow, went forward and received the reverend gentleman with a hearty jocular urbanity.

"Warm weather, Doctor, this," said he; "never felt the heat more oppressive in Bengal, except a day or two during the hot winds, but even there you can keep it out by means of tatties, you know. Here, in Europe, we are still very far behind. Houses are very good for winter and wet weather, not at all adapted for the summer climate; but when I have once got Nawaubpore in proper order, I'll make my own climate, as the Nawaub of Lucknow told Lord Wellesley—I'll have a subterranean parlour for the hot season. But hadn't you better take some sherbet, or a glass of sangaree, after your walk? My aubdaar will cool it for you, with a whole seer of saltpetre: for my ice-house has gone wrong, you know, by the mason leading the drain wash-house through it, like a d—d old fool as he was.—I beg your pardon, Doctor—"

Dr Lounlans had evidently prepared himself for the interview: his manner was dry, cold, and almost repulsive, as he said, "No offence to me," dwelling emphatically on the last word, and adding—

"The business, Mr Rupees, which has induced me to postpone a journey until I could see yourself, is very urgent, and I hope it is convenient to let me proceed with it."

The Nabob was somewhat taken aback at the abruptness of this commencement, but, significantly winking to me, requested the Doctor to be seated; and, throwing himself down on a sofa, he lifted up one of his legs upon it, and said, "I am all attention, Doctor."

Prepared as the young pastor was for his undertaking, this nonchalance somewhat disconcerted him, but he soon recovered his self-possession, and replied,

"When I came into this parish, I understood that Mr Mailings, your neighbour, was one of your most particular friends."

"Well, and what of that?"

"And now I understand," resumed the minister, "that without any fault on his side, but only the misfortune of having borrowed your

71

money, you have instituted proceedings against him of unusual severity."

"Well, and what then?" responded the Nabob, winking at me.

"Such rigour, in such a case," replied the Doctor, "cannot, Mr Rupees, have proceeded from the dictates of your own feelings, but must be the effect of advice, in which your long absence from the usages of your native land has been employed as much to the disparagement of the goodness of your heart, as to the prejudice of the solitary old man, your unfortunate debtor."

The Nabob, putting down his foot, and assuming an erect posture, looked a little more respectfully towards the Doctor, as he said with cordiality—

"I suppose, Doctor, you think that the people of India are less liberal than those of Europe, but they are a d—d sight more so—I beg your pardon, Doctor. For myself, I never pretended to be a philanthropist, but I have often given fifty gold mohurs to an officer's widow, when people of the same rank in Europe would have thought a guinea prodigal. In this very case, did not I lend the old Guddah £3000 at 4 per cent, when consols were at 73, and when I might have had ten in Calcutta from my friend David, bear as he is?"

"Your kindness in that respect, certainly," replied Doctor Lounlans, "is not to be disputed; but to exact a repayment at this particular time, is turning your former favour into a misfortune."

"Who says so?" exclaimed the Nabob, resuming his recumbent posture on the sofa; "I have not yet asked for my money, though the last half year's interest has not been paid."

"Then you are unjustly suffering in public opinion, for it is universally reported that you have given instructions to your man of business to demand repayment, and in the event of refusal—the poor debtor must of necessity refuse—it is also reported, that you have ordered every measure of law to bring his estate to sale at this time, when it is morally certain that it will not sell for half its worth."

"Dr Lounlans," said the Nabob, looking loungingly over his shoulder, and then winking at me,

—"The worth of any thing[1]
Is just whatever it will bring."

The Doctor turned to me with dismay in his countenance. He was

[1] "*The worth of any thing . . .*": *Hudibras*, lines 465–6, altered somewhat, as the Nabob (and Galt) are, as usual, quoting from memory.

conscious that argument could make no impression, and apprehensive that entreaty would prove equally ineffectual; but nevertheless he again addressed the Nabob, in a firmer tone, however, than he had hitherto employed—

"Sir, such proceedings are not in unison with the feelings of this country. Mr Mailings is the representative of an ancient family; the habits and affections of the people of Scotland are still strongly disposed to take the part of a man of his condition when he suffers from oppression."

"They were," replied the Nabob, drily; "but now, I suspect, they are quite as well disposed to esteem those who, by their own merits, have made their own fortunes, and have brought home from other countries the means of improving their native land. I have myself spent more money here, Dr Lounlans, on Nawaubpore, than all that the Mailings, since the Ragman's Roll, have had to spend, whether got by thieving in days of yore, or by rack-rents and borrowing in our own time."

"But, sir," replied the young minister, fervently, "the day is yet far distant, and I hope will long remain so, when the honest people of Scotland will look tamely on and see mere wealth and ostentation treading down their ancient gentry."

"Ay, honest! Ah! that's but a small portion of the nation, even including the General Assembly of the Church and the College of Justice. But if they were as numerous as the daft and the imbecile, who, you will allow, are not to seek among gentry of the landed interest, as, indeed, in my opinion, they constitute the majority of the nation at large; for, you know, that every man of sense and talent seeks his fortune abroad, and leaves only the incapable and those who are conscious of their deficiencies at home—"

Apprehensive that the conversation might become a little too eagerly pointed, I here interposed, and said, to turn aside the sarcasm which I saw Dr Lounlans was preparing to launch: "Your observation, Mr Rupees, explains to me why it is so difficult to give any correct exhibition of Scottish manners, without bringing Tom o' Bedlams on the stage. In the Parliament House of Edinburgh you may see—"

"I beg, sir," said Dr Lounlans, interrupting me, "I beg your pardon. —Am I then to understand, Mr Rupees, that you are determined to persevere in your rigorous proceedings?"

"I intend to do no more than the law permits me to do. I will do nothing contrary to law; and if there is any rigour in the case, the fault is in the law, not in me."

"But," replied the Doctor, "consider public opinion."

"D—n public opinion," responded the Nabob—"I beg your pardon, Doctor."

"But, Mr Rupees, reflect on the prosperity with which it has pleased Heaven to crown your endeavours."

"Well, sir."—A short pause here intervened, as if the Doctor felt in some degree deterred from proceeding; but presently he rallied, and replied—"The same Power that has filled your cup to overflowing, hath seen meet to empty that of your ill-fated neighbour, and you should—"

"Should," interrupted the Nabob, sharply; "would you have me fly in the teeth of Providence?"

It was now evident, that, notwithstanding the popular eloquence and many excellent qualities of the Rev. Doctor, he was not possessed of stamina sufficient to stand a contest with a character of so much energy as the Nabob, whose original strength of mind had been case-hardened in the fiery trials of Indian emulation and ambition, and whose occasional liberality sprung more from ostentation and the feeling of the moment, than from any regulated generosity or sense of duty.

The Doctor rose somewhat flushed, and coldly wishing the Nabob good morning, immediately left the room. I also rose and followed him. The Nabob at the same time had likewise risen; and as I was going out at the door, patted me on the shoulder, and chuckling with triumph, said in a whisper, "Haven't I done for him; did you ever hear such a fellow? Canning, I'm told, calls my friend Sir John, Bahaddar Jaw,[2] but our worthy Padre would better merit the title."

[2] *Bahaddar Jaw*: a bilingual pun. The Sir John (Malcolm) referred to was a well-known soldier-diplomat (d. 1833). He was 'Bahadur Jah' (an Indian title: 'very gallant') and 'Jaw' (for his loquacity).

CHAPTER XVIII

On leaving Nawaubpore, having bid adieu to Dr Lounlans at the gate, I walked leisurely, in a mood of moral rumination, towards Auldbiggings.

It seemed to me that there was no chance of mitigating the dispositions of Rupees, nor any mode by which the old Laird could be extricated from his unhappy situation, save only that which Mrs Soorocks had, as I thought, so impertinently suggested. The more, however, that I reflected on her suggestion, ridiculous as it had appeared in the first instance, the more I became persuaded that it was not only plausible, but judicious; and accordingly, before I reached the avenue of the Place, I was resolved to do all in my power to further and promote the marriage. Fortune favoured the benevolent intention.

On approaching the house, I discovered the old man seated, as his custom was about that time of day, on his own louping-on stane. He seemed more thoughtful than usual; instead of looking anxiously towards the high road to see who was going to, and who coming from the town, his head hung dejectedly drooping, his hands, the one within the other, rested on his knees. He was indeed so rapt in the matter of his own thoughts, that he did not observe me until I was close upon him.

After the customary interchange of morning civilities, I told him that I had been with the Nabob, whom, with a prospective view to the matrimonial proposition which I had determined to urge, I described with lineaments certainly as harsh as those which he had shown in the conversation with Dr Lounlans.

"Deed, sir," replied the Laird, with a sigh, "it's a' true that ye say: he's as boss in the heart, and as hard, as a bamboo cane; but what can ye expect frae the like o' him, or o' them, as the worthy Mr Firlot used to say, "beggars whom the Lord had raised from the dunghill, to set among the princes of his people?" Set him up indeed! Before his mother's brother sent him to Indy, I mind him weel a dirty duddy do-nae-guid, that couldna even tak care o' his father's kye; for ae day he was sae taen up on the brae wi' getten the multiplication-table by heart—(weel has it taught him baith to increase and to multiply)—

75

that he left the puir dumb brutes to tak care o' themselves, and ane o' them, a silly stirk, daunert o'er the quarry-craig, and was brained. But what am I to do?—to fight in law wi' this Great Mogul, wud, wi' my light purse, be as the sound o' the echo to the pith o' the cannon-ball. Gude help me, I maun submit! And what's to become o' me, wi' thae feckless auld hands, unhardened by work, and the book o' my life but half written? I may sing wi' Jenny in the sang—

> 'I wish that I was dead,
> But I'm no like to dee.' "

To such despondency it was not easy to offer any immediate consolation, but I said, "It is much to be regretted, Mr Mailings, that at your time of life you have not the comfort of an agreeable companion to cheer you. A man of your respectability, I think, might do worse than look out for a helpmate to lighten these cares that have fallen in evil days on your old age."

"I have had my thochts o' that," replied he, "but I fear I'm tyke auld, and November's no a time to saw seed. But between ourselves, I'm no overly fond o' the rule and austerity o' a wife, after the experience that I hae had o' the juggs o' matrimony that Mr Firlot set me in for the business o' Babby Cowcaddens, 'cause she had got an injury and wyted me."

"You don't mean to say that the late Mrs Mailings was a woman of that description? I always heard her spoken of as one to whom you were greatly indebted for the order and frugality with which she managed your domestic concerns."

"It would hae been an unco thing an she had been in a faut," replied the Laird. "Nae dout she rampaged up and down the house frae Monday morning till Saturday night like a roaring lion, cowing the lasses, and dinging me about as if I had been nae better than a broom besom, by the whilk we grew rich in napry and blankets. But O, she made dreadfu' saut kail on Sunday!"

"But, Mr Mailings, is it the case that you had been gallant to her before marriage?"

"I canna deny but I might hae been, but she was leed on if she wasna thranger wi' a Captain Gorget that was recruiting in the toun."

"Who was she?"

"Oh, she was weel eneugh in respec of connexions, for she was the only daughter o' Cowcaddens of Grumphyloan; she had lost her mither vera young, and so, being edicated amang the giglin hizzies and rampler lads o' the neebouring farms, she was—But, to make a lang tale short, Mr Firlot said, that if I didna marry her, she being o' sae respected a family, he wad gar me repent in the bitterest manner he could; so that rather than be sae disgraced, o' the twa evils I chose the least. But she's quiet noo, and her bairn lies by her side, and has, I trust, found a father on high, though its parent, by the father's side, in this world, sure am I, must hae been a matter o' doot when it was laid to my door."

"Well, but, Mr Mailings, though your first marriage was not a happy one, might you not now, in your maturer years and riper judgment, choose for yourself? There, for example now, are the ladies of Barenbraes, excellent gentle-women, rich, and of the purest character;—could you, Mr Mailings, do better than make up to one of them, and thereby obtain a careful and kind companion, and free yourself from the thraldom of the Nabob's oppression?"

"That meddlin woman, Mrs Sourocks, was here yestreen, on ane o' her sympatheezing visitations, and really spoke sensible on the vera same head; but ye know that baith the sisters are past the power o' posterity, which is an objection, even if my heart didna tell me that I ne'er could like either the tane nor the tither o' them: they're no for a man that likes a free house and a fu' measure: a' might be pushon that's aboon the plook wi' them,* and that, ye ken, wad never do for the hospitable doings o' the house o' Auldbiggings."

"Laird, better small measure than no drink."

"That's a gude's truth; but Miss Shoosie's very ordinar, and Miss Girzie ne'er was bonnie—I grue at the thochts o' either o' them."

"Mr Mailings, take the serious advice of a friend, who feels for your situation, and do not allow the fancies that may be pardonable in a young head, to bring your grey hairs down with sorrow to the grave."

At this moment Jock came running towards us with a paper in his hand, crying,—

"Laird, Laird, here's news, the king's greetin."[1]

* Scotch pint-stoups, before the reformation of the imperial measure, were made to hold something more than the standard quantity, but at the point of the true measure a small *papilla* or plook projected, the sapce between which and the brim was left for an *ad libitum*, an exercise of liberality on the part of vintners and other ministers to haustation. When, however, measure was regulated by the *scrimp* rule, it was said proverbially of those who did so, "that of their liquors all was poison abune the plook." [Author's note.]

[1] *the king's greetin*: 'the king's greetings' (i.e. a summons). But the Laird can only understand the phrase in its Scots sense ('the king's weeping').

"What's he greetin for?" said the Laird; "I'm sure I hae mair cause, and it'll be lang or ye'll see me greet."

I took the paper from the servant's hand, and saw that it was a summons raised at the instance of Hugh Caption, notary public, for an assault.

"This," said I, "Mr Mailings, should put an end to any scruples that you may have to the ladies of Barenbraes; and therefore, with your permission, I will go to them before returning home, and declare your desire to throw yourself at the feet of one of them. If you would take my advice, your affections should be set on Miss Shoosie, for she's the eldest sister."

"If I maun consent, I maun—there's nae help for't; and so ye may just choose for me. It's a sore thing for a man to be frightened into his first marriage by the bow wow o' a kirk session, and driven into a second by a coorse o' law."

CHAPTER XIX

On arriving at the house of Barenbraes,[1] I could not help feeling that my mission was one of peculiar delicacy. It required, indeed, all the consciousness of the benevolence and rectitude of my intentions to reconcile me to the task of confidant, or blackfoot, as it is called in classic Scotch, to such "a braw wooer" as the Laird.

I hesitated before entering at the dial on the green—took out my watch, saw that there was a difference of several minutes between the time of the gnomon and the chronometer—adjusted the latter—placed it to my ear to hear if it was going—not that my resolution to perform the duty I had undertaken was in any degree weakened. I only doubted as to the manner and terms in which I should, as proxy, declare a passion at once so ardent and refined.

As I was leaning against the dial, I overheard the voice of Mrs Soorocks with the sisters resounding from the parlour. I went forward to the door, which was open. I again halted there, for the ladies were engaged in a vehement controversy on the very subject of my mission. No member of the *corps diplomatique* would lose the opportunity of listening to the cabinet councils of the court with whom he was to negociate, if he had it in his power and therefore I stood still.

The first words I distinctly made out were from Miss Girzie.

"Deed, mem," said she, addressing, as it would seem, Mrs Soorocks, "the old gentleman has his failings, that ye must alloo."

"Failings!" replied Mrs Soorocks, "havena we a' our failings? and between friends, Miss Girzie, ye hae your *ain* infirmities likewise."

Here Miss Soorocks interposed with a declaration to the effect that Mr Mailings would never be the husband o' her choice.

"Choice, Miss Shoosie!" exclaimed the Laird's advocate, "Choice? Mony a far better woman than ye were in your best days never had a choice.—Really, at your time o' life, Miss Shoosie (You're aulder than your sister) you ought to be thankfu' to providence if ony thing in the shape o' man is even'd to you."

[1] *On arriving at the house of Barenbraes*: The MS begins at this point. Samples of Moir's readings and alterations will be noted.

The widow made nothing by this taunt for the indignant spinster retorted,

"It would be gude for us a' if we saw oursels as ithers see us; but if I could hae demean'd mysel to tak up wi' sic men as some folk were glad to loup at, I might noo hae been in my widowhood. O but ye hae been lang obliged to thole that dispensation, Mrs Soorocks—that was your ain choice, nae dout."

"Sister," said Miss Girzie, "shurely ye forget that Mrs Soorocks has aye been vera obliging to a' kinds o' wanters suitable to her years."

"O aye," replied Miss Shoosie, "we hae baith heard o' mair than ae instance o' her condesention."

"There was Dr Pestle," said Miss Girzie, "hi! hi! hi!"

"And Mr Grave, the relief Minister, ha! ha! ha!," responded Miss Shoosie.

"It was said you were particular to auld Captain Hawser o' the press gang," added Miss Girzie, "was that true, Mrs Soorocks?"

"Was that true, mem?" subjoined her sister "I'm sure ony woman maun hae had a cheap conceit o' hersel that would hae thought o' sic an objik—and only three parts o' a man too, for he had a timmer leg."

To all this Mrs Soorocks replied with her wonted candour and suavity.

"It's vera true, that there was a time when I was inclined to have changed my condition,—I'll ne'er deny't; but no one could ever impute to me a breach o' discretion—we live, however, in an ill-speaking warld, Miss Shoosie; and was na there a time, my dear, when folks were na slack—they ought to have been poonished, Miss Shoosie, for cooming your character in the way they did. But ye had great credit for your bravery. I did na think it was in the power o' woman to have sae face't it out in the way ye faced it out. It was to be sure a maist improbable thing that a young woman o' a genteel family would hae foregathered in a glen by appointment wi' an ill faur'd, knule kneed, intaed, blackavised, pocky-aurr'd Potato bogle o' a dominie. For my part, I aye thocht the meeting maun hae been accidental and so I said at the time, Miss Shoosie, to Mr Firlot when he consulted me about sending the elder to test the fact. Ye might hae been the first lady to hansel the cutty in our parish for I have nae dout the Session would hae been at the expense o' a new stool for the occasion, considering it was for an heritor's dochter; but naething could be proved for there was nae leeven witness—at least that ever I heard tell o'."[2]

[2] *an ill faur'd, knule kneed . . . ever I heard tell o'*: Moir altered this passage considerably.

Here a yell so alarmed me, that I could not resist rushing into the room, where the amiable disputants, in the warmth of argument, had started from their seats, and were standing in the middle of the floor.

The aspect of Mrs Soorocks indicated the most resolute calmness, and a sweet smile played round her lips, and no one could have traced the storm of passion raging within, but by the lightning that flashed from her eyes.

Miss Shoosie, a tall meagre heron-necked anatomy of womankind, was standing as stiff as Dr Gaubins, of Glasgow, of whom Beeny Hamilton said, that he looked as if he had swallowed decoction of ramrods—Her hands were fiercely clenched, her cheeks pale, and her lips quivering, her teeth grinding, and her small greenish grey eyes sparkling, as if they emitted not constellations of fire only, but visible needles and pins.

Miss Girzie had thrown herself between them and was pushing her sister back by the shoulders, evidently to prevent her from fixing her ten commandments[3] in the imperturbable tranquillity of her antagonist's countenance.

On my appearance the storm was instantly hushed; the sisters hastily resumed their seats, and Mrs Soorocks with ineffable composure addressed herself to me.

"How do you do, Sir, me and the leddies hae been just diverting ourselves, talking o'er auld stories, till we hae been a' like to dee of laughin. Miss Shoosie there ye see has na got the better o't yet—O! Miss Girzie, but ye're gude at a guffaw; as for your sister, I'll no forget the way she would joke wi' me. I hope ye havena taen't ill, Miss Shoosie? I was just reminding her, Sir, o' a wee bit slippy in the days o' her youthfu' daffin—"[4]

The insulted virgin could stand no more. Bouncing to her feet she gave a stamp that shook the aged mansion from roof to foundation and raising her clenched hands aloft, she screamed through the throttlings of rage—

"It's false—it's false—as false as hell!"

And so in verity it was, for the whole insinuation, with all details and particulars, was only an invention got up by the ingenious Mrs Soorocks, on the spur o' the occasion—having no other material wherewithal to parry the cutting insinuations of her acrimonious

[3] *her ten commandments*: her ten blood-thirsty talons (Moir).
[4] *wee bit slippy in the days o' her youthfu' daffin*: wee bit daffin in the days o' her youthfu' thochtlessness (Moir).

adversaries—The widow, however, took no notice of the judge-like energy of the denial, but said,—

"Good day, my old frien's, and tak an advice from me, put a briddle on the neck o' your terrible tempers. Miss Girzie, I may say to you, as Leddy Law said to ane like you, 'May be if ye would shave your beard, it would help to cool your head.' "

With these words she swirled meteor-like out of the room, with a magnificent undulation or curtsey in motion before Miss Girzie could discharge the bomb of her retort. That it might not, however, be lost, but strike, as the artillery men say, by *recouchet*, the infuriated virgin turned sharply to me and said,—

"She's ane, indeed, to speak o' shaving faces—she ought to be taught to scrape her ain tongue. But it's beneath me to discompose mysel for sic a clash-checking clypen kennawhat. She's just a midwife to illspeaking."

Miss Shoosie, who had by this time in some degree rallied, exclaimed,—

"Sister—I beg, sister, ye'll say no more about her, for I'm determined to take the law," and with these words she burst into tears.

CHAPTER XX

When, after some desultory conversation, in which, with all my usual tact and suavity, I had in a great measure succeeded in soothing the irritated feelings of the ladies, Miss Girzie, "on household cares intent," had left the room, and I found myself alone on the sofa beside her sister, I began to throw out my feelers with a view to ascertain in what manner the negociation should be opened.

"Miss Shoosie," said I, gravely, "it is the misfortune of your sex to stand in need of a protector. Without some one of ours being interested in your happiness, the variety of insults and vexations to which you are hourly exposed—to say nothing of the value of a male friend in affairs of business—renders it the duty of every prudent woman, at some time of her life, to clothe herself with a husband."

In saying this, I laid my hand upon hers, to give the greater emphasis to my persuasion, but the look with which she considered the movement was to me truly alarming.

"It's a vera just observe, Sir," replied she, sighing, and endeavouring to look amiable. Such particular manifestations brought me at once to the point, and I resumed,—

"You are sensible, Miss Shoosie, that no man can take a deeper interest in the happiness of his friends than I do. And as you are a lady of sense and knowledge of the world, I acknowledge to you that my visit this day is for a very special purpose."

Here I felt her thumb, as it were, fondly disposed to turn up and embrace mine and I was therefore obliged to be quick with the declaration, for I saw that we were running the risque of coming into what the Laird would have called a comical situation; so I added,—

"I have been this morning with our friend Auldbiggings, and have had a very earnest conversation with him on this very subject."

Miss Shoosie withdrew her hand, and taking hold of her elbows, she erected her person and said dryly,—

"Well."

"He spoke of you with great tenderness, lamenting that the circumstances of his first marriage had prevented him in the ardour of youthful passion from throwing himself at your feet."

83

"Did he really say so?"

"Nay, I assure you, that it would offend your delicacy were I to repeat the half of what he said; but I can assure you, that his youthful feelings towards you have undergone no change."

"No possible!" said Miss Shoosie, relaxing from her stiffness.

"It is, however, true, my dear Madam, and surely it is much to be deplored, that two persons so well calculated to endear themselves to each other, should by the malice of Fortune have been so long kept asunder. What is your opinion, Miss Shoosie, of Mr Mailings?"

But instead of answering the question, she said—

"Do you know, Sir, that Mrs Soorocks, when ye came in, was talking in very high terms of him? And certainly I never heard that he was guilty o' ony indiscreetness, sept in the misfortune o' his marriage; but in sic things the hizzie[1] is aye mair to blame than the man, and there have been folk that said Mr Firlot, the minister, ought not on that occasion to have, in a manner, as they said, forced the marriage; but ever since Mr Mailings has been a widower he has conducted himsel, I will alloo, wi' the height o' discretion."

"But how has it happened, Miss Shoosie, that you and him never meet?"

"It's no my fau't," said she; "for ye ken that my sister and I are very retired; it's no our custom to wear other folk's snecks and hinges like Mrs Soorocks; nor would it become women in our situation to be visiting a wanting man."

"Upon my word, Miss Shoosie, I do not see that there would be the least indecorum in your asking Mr Mailings and myself, on a Sunday afternoon, to a sober cup of tea."

"I would have nae objection," was the answer; "but what way could it be brought about wi' propriety?"

"It's quite refreshing," replied I, "to converse with a sensible woman —Had you been Mrs Soorocks, Miss Shoosie, the chance is, that instead of the refinement and sensibility with which you have accepted the offer of my worthy friend the Laird's hand—"

"Offer, Sir, I never have had an offer."

"O Miss Shoosie! what then is the purpose of my being here but to make you an offer?"

"You don't say so!" said she with a simper, looking away from me, and turning down the side of her head as if she was hiding blushes.

---

[1] *hizzie*: woman (Moir).

"I do, Miss Shoosie, and I think you most singularly fortunate in receiving such an offer from the man on whom your affections have been so long placed."

"Are you really sincere, Sir? because if you are, I'll ne'er deny that I have long thocht that with proper management Mr Mailings might make an excellent husband."

"Then, Miss Shoosie, why delay your felicity and the felicity of the man of your choice?"

"Oh, sir, you would never advise that I should take such a rash step as to change my condition without consulting my friends. Our sister Lady Chandos is at a distance—"

"I hope her Ladyship is very well," said I, falling into the humour of Mrs Soorocks—"when did you hear from her last?"

"My sister was never gude at the writing."

"But her man of business, when he draws on you for the rents, surely lets you know of the welfare of her Ladyship and the young heiress Miss Clauson, I understand, is about coming of age. It will be a most fortunate thing, Miss Shoosie, both for you and Miss Girzie, to have the assistance of a husband like Mr Mailings, when you come to settle accounts with the executors of your brother-in-law."

"To be sure, there is no needcessity that I should consult Lady Chandos, for when she was married she never consulted me; but I can give no answer to the proposal till I have conferred wi' Girzie."

"Then let us call her into the room, and settle the business at once, I shall return to Auldbiggings with a light heart, conscious that I have this day been instrumental in establishing the happiness of two persons worthy of one another."

"But, sir," replied Miss Shoosie with solemnity, "is there no glammoury in what you hae been saying, for ye ken it would be thocht a most extraordinar thing were I to confess a preferrence for Mr Mailings, and nothing to come o't—"

I assured her that I was fully accredited to make the proposal, adding,

"Indeed, Miss Shoosie, you are highly honoured, and your marriage cannot fail to be a happy one since like a princess you are courted by proxy. Let us call in Miss Girzie, and as the day is warm and I am tired with my walk, I hope on such a blythe occasion you will not refuse me a glass of your delicious currant wine and water."

"That you shall have, Sir, without delay,—but you must leave me and my sister to confer in private."

"Am I then to give my friend any hopes?"

85

"I dare say you may say he needna despair."

"Miss Shoosie," I exclaimed, "you are a pattern to your whole sex, and I cannot but envy my friend that the disparity of our years, and the fidelity of your affections to him would, even if I were willing, allow me no hope of success as his rival."

"O Sir, O Sir!" said she with a self-congratulating titter, "ye gar me doot—I wish ye may hae a' this time been o' a true sincerity."

"Miss Shoosie, a marriage made up without jocularity was never a happy one; 'a dull bridal and a scrimp infare,' as the old proverb says, 'bodes quencht love or toom pantries.' Bring in the wine and let us drink—May there ne'er be waur amang us."

CHAPTER XXI

When I returned home in the evening I sat down to the full enjoyment of those agreeable reflections which are sometimes all the reward that kind hearted people like me receive in this world for the trouble of doing good and charitable actions.

The day, as I have already mentioned, had been uncommonly warm, but the twilight was cool calm and clear. The moon was just above the horizon, and so directly behind the high church and steeple of "the canny town," as King James the Sixth used to call Paisley, that they appeared like an apocalyptical vision dimly on her disk. I heard the faint far off sound of the bell at intervals—now and then the bleating of the sheep on the whinny knowes, accompanied with the occasional bark of their guardian colley—while the sound of a flute from a neighbouring grove, as Hervey[1] says in his Meditations, came upon the ear with "auricular fragrance," as a Lake poet describes the dashing of oars during the night on the bosom of Windermere in his amiable poem of the "teamster."[2]

As I was sitting by the open window of my study, tasting the freshness of the evening air, and listening to the soothing harmony of those mingled sounds, I observed the shadow of a man on the moonlight wall of the garden, coming by the footpath towards the house, and presently Mr Tansie the schoolmaster emerged upon the lawn from behind the shrubbery—I immediately ordered candles and by the time they were lighted he was admitted.

"You have come in a happy moment," said I to him: "I have been enjoying the delicious tranquility of this still and fragrant night. The spirit of contentment is abroad and there is a pleasing augury of peace and repose in the aspect of universal nature."

I knew that these euphonious phrases, imitated from the style of my friend Lockhart's "Omen",[3] would soon set the enthusiasm of the

---

[1] *Hervey*: See note to page 2.

[2] "*the teamster*": clearly a reference to Wordsworth; but Moir read 'teamster' as 'Hoxter' and made nonsense. Galt fuses memories of the 'dashing oar' of *Evening Walk*, and the Windermere of *The Waggoner*.

[3] *my friend Lockhart's "Omen"*: a private 'in' joke. Galt's *Omen*, 1825 was assigned

mystical dominie agoing, and so it happened for when he had seated himself he thus began—

"Call you it a happy time, when everything indicates a crisis—the sun hath for the season reached the maturity of his power; he sent forth a heat which the memory of the oldest person in the parish cannot parallel; and from this day his glory will begin to decline, into the ineffectual lustre, which illuminates but warms not the dreariness of winter—The moon is in this very hour at the full, and already hath begun to dwindle and to wane—The grass hath been cut down—the sheep are shorn of their fleeces, the sweet influences of the spring are over and gone, and the Summer pauses in the weaving of her garlands, as if she had twined enough for the use of the year—all gives the sign of mutation, and the fortunes of men are in unison with the condition of things. We shall hear rumours of strange matters that will speedily ensue. The green boughs of prosperity will soon be seen with the sere and yellow leaf—Tidings of change and decay will come among us, and proud hearts will be moved with disasterous fears."

This sort of Almanack prognostication of the good and simple man derived an impressive emphasis in its meaning from the events of the day; insomuch, that although I had set him off in the mere playfulness of the moment, it had yet considerable effect upon my feelings, and I replied,—

"There is something of a vague and hazy truth in your observations —but I have heard as yet of no particular occurrence to convince me of the existence of that astrological reciprocity between the course of moral actions and celestial signs which you so often maintain. On the contrary, I have this day myself sown the seed of an event which cannot fail to be of prosperous issue."

The philosopher looked serious, and said,—

"Modesty requires that you should add to the bravery of such a boast an 'if', like as if no unforeseen accident comes forth to blight it— but whatever experience, Sir, you think you have had of a contrariety to my doctrines, I myself have met with a wonderful instance of their truth. This very day, a man and a child have come to Renfrew, and are abiding at the public there. What I have heard of them and of the jeopardies they have come through, convinces me that they are unconscious agents to bring about some singular mutation that is ordained

by many (including Scott) to Lockhart. Galt is slyly appearing to agree. Blackwood (22 Aug. 1826) wrote Galt that the passage was 'in bad taste'. Moir completely altered it.

to come to pass in this country side. They have come here, as I am told, from a foreign land, in quest of great wealth that appertains to the child whose parentage was burned at sea. More I have not heard, but hearing thus much, I could do no less than come to tell you for knowing how well gifted you are with the faculty o' curiosity I am sure that you would lose no time in going to Renfrew the morn's morning, to satisfy yourself, by sifting all the particulars and doing your utmost to help the friendless in this to them strange land."

"I beg your pardon, Mr Tansie, I am not a man of such curiosity as as you seem to think, but only actuated by a liberal spirit of enquiry, the love of truth, and a constitutional *penchant* for facts."

I was indeed not quite pleased to hear myself so considered, notwithstanding the compensation in the just acknowledgement of my benevolence.

Our conversation was here interrupted by the arrival of a messenger from Mrs Soorocks, in "the form and pressure"[4] of one of her servant lasses. That lady was always particular in the choice of her handmaids, both as to character and personal appearance, and therefore I desired Leezy, as the girl was called, to be sent into the room, that I might hear the message from her own lips; at the same time, I requested the Dominie to sup with me, begging him to have the goodness, for a minute, to take one of the lights and go into the dining room, giving as my reason that I knew the business, to which Mrs Soorocks was desirous I should attend, was private and confidential.

The Dominie accordingly left the room and Leezy came forward.

She was of the better order of Scottish housemaids, a ruddy lively girl of twenty, and habited as befitted her condition—Her ancles, which is the next thing one is apt to look to in a woman after her face, were well turned, stockingless, it is true, but, even by candle light, of a fresh pink colour, which finely contrasted with her neat black shoes; her pettycoat was of chocolate coloured calimanco and of an engaging brevity, and she wore a white dimity short gown, with a many-coloured silk handkerchief over her full bosom; her hair, saving the front locks in ringlets, was closely smoothed back, and gathered within a kipplin comb.

"Weel, Leezy," said I, "which o' your sweethearts has led ye sae far a-field the night?"

4 "*the form and pressure*": *Hamlet* III, ii, 25.

"Sweethearts!—the last sweetheart I had was a gingerbread faring and I ate it."

"O had I been made o' gingerbread, and in such lips!" replied I, in the tone of Romeo, wishing himself a glove.

"Ye would hae been o' some use," retorted Leezy; "but I have na time the night to haver wi' you, for my mistress tell't me to come straight back, and she aye threeps that I lose her time when I forgather wi' you,—she's just been wud wi' a passion o' haste the night."

The spirit of enquiry was roused within me by this remark, and I exclaimed—

"What has happened?"

"How can I tell you? Ye ken best what trafeckin has been between you and her—but she bad me gi' you her compliments and to say that she wished ye would come the morn after breakfast and convoy her to Mr Roopy's, on the bizzness that ye ken o'."

At that moment, Mr Tansie with the candle in his hand, looked in at the door and said,—

"I thought she was away."

"Ah Mr Tansie", cried I, "Ours is a very innocent conjunction[5]—it will bring forth no trouble to you as session clerk". Then turning to Leezy I added "Give my compliments to your mistress and say I'll wait upon her; but take care of yourself with the young lad that's waiting at the gate for you."

"He'll wait lang that I care for", replied Leezy and as she quitted the room she slyly said in passing the Dominie "When, Mr Tansie, are ye going to make another clipse o' the moon?"

[5] *a very innocent conjunction*: Moir re-wrote the final two paragraphs, deleting the sexual innuendoes.

CHAPTER XXII

According to appointment I went over immediately after breakfast to Keckleton, the residence of Mrs Soorocks, whom I found sitting with her pelisse and bonnet on waiting for my coming. The instant I entered her neat well-ordered parlour, she snatched her gloves and parasoll from one of the shining mahogany tables—and—"I'm ready and been expecting you—for I fear if we dinna mak haste, that the ill you and Dr Lounlans hae done will be past reparation. Bonny ambassadors ye hae shewn yoursels! But come awa."

With that she took my arm and hurried me out of the house.

"My dear Ma'am," cried I, "but tell me first how you intend to proceed—"

"Dinna ye fash your thumb aboot that—ye'll see that I'll no let a wark o' needcessity slip through my fingers like a knotless thread."

The rest of our conversation till we reached the verandah of Nawaubpore was not worthy of particular preservation, although pertinent enough to the matters in hand—namely the concerns and characters of our neighbours.

Our reception by the Nabob was particuarly courteous, to the lady he was indeed all smiles and gallantry.

After we had been seated a few minutes, he shouted with a voice that made us both start, "Q'hy," which brought into the room one of his Indian servants, to whom he said something in his own language touching tiffin.

"What an elegant creature that is!" said my companion, "for though his face is the colour o' a brass jeelly-pan, and his dress like a man's on a tea cup, has na he a genteel manner about him?"

By this I discovered to what key she had modulated her meditated performance.

"Your remark is perfectly just, Madam," said the Nabob, "there is a natural grace even amongst the lowest of the Asiatics which no European unless he has been very long in the country can acquire. I have seen a Metranie throw on her Capra in a style that an English princess, whom you would call here the ornament of society, would have given half her dignity to be able to imitate."

"O Mr Roopy—Nawaubpore, as I should rather ca' you—I always heard that ye gaed very young to Indy."

"Yes, Ma'am, I certainly did, but besides that I had the good fortune to be early attached to our residency at the court of Delhi, where I had an opportunity of frequently associating not only with the first native society in India, but with the princes of the blood of Timour."

"Nae wonder, that wi' such advantages o' Education, you hae the fine taste that everybody's speakin about—O but that's a lovely picture, and what a handsome young gentleman that is there, on the back o' the elephant—Weel I never thocht that an elephant was just a grumphy—but dear me Mr Roopy—Nawaubpore, I should say—I think that bonny lad on the beast's back must hae been a relation o' yours, for he's really very like you—it's weel seen that he has been amang superior folk—Nane o' our hamewart gentry could sit wi' sic an air o' composity in the middle o' a stramash like that.—Did the teegur there really rin awa wi' the blackamoor?"

"He would have done so," replied the Nabob, "had it not been for the trueness of my aim for I'm the young man in the houdah that you have pleased to compliment; and it was considered in those days a very good likeness."

"In those days, Nawaubpore? That canna hae been vera lang ago. But I have heard that you have a wonderfu' fine collection o' pictures. I hae a great inclination that way mysel, ever since I saw Daniel in the lion's den in Hamilton Palace, and that was on my marriage jaunt to the Falls o' Clyde. It's an auld story, Nawaubpore. Ye were then a young man, making conquishts o' the yellow ladies I doot na in that great Mogul toon, where ye learnt manners."

I had begun at this to be afraid that the lady's curry would prove too rich even for the oriental palate of the Nabob but the complacent smile which played over his turmeric coloured countenance soon convinced me of the capacity of the Indian temperament for adulation. But it would seem that there is something in the influences of the sacred Ganges that generates an inordinate craving for flattery, as well as the hepatic maladies—there have been cases of this disease even late in life, a noble instance of it very recently, where the symptoms so insatiable in India are said scarcely to have been mitigated by impirical dozes of the *Leadenhall* faculty.

"My pictures," said the Nabob, "are not very remarkable—some people, however, have thought well of them—but Ma'am, allow me the gratification to show them to you, such as they are."

92

"Na," said Mrs Soorocks, taking his offered arm, "this is politeness," and as they walked out of the room I followed them.

All she beheld filled her apparently with the most extraordinary delight. On entering the principal drawing room, she exclaimed—

"O Mr Roopy—Nawaubpore, as I should weel ca' ye—you and me are just like King Solomon and the Queen of Sheba when he was shewing her all his wisdom, and the house that he had built and the meat of his table."

"That you shall see presently," said the Nabob laughing, "for I have ordered tiffin in the dining-room."

"And I see, like him, ye hae sitting servants too," rejoined the lady. "All this must hae cost a power o' money, Nawaubpore—"

"It did cost a few lacks, a great deal more than I could well afford."

"Weel I'm vera sorry indeed to hear that—it accounts for what I have heard; for sure am I a gentleman o' your extraordinar liberality, had ye no straightened yoursel wi' this grandeur, would ne'er hae thocht of molesting that poor silly doited do-naething Auldbiggings about his wadset."

"O not quite so bad as that neither, Ma'am, for all his debt would be but a drop in the bucket in my affairs," said the Nabob.

"Weel I was sure o' that and I so said to them that told me, and I said likewise, that you had been very ill used, for if Auldbiggings did na insult you himsel, he egget on the misleart creature his servant man to break your land surveyor's implement and that it was na the worth o' the money that gar't you persecute him if it were sae, for that ye were a man far aboon heedin whether ye were pay'd at this time or seven years hence especially as you could not but know that the property would come vera soon to you in a natural way—the feckless body being in a deep decline, wi' a great host and a sore defluction o' the chest."

"I have long known," said the Nabob, laughing, "that his *chest* was out of order."

Here the lady burst into a most immoderate guffaw, in which the Nabob heartily joined. At the conclusion she exclaimed,—

"Really Nawaubpore ye're as funny as ye're wise; but it's no christian-like for you and me to be gambollan ouer the weak man's infirmities—could na ye just let him be? I'm sure if I had but the tenth part o' your forton and no the half o' your generosity, rather than hear the clash that's bizzen about a' the kintra side concerning you and Auldbiggings, I would put his heritable bond in a blank cover, I

93

would na demean mysel to write the body, and send it to him wi' my contemps."

I thought Mrs Soorocks truly like the Queen of Sheba for her management in this instance, especially when the Nabob, with a slight shade of thoughtfulness, replied, he was sorry to hear that there was so bad an account of himself in the country.

"But," replied she, "I never believed it, and ye need na fash yoursel as ye ken it's no true—it's a soogh that soon be ower."

"Every thing, my Dear Madam," said the Nabob, "is in this world misrepresented and much exaggerated—That hectoring lecturing prig of a fellow, padre Lounlans, came here dictating to me what I should do—"

"He's a self-conceited man, Dr Lounlans," interrupted the lady, "he would rule the wisest in the Parish if he could and for your own dignity, Nawaubpore, you who have seen so much o' the great world, could na suffer yoursel to be governed by the likes o' him. It will, however, be a pity if you let your scorn o' a meddlin minister hurt your ain character. If I was in your place, noo that the Doctor's awa to be married, I would shew the world that I would do muckle mair o' my ain free will than I wad do either for fleechin or preachin."

The Nabob was now evidently thawed, and said,—

"You think my own thoughts, Ma'am—I have been for some time intending to stop the proceedings which my man of business had advised me to institute."

"But," said Mrs Soorocks, "if ye stop the proceedings which is as much as can be expected of you I would nae advise ye to gie up your heritable bond—for if ye dinna get the property at his death, somebody less deserving will."

"I'm sure, Mrs Soorocks," said the Nabob, "I shall do anything you like in the matter; I am too happy in having made the acquaintance of a lady so judicious to refuse her any wish in so trifling a matter— allow me the honour to show you the way to the dining room."

CHAPTER XXIII

Having bade adieu to the Nabob at the Fakeir gate, or, as Mrs Soorocks called it, "The Beautiful Gate," to which he had accompanied us, we walked on together, congratulating each other on the success of our undertaking.

"Weel," said the Lady, "ye see how a thing may be done, if folk kent how to set rightly about it—To be sure, considering that Dr Lounlans is a young man, no experienced in the ways o' the world, and that ye're but an authour, which, in a certain sense is only a something between a dominie and a bookseller, and that Nawaubpore is a man o' abilities (though a thocht vain o' them, that maun be alloo't)—it was none surprising that ye baith cam sae little speed—Folks say that the Nabob's proud, but, for my part I think he's a man o' condesension and has na he a fine style o' manners? It will be lang in the day or ye'll see ane o' our stirks o' country gentlemen linking a leddy about his house, and shewing her his plenishing and other curiosities. Poor bodies! they ne'er hae a greater curiosity than themselves—He maun indeed be a rich man yon—I said he was like King Solomon in all his glory, and like Solomon he has his weak side too; but I couldna help thinking, as he shewed me his gold and silver and his precious stones— did na ye think the big chiny jars maist handsome—that he was mair like Hezekiah shewing the men that brought him the present after he was no weel from Berodoch Beladin, the son of Beladin King of Babylon—It's surely a neglect in the Scriptures no to tell us what the present was for no doot it was some very fine thing—I hope, however, that what Nawaubpore has shewn to us this day of his precious things, his spices and his ointments—There was rather an overly ostentation of spice in yon Mugglecatauny Soup—But we should na look a gien horse in the mouth, so I hope that the pride of the Nawbob's heart is no to be dismayed wi' the sight o' his veshels o' gold and his veshels o' silver carried away captive, as it were, to the Babylon o' Glasgow, to be put in the fiery furnace o' William Gray's melting pot."

This speech dishevelled and ravelled as it was reminded me of the schoolmaster's prediction and I told Mrs Soorocks of the strangers who had come to Renfrew and of my intention of then going there to see them, advising her, at the same time, to proceed to Auldbiggings to comfort the Laird with the tidings of our achievement.

She was greatly struck with the coincidence of the Stranger's arrival at the time of what she called the Nebuchadnedzar vanity of the Nabob, about the great Babylon he had built and she would willingly have accompanied me to see the bottom of such "a judgement-timed event", using many ejaculatory terms concerning what might come to pass—I had, however, enjoyed enough of her company for one morning, and shook her off with as much civility as possible promising to call on her as I returned home, to tell her all the particulars. We accordingly separated where the roads diverged—I for the Royal borough, and she for the Laird.

I had not parted from her more than two or three hundred yards, when I met Jock the Laird's man coming leisurely from the town.

"Where have you been this morning, John?" said I, "and how is your master?"

"He's like a lying-in wife," replied Jock, "as weel as can be expecket and I hae been gettin for him a cordial o' mair efficacy for his state than the drogues o' a Doctor's bottle."

"Indeed! and what may that be?"

"Ye ken his malady's a sore disease—the want o' siller, the plague o' the present time."

"The want of money, do you mean? What's your remedy, John?"

"I had hain'd three and twenty shillings and fivepence hapeny out o' the wage that was pay'd me twa year bygane, and I barrow'd four shillings and sixpence from Jenny Clatterpans—ye'll ken her, she's yin o' our lasses. Wi' that and a bawbee that I saved out o' twopence that the Laird sent me to waster on snuff for him—isn't it a daft like thing for a man to create an appetite in his nose, when he's sae fash'd to get the wherewithal to satisfy his mouth—Wi' the aught and twenty shillings I hae bocht a sixteenth, and when it comes up a prize o' therty thousan pounds, me and the Laird intend to go o'er the knowes to the Great Mogul and pay him his wadset, plack and bawbee, sine snap our fingers in his face—

"But O Sir, sic a straemash is in the toun o' Arenthrew[1]—the bailies are rinning about like dogs wi' pans tied to their tails, and the provost's wife is sitting at her 'bower window high' wringing her han's and singing—

[1] These pages of 'stuff about Renfrew' were deleted by Moir.

'Wally wally up yon bank
  And wally wally doun yon brae'
for the toun has been afrontit and the steeple misca'd.''

I prick'd up my ears at the mention of the calumniated steeple, for I have ever entertained a particular affection for steeples. In my nonage, their principal charm to me consisted in their height—after that I began to feel interested in their shapes, and of late years—no doubt a forerunning symptom of age—I have thought of them as monuments, and have in consequence resolved that all those which "point to Heaven along the banks of Clyde"[2] shall be so many witnesses to my immortality.

It is true that the idolised ornament of Port Glasgow bears but oblique testimony and that having in an unguarded moment called the one on Hutcheson's hospital in the maternal city—a potatoe beetle, I may not hope for much renown amidst the murmurs circling round its base but I shall endeavour to conciliate all its neighbours from the bodkin of St Enoch's, the Laigh Kirk dibble, to the pepper box of St Andrews, nor shall the old one with its four young steeplings or the tower of St George's be forgotten. The only perfect steeple that I have ever heard of—is the Greenock steeple—every other has either a story too many or too few—but such excellence is not to be wondered at when one considers the "deevilish cleverness" of the Greenock folk. However—to return from this steeplechase—I said to Jock,—

"And who is it, John, that has spoken ill of the poor steeple of Renfrew?"

"Na, they were na content wi' that—They threatened to tak it awa' to Paisley on a hand-barrow."

"Who threatened, John?"

"A wheen Paisley hempies that came doun yesterday to the fishing— for ye ken it's their preachings—and they filled themselves fu'— Government has muckle to answer for since it made the whisky so cheap—and so being fu' they came to the Cross and seeing the harmless ill-used thing there, they began to be jocose aboot it, and syne to wag their heeds and guffaw at it, till they ga'ed the length o' ca'ing't a pint stoup when ane o' them—a thickset stighy ne'er-do-weel wi' a muckle toosy round red head and a face like a norwast win', said, meaning the creditable toun o' Arenthrew—'It's no their steeple—it's our

---

[2] Contemporary prints of Glasgow, viewed from the South bank of the Clyde, shows a 'steepled' skyline, not unworthy of Wren's London. Like the Laird, it has long vanished.

steeple for their toun council borrowt the siller frae Paisley to big it and as they hae never pay't it back, we'll tak it hame wi' us.' "

"Indeed, John, and how did they set about that?"

"They gaed in queesht o' a hand-barrow—and fell in wi' the trams o' an auld cart which being stronger they took up and, laying twa stabs across them, they came yellyhooing and triumphing down the crown o' the causway, which caused a dreadfu' cry and alarm to rise in the loan. Windows flew up and doors were opened and out came young and out came auld and out came a' thegither. An angry man was the provost when heard o' the mented removal of their darling Dagon and he gar't summon the council and town officers to bring the reprobates before him.

But when they were there they showed no respeck to his dignity—ane o' them frae the very bar o' guiltiness, where they were a' placit on trial, raxed o'er his hand and took a pinch o' snuff frae a Bailie's box wi' as meikle cordiality as if they had been marrows. But I true he was soon taught to know the difference between a magistrate and a malefactor—For the provost startit out o' his chair o' state and gieing a stamp wi' his foot that gart a' the Tolbooth dirl, said wi' a voice that would hae dauntit Goliah—'I'll no sit and see sic blasphemy', and wi' that he sent them to the stane chaummer[3] in the vera steeple they were daring to steal."

"I never in all my life, John, heard of such a business—"

"Nor did any christian man, Sir—but th're lost creatures yon—a' night they did naething but laugh and sing sangs—psalms would hae been in mair conformity wi' their deplorable situation—and ye'll see them when ye gang to the toun, for I see y're on the road, looking through the airn stinchers o' the wicket holes making faces and jeering the crowd in the streets, Mrs Paterson, the Dean o' Guild's[4] leddy, said to mysel that they would come to untimely end—she should ken something of what their sentence will be. Past-bailie Given's wife has taen to her bed wi' the fright, and it's thought will ne'er get the better o't. But Mrs Orr—her gudeman's deacon o' the tailors—she's just wud. You'll see her afore the tolbooth knocking her neives and girning wi' her teeth, crying to the pannels 'tak it awa' noo! Tak it on

[3] *stane chaummer*: stone chamber (i.e. prison cell). The Tolbooth in Galt's Scottish scene retained its old combined functions: town council chambers; magistrate's court; jail.

[4] *Dean o' Guild*: one of the senior offices available to town councillors and a source of quiet profit. See *The Provost*, chap. 4.

your backs and mak a Will-Dick's show o't in the snedden if ye can'.

"O Sir, there *is* an occasion yonder and what's to be the upshot no man can tell, but we live in fearfu' times—ae day the King's Greeting at a 'stated gentleman o' family being obligated to answer to the Law for a bit tig that his servant gied to a brass whirligig and the vera neest a band o' robbers coleaguing to steal a steeple and frae a tolbooth too—in broad daylight. But I'm taigling you when your help by head or hand may be wantit in yon afflictit toun—so I'll wish you a very good morning."

On my arrival, however, I found the panic had subdued. The bailies were pacified and the provost on the application of their worthy representative, my friend the Colonel, had set the captives free. The boys of the town, however, justly incensed at the indignity which had been offered to the whole community followed them with showers of stones and proved what hearts and hands were strengthening for the defence of the dearest rights of Renfrew.

CHAPTER XXIV

I found the stranger with his young ward in "the inns," and, upon requesting to see them, was shown into "the best room up the stair," where they were then sitting.

Mr Coball, for so the stranger was called, was a plain, but respectable elderly person of a tropical appearance; the little boy wore also the impress of the Indian clime for though in vivacious health, his face was colourless, and though his eyes sparkled with the morning light of life, his cheeks were untinged with any of its vernal bloom.

It was not easy to explain the motives of my intrusion but I got through the ceremony of self-introduction tolerably well and without much embarrassment; for instead of affecting to offer any apology, I professed to offer my services, at the same time assuring Mr Coball, that although I should have much pleasure in showing him every thing interesting about the town, there was in fact nothing worthy of a traveller's notice *in* it.

"I'm not here," he replied, "in quest of those things which attract travellers—but as it were by accident—yesterday I was landed at Greenock from America, and was on my way to Edinburgh for the purpose of instituting some enquiry to discover the relations of that poor child, when I happened to hear the name of a gentleman mentioned who is probably the chief person I am so anxious to find. He left India two or three years ago—that is if the same whom I believe he is, and I have halted here to call on him, which I propose to do in the course of the day."

But not to dwell on uninteresting particulars, it proved that the gentleman in question was the Nabob, and that he was supposed to be either nearly related to the boy, or acquainted with his friends—if he had not been executor to his father, who died about five years before, leaving a wife and three children.

"They were coming home," said Mr Coball, "in the same ship with me, but by the terrific calamity which befell us, and our subsequent disasters, all the evidence (with the exception of a few seemingly unimportant letters) has been lost, by which the unfortunate child may be identified to his relations."

He was too much moved by the recollection which this incidental allusion to his misfortunes recalled, for me to interpose any question, but as his emotion subsided he began to describe his sufferings, till he insensibly came to talk of the catastrophe of the ship.

"It happened," said he, "on a Saturday night—we had been all merry, according to the custom at sea and had retired to our respective cabins and births, in the hope of making the Cape in course of a day or two—I had just fallen asleep when a sudden and strange noise roused me from my pillow—I listened, and a wild cry of fire was instantly echoed by many voices. I started up and ran on deck—I could see nothing but only a steamy white smoke issuing from the forehatchway—In a moment every soul on board was around me.

"The captain with undismayed coolness ordered all to prepare for the worst, and the other officers with their trumpets were immediately at their posts directing the crew in the attempt to extinguish the flames. The night was calm—the heavens above were all serene, and the sea lay so still around that the ship appeared to hang in the centre of a vast starry sphere, so beautiful and bright was the reflection of the skies in the unbounded ocean.

"I may not describe the dreadful contrast which the scene onboard presented to that holy tranquillity. There was distraction, and horror, and wild cries and fearful screams, and hideous bursts of delirious laughter. Then there was a crash below and silence for a moment—and then the busy troubled sound of the consuming destruction, felt as well as heard, gnawing and devouring the inward frame and beams of the ship, still growing louder and fiercer.

"In the meantime the boats were lowering—the first that floated was instantly overloaded and she sank with a horrible throttled cry—every soul who had so wildly leapt aboard perished.

"The rage of the burning still increased—It was no longer possible to go below without the risk of suffocation.

"Another boat was launched—One of the officers leaped onboard, and sword in hand, shoving her from the ship's side, suffered no one to follow until water and provisions were handed in—But notwithstanding his prudent endeavours she was soon filled both with the sailors and the passengers. The mother of this orphan was standing on the gangway with her three children, she looked as if she too would have leapt into the boat, but the babies clung to her, and so hung upon her arms that she could not disentangle herself from their fond and frantic embraces.

"I tore this poor boy from off her—she cried, 'O save him if you can!' —the third boat was by this time in the water—I flung him to a sailor onboard. She snatched up the other two beneath her arms and with a shrill dismal shuddering shriek, which made every one that hung clustered about the shrouds and gangway look round, she rushed into the smouldering cabin and shut the door.

"Her madness infected all who witnessed it—the boat was pushing off—there was no other chance for me—I leapt into the water and was taken aboard—many followed me but the officer, with a terrible compassion for those who might be saved, hewed off their hands with his cutlass as they laid hold of the gunwall—'Row,' he cried to the sailors who had seized the oars, 'the fire is making towards the maga- zine—Row, off or we shall be blown to pieces.'

"The sailors rowed with their utmost vigour—as we left the ship a cry rung from all the unfortunate wretches who were abandoned to their doom—so frantic, so full of woe and despair that it made even the firm minded officer exclaim, 'Good God, what is that!'

"I covered my ears with my hands and bent my forehead to my knees that I might neither hear nor see.

"When we had rowed to some distance the men at the oars paused—I uncovered my ears and looked up—a deep, low, hoarse, mumur- ing and crackling noise came from the ship, and now and then a human cry. As yet the flames had not appeared—but all around us, save where those dread and dismal sounds arose, was stillness and solemnity—and the smoke from the devoted vessel appeared like the shrouded form of some incomprehensible and tremendous phantasma ascending from the sepulchres of the ocean to the dominions of omens and powers.

"We looked at the spectral sight with terror and in silence—The orphan was clinging to my knees—at last the fire began to break out. The flames showed themselves at the cabin windows—in a moment they whirled up the rigging—The sails blazed and the ship was for the space of a minute like some unblest apparitional creation of sorcery.

" 'It is all over,' said the officer and his voice sounded hollowly over the mute echoless ocean. 'The fire is in the gun-room! Ha!'

"At that instant a vast sheet of flame filled the whole air, and like an angry demon unfurling his wings scattered meteors and malignant fires against the stars. The black forms of many things hovered like motes in the sunbeam for a moment in the blaze. I distinctly saw an anchor, and many like men with outspread arms.

"That momentary and indescribable vision of fires and fragments

102

was succeeded by a booming roar as if an Earthquake had raised his voice from the abysses of the silent waters, and then there was a numerous plashing noise of many things falling around us into the sea, but that too soon passed, and then there was darkness and silence.

"At that moment a cold wet hand caught mine, which was hanging over the boat's side—and a man from the sea cried in a homely Aberdonian voice, 'For Christianity, will ye no tak me up?' The officer heard him, and relenting from his firm and merciful purpose ordered him to be taken onboard—'Na, na', cried the Scotchman, 'tak my bag first,' and he held up to me a small haversack which I grasped and lifted in—but in the same instant, an undulation of the sea came rolling from the whirlpool where the ship had sunk—The boat rose on the swell, the fated wretch lost his hold, and sank beneath her for ever."

After a short pause Mr Coball added, "It pleased Providence to rescue us next morning from our perilous situation—a ship bound for the Isle of France had seen the glare of the burning during the night, and steering towards it when the wind freshened came up to us by day break and took us all onboard. As the orphan (whose name is Charles Bayfield) still hung about me I undertook if possible to restore him to his friends. He is a singularly sharp boy for his years and in the Aberdonian who had strangely preferred his bag to his life, he had recognized one of his mother's servants—The contents of the bag were in consequence adjudged to belong to him and assigned to my custody. They consisted of the letters I have mentioned—besides several packets of valuable pearls and other costly trinkets, which may help me to discover his friends. But I hope the Mr Rupees of this neighbourhood is the same gentleman of that name who by the letters appears to have been the executor of the deceased Colonel Bayfield, the child's father."

Our conversation after this became general. Mr Coball mentioned several things the knowledge of which he had acquired from the letters in the bag and which convinced me that the Mr Rupees he was in search of could be no other than our Nabob. But I became uneasy when he stated that by some of the letters it appeared Colonel Bayfield had died very rich and that the bulk of his fortune was in the hands of his executor from whom his widow had not been able to obtain any satisfactory information concerning it. I did not, however, divulge what I feared, but only advised Mr Coball to see the Nabob as soon as possible, adding, "If you find the assistance of any friend necessary make no scruple of calling on me, for you have both interested my feelings and awakened my curiosity." I then took my leave.

Thus it came to pass that what with the Laird's affairs and this new adventure, I, good easy man, who never meddled with any other body's business—for my innocent curiosity can never be called meddling—had as much toil for my feet, work for my hands, and talk for my tongue, as Mrs Soorocks herself—mine, however, was owing to the purest and most disinterested motives, while her visitations spring as I do think from a prying disposition and an unaccountable desire to have a finger in every pye baked in the neighbourhood—the neighbourhood did I say!—I might well say the county—I have indeed often wondered that she did not remove herself to the multifarious field of Glasgow, but her reason was excellent,—"Because," said she, "nobody in a populate town cares for one another, and I would die if I did not ken something about my neighbours—It's no a field for dispensing the workings of grace or the exercise of a mind void of offence, for I love to do good especially to my friends in affliction." How blind some people are to their most obvious defects!

CHAPTER XXV

Fatigued with my long walk, the heat of the day and the influence of my dinner, I had thrown myself on the sofa to indulge in a short siesta before going, as I had promised, to tell Mrs Soorocks the result of my journey to Renfrew. I had not, however, stretched out my limbs many minutes when that indefatigable personage was herself announced.

"I thought," said she as soon as she had entered the room, "I would spare you the trouble of coming to me, for although I was just curious to hear the discoveries that ye hae made I could better spare hearin o' them than refrain frae telling you o' the tribulation we are baith likely to be put in for the pains we hae taken, out o' a sense o' religion to help the Laird in his jeopordies."

"What tribulation? What has happened?"

"O, the swine's ran thro't!" exclaimed she, "no sooner had I told the auld gaumeril that Nawaubpore was a perfec gentleman and was disposed not only to treat him with mitigation, but to allow him to live on the estate upon easy terms for the remainder of his life than he began to hum and haw and to wish that he hadna geen authority to you to bespeak ane o' the Miss Minnigaffs to marry him—Did ye ever experience such blank ingratitude?"

"You do not say so, my dear Madam—if he draws back what shall I do? I have pledged my honour for him to Miss Shoosie."

"I see nothing for't but to tak her yoursel," said Mrs Soorocks laughing.

"It is no laughing matter to me, Mrs Soorocks, after the praises I have bestowed on Miss Shoosie which though they carried no offer, might yet perhaps by the help of Edinburgh advocacy be screwed into as much as, if it did not draw damages, would draw from my pockets the fees both of advocate and writer, and worse than all make me be talked of as a perjured wretch in all the boarding schools of Athens—Even though the case should happen to be accurately reported in that amusing periodical Shaw and Dunlop's[1] Decisions of the Court of Session."

[1] *Shaw and Dunlop*: Patrick Shaw and Alex. Dunlop produced from 1824 in Edinburgh a series of legal reports under the title *Cases decided in the Court of Session*. Galt ironically reduces its pretensions by calling it a 'periodical'.

We were here interrupted by my servant coming into the room, saying that the ladies of Barenbraes wanted to speak a word wi' myself in private.

"They'll be comin to consult you anent takin the law o' me," said my visitor endeavouring to smile and she added "Oh but this is a treacherous warld! Howsever, you can go, Sir, and see what they daur to say and I'll bide till you're done wi' them. I redd ye, Sir, tak tent ye dinna straik them against the hair."

I accordingly left her and went to the ladies who had been shown into the drawing room and were sitting on the sofa with pink silk scarfs like twin cherries on one stalk. Miss Shoosie was doing amiable with bridelike bashfulness, her eyes perusing the carpet while she played with her shoe toe with the point of her parasol. Miss Girzie had less of conscious delinquency[2] in her appearance. Her parasol lay across her knees and was resolvedly grasped at the extremities while her countenance indicated both fortitude and intrepidity.

"We have come, Sir," said she, "having considered the proposal ye made to my sister yesterday—"

The "ye maun tak her yoursel" of Mrs Soorocks still ringing in my ears, I exclaimed, "Proposal, Ma'am! I made no proposal!"

"Sister!" cried Miss Girzie, "Sister, is it possible that you could be mistaen?—but I told you that it was ower gude a godsend to come to our door, especially as Auldbiggings has done sae lang without a wife."

This speech relieved me in one respect: that is, in as far as I thought myself implicated, but considering what Mrs Soorocks had told me of the alteration in the Laird's views, I began to feel as if I had only got out of the frying-pan into the fire, nevertheless, I mustered self possession enough to say with some shew of gaiety—

"Well, ladies, and what is the result of your deliberation?"

"I told my sister," resumed Miss Girzie, "that there could be no objection to Mr Mailings as a man, which was quite her opinion: but I thocht it would na be prudent of her to give her consent to an acceptance of his hand until we both knew what sort o' settlement he was disposed to make upon her."

"Settlement! Miss Girzie," cried I, glad to find any loophole— "Settlement—surely, ladies, you must have long known the embarrassed state of Mr Mailings's affairs—were times to mend, as we hope they will do, doubtless he may have it in his power to make a settlement,

---

[2] *conscious delinquency*: downcast modesty (Moir).

but really under existing circumstances any thing like a regular settlement ought not to be expected."

"Is't possible," replied Miss Girzie, "that you could suppose my sister would marry ony man without a provision for a family? I'm sure she could ne'er hae my consent to such undiscreetness."

Glad to find the venerable spinster in so sturdy a humour, I grew a little bolder and said,—

"Whatever your sentiments, Miss Girzie, may be, I have always had a very high opinion of the disinterestedness of your sister, and will say so before herself there where she sits. But if I thought that in an affair of the heart, after the great tenderness and affection shewn by my friend Mr Mailings, she could be so mercenary as to make any such sordid stipulation, I would advise him to have nothing further to say to her."

Here Miss Shoosie said with a plaintive accent, "I'm no o' a mercenary disposition and so I told my sister when she first spoke o' settlements."

This was alarming, and I was completely perplexed when Miss Girzie subjoined—

"It's vera true, Shoosie, but when a thoughtless young couple's coming thegether it behoves their friens to see that the solid temporalities are no neglected in the delusions o' love."

"Indeed, Miss Girzie, you are quite right and you would be wanting in sisterly affection if you did not see a proper jointure secured. At the same time I will be plain with you, as the friend of Mr Mailings I will set myself against everything of the kind. I am very sorry, ladies, that so unsurmountable a bar should have arisen to the completion of an union every way desirable."

Miss Shoosie moved as if she would interpose to prevent me from proceeding but I was so apprehensive of a more frank avowal of her willingness to accept the Laird that I raised my voice and continued—.

"It cannot, however, be helped. I cannot see a gentleman's affections treated as no better than saleable commodities. You will excuse me, ladies, but my feelings are strong on the occasion. I do not blame you, however, Miss Girzie, you are but doing your duty as I am doing mine—I will tell Mr Mailings of what has passed and as a lady is waiting for me on particular business in another room, you will pardon me for so abruptly wishing you good afternoon."

Miss Girzie at these words started up, and said, "Sir, Sir, just ae minute."

"I can hear no more," cried I, "it is plain you intend to make a bargain with my friend. No abatement of expectation, no retractation of opinion on the subject, can change my mind. I may seem to you warm, ladies, and I am so; who can help it? when one hears of a gentleman's heart and hand regarded as of no value, unless the hand be filled with glittering trash."

The tone in which I expressed myself had so sounded through all the house, that Mrs Soorocks came rushing into the room, crying, "Gudeness me, have they flown upon you too?"

At the sight of that lady the two sisters rose and making a formal courtly curtesy moved towards the door while she returned the recognition by another so profound, that she seemed to have fairly seated herself on the floor, setting up at the same time a guffaw, that made them tottle out of the room with short nimble steps, supporting each other as if some horrid monster was bellowing at their heels.

CHAPTER XXVI

When I had told Mrs Soorocks of what had passed with the ladies and related to her the conversation I had held with Mr Coball—when we had mingled our opinions respecting the demand which was likely to come so suddenly on the Nabob and when I saw the interest which the doubtful situation of that gorgeous personage had excited in the sympathy of my visitor, I ordered tea for her that we might discuss at leisure the course we ought to adopt in a case so singular and important but before the kitchen, *anglice* tea-urn, was brought in, the Laird made his appearance evidently dressed for some occasion of ceremony.

His coat and waistcoat were of the same snuff colour; the latter with flaps after the manner but of greater amplitude than the style of the court dress—His breeches of black silk rather short and scanty were adorned at the knees with heir-loom buckles of Bristol stones set in silver—his stockings were also silk of a bluish tinge and a cottonial dimness, the effect of many lavations—his shoes, cleaned by his man Jock, though jet black yet were more of a lacklustre clothy appearance than of the satin-like brilliancy of Day and Martin—contrasting finely, however, with the radiance of his richly-chased massive Patagonian silver buckles—he wore his best wig well powdered, a demi-forensic structure of a middle and anomalous architecture between the prim tye-wig, with Ionic volutes over the ears, of a snug and debonair citizen, and the wig of wisdom, luxuriant with Corinthian curl, which distinguishes the upper end of a Lord of Council and Session. In the one hand he carried his Sunday hat—a fabrication of the last century, silky and sable—the sides half looped up towards the crown indicated that it had been formed in that equivocal epoch when the aristocratic cock, yielding to the progress of taste and the march of intellect, was gradually relaxing into the philosophical fashion which ornaments the craniological organization of the present enlightened age. The other hand grasped his tall malacca cane crowned with gold and shod with brass. A tassel of black silk which dangled from the hole[1] above his hand, by its centrifugal force, swept the air with

[1] *hole*: whole (Moir).

109

magnificent oscillations as he came staffing his way into the centre of the room.

The first impression of this ceremonious appearance led me to think that the old gentleman had so adorned himself for the purpose of paying a visit of gratitude to the Nabob; and Mrs Soorocks, it would seem, had formed the same opinion for before even the common salutations were exchanged; she said,—

"Dear me, Mr Mailings, ye can never be going to Nawaubpore's at this time o' day? he'll be at his dinner—eating his dishes gude for the liver complaint—to be sure, he may excuse the intrusion of an auldfashioned man, a hame'art gentleman, who has never seen the world nor gallanted like him, wi' the yellow ladies in yon palaces o' delight in Indy."

"Dinna lift me before I fa', Mrs Soorocks," replied the Laird, evidently not entirely pleased with her observation, adding, "I am not going to Nawaubpore, but to pay my respecs at Grey Stane."

"Grey Stane, Laird? I did na ken that you and the family were on visiting terms," said Mrs Soorocks. "Mrs Luggie is certainly a pleasant woman, and they say Miss Jenny, who cam last week frae the boarding-school at Edinbro', is grown a perfec beauty, and can play on the spinett and paint red cabbages and kail blades upon paper. It was a better world when a Laird's doughter learned to play on the spinnin wheel, and kent the wholesome use o' kail blades; but nae dout your visit's a curiosity to see the beauty."

"Ye're a woman o' sagacity," replied the Laird, "and I'll no deny the truth among friens, for ever since ye pointed out to me the disconsolateness o' my situation without a help-meat, I hae been seriously thinking that I would be the better o' a wife."

Here I interposed, exclaiming, "My gracious! Mr Mailings, did you not authorize me to carry a proposal to the ladies of Barenbraes?"

"And," cried Mrs Soorocks, "when I shewed the need that ye stood in, o' somebody to take care o' you, did not I tell you that Miss Shoosie was the fittest woman in a' this country side for that purpose?"

"But ye ken," said the Laird, addressing himself to us both, "that my heart grewed at the thocht o' ony yin o' the twa reisted auld frichts—crined in the flesh, wi' hides like the skin o' a pouket guse, and hues like yeleranes—denty lions I mean."

"But, Mr Mailings," said I, "I have done my duty and fulfilled the sacred trust which you confided to me—Miss Shoosie has consented to accept your hand and share your fortune and although her sister has some scruples of a mercenary nature, yet your faith and truth are pledged and to retract now would be most dishonourable."

"Dishonourable!" exclaimed Mrs Soorocks, "it wad be even doon perfec perjuration—if Dr Lounlans were at hame, and siccan a sinfu' abomination to be committed within the bounds o' the Parish, he wad set the Session, wi' its seven heads and ten horns, upon you and ye hae had some experience o' what it can do. Oh, Mr Mailings, to betray another young woman[2]—Whare div ye think ye'll gang when ye dee?"

The Laird, raked by this cross fire, fell into confusion, and instead of parrying the attack replied with humility,

"I aye thocht that a man had a richt at least for yince in his life to please himsel."

"Please yoursel to be sure," said Mrs Soorocks, "but wi' a discretion—And what discretion would there be in a feckless auld man, so well stricken in years as ye are, to marry a gallopin, gallantin, gigglin Miss in her teens, and to forsake a sober, douce, sensible, agreeable, judicious woman?—I may weel say to you as Mause in Patie and Roger[3] says to Bauldy,—

'Vow and loup back! was e'er the like heard tell?
Swith tak him, Deil, he's ou'r lang out o' H—.'

Deed, Auldbiggings, ye had better repent and sin no more or ye'll maybe hae Miss Shoosie's death well laid to your door for she's a kind gentle creatur, and canna miss but to die o' a broken heart, and what'll come o' ye then, when like the ghost in William and Margett[4] her spirit appears at your bed fit with a lilly hand and a sable shroud?"

"But," rejoined I, "it is not to the Session only he shall answer—It is not only before the injured spectre o' Miss Shoosie that he will lie quaking at the dead of night—he must answer to me. I will not submit, after having been so entreated to negociate the marriage, to see it so lightly broken off, and for what!—a young girl that has nothing but flesh and blood to recommend her!—Mr Mailings, I consider myself exceedingly ill used."

"Na!" cried Mrs Soorocks, "I canna see hoo ye can be aff fechtin a duel wi' him—and a bonny sicht it would be to see him brocht hame on a barn door, after getting his head shot aff, and Jock, poor cretur,

---

[2] *to betray another young woman*: Moir rewrote, to conceal the seduction.

[3] *Patie and Roger*: The first episode of Ramsay's *The Gentle Shepherd* 1725, often used as a title for the whole work. Cf. *The Entail*, i, chap. 26.

[4] *William and Margett*: the ballad 'William's Ghost' (Herd, i. 76).

greetin, and following the mournful procession carrying the head by the lug, as if it was no better than a sheep's gaun to the smiddy to be sing't."

The consternation of the Laird was continuing to increase and looking first at me and then at his ruthless tormentor, he exclaimed,—

"Hae I fallen into the hands o' the Philistines?"

"Philistines!" cried Mrs Soorocks—"Surely ye're an uncircumceesed as weel as a mansworn deceiver. Had I no molified Nawaubpore, there would hae been less daffin in your head the night; for instead of dressing yoursel out like a squire o' high degree and singing—'I kiss'd and I prattled with fifty fair maids,' to mak conquests o' bits o' lasses, ye would hae been sitting in your forlorn chair, confabbing wi' Jock, about whether by rope or gun was the easiest way o' deeing. But I'll go to the Nabob this precious minute—I'll let him ken what a false deluding man ye are—I'll tell him o' the plague ye were to the Kirk Session, before Mr Firlot got you to right that amiable ill-used woman your first wife, and the wrongeous ye would noo do to the sweet girl whom Providence has made me an instrument to choose for your second."

This last threat finished the Laird; he lay back in his chair with his eyes fixed on one of the bell cranks, his arms hanging as it were powerless by his sides, and every feature of his face relaxed with helplessness.

"I canna," said he, in soliloquy, "warsle wi' this—I hae lang thole't the conspeeracy that has rookit my rents—I hae endur't the loss o' my first love, Annie Daisie—I quietly submitted to my wife till it pleased Providence to quench her—I hae seen the lands o' my forefathers mouldering awa—I hae known the terrors o' the law, and the judgment o' a wadset—I hae had sickness o' heart, and the rheumatics, and the toothache—Weel may I say wi' the play-actor in the show that I alloot in our barn,—

'But it's this too solid flesh which makes the calamity of life,
For who would bear the pangs of despised love—
The oppressor's wrong—the insolence of Law.'

The Deevil tak Hugh Caption and all the other ills that flesh is heir to—I'm ruin't beyond redemption—Mrs Soorocks and Sir—I gie myself up into your hands—be pityful if ye can."

CHAPTER XXVII

After the departure of the Laird and Mrs Soorocks, I set myself quietly down to read the *Literary Gazette*[1] of the preceeding Saturday, but either from the interuption of my siesta or from the influence of my erudite and particularly accomplished and elegant friend the Editor I fell asleep.

Mr Jardine or, as Mrs Soorocks calls him, Mr Jordan ought to exert himself more to enliven his readers but no doubt he does his best. He is nearly related to that lady she has often assured me herself. However though she says she taught him the English language he had never either her smeddum or her talent. "He's just," says she, "like the Laird, aye maundering about taste and gude morals, as the other puir feckless body does about taxes and polotic economy, and to hear him speak he wad gar ye true that he and Mr Canning were kippled together in a leash, ganging together frae Dan to Beersheba worrying the reformers, and making spade shafts bear plums in some howff they ca' the Royal Society o' Literature—"

But the worthy nation does not execute justice on her kith and kin, for my friend Jerdin is really possessed of a modicum of talent and if he would write less himself and procure other correspondents his periodical would soon become respectable. He is certainly a little vain of his familiarities with "the accomplished secretary" but he has sense enough not to pretend that he has assisted the Right Honourable gentleman either in the composition of his speeches or the improvement of his dispatches, though I have no doubt he has sometimes either in the way of cause or effect helped him to flourish a *bon mot* or launch a sarcasm—

But as I intend to vindicate the many remarkable qualities of the Brompton Apollo in my poem with copious notes "the Helicon of Hans Place" I shall spare his modesty from my further commendations at this time, it being more germaine to the present matter to relate

---

[1] *to read the Literary Gazette*: Blackwood considered this satirical attack on William Jerdine, the editor of the *Literary Gazette* 'in bad taste' (22 Aug. 1826) Moir deleted the entire passage and wrote a new opening for the chapter, the narrator merely reading 'the newspapers'.

that I was aroused from the deep sleep into which the wizzard or as you will—the warlock—of the *Literary Gazette* had enchanted me by the thunder of the Nabob's chariot at my door.

I was much surprised at this avatar and no less by the friendly and familiar courtesy the Burrah Sahib addressed me.

"I have come to talk to you," said he "about a very comical affair, in which I may stand in need of some advise, and you are the only man of any *nous* that I'm acquainted with in the county."

"Then you have never been in Greenock, I presume?"

"O yes, I have though! a very good sort of a town—plenty of punch and much jaw—quite edifying to hear the excellent character every one there gives of his neighbour—They have some fun too among them— one John Esdaile has long served them instead of Joe Miller—But I have no time at present to send for my friend the Bailie—besides he's not very portable and I have left all my elephants in Bengal, where I had one that could have carried *him*."

I was here so shocked at this personality, that I almost fainted. I entreated him to forbear, to recall him from the digression into which he had so much the habit of falling although he might have excused the objectionable expression by making an apology, as is usual on such occasions.

"Why, the business," said he, "is nothing less than a claim on more than half my fortune. I had a friend in India, one Tom Bayfield, who rose to the rank of Colonel in the Company's service; he married one day a very pretty girl, the daughter of my old chum Dick Campbell— they were very happy, and got three children between them—Tom was a devilish clever fellow, made upwards of ten lacs—and died suddenly— I was in Europe at the time but in making his will he left me his executor and, failing his own children, his heir—for I had lent him a helping hand when he was only a cadet. Somebody, however, put mischief into the widow's head against me, as if her children had been cheated by this settlement, and she wrote me such vixen letters that I told her, but in polite terms, that she might go to the D—l; although out of regard for her husband I did intend to adopt her son. Well, as ill luck would have it, on receiving my letter, she was advised by some of her nincompoop relations in Bengal to ship herself and family for Europe; when if she had staid till a decent time after her husband's death she would certainly have got married again—but the ship was lost at sea, and it was supposed that every soul on board perished, so that I administered as heir to the Colonel. But the deuce is in't, there has been with me this afternoon a confounded impostor as I think, who says that he was in the ship with Mrs Bayfield and her family; that the vessel was not lost, but burned and that he had saved her son Charles whom I had intended to adopt and what do you think? he brought a great lubberly boy with him, whom he called Charles and who was no more like the babe that I saw in the arms of the Ayah when I left India, than an arab is like a caffrè; but certainly considering the time that has elapsed since I saw the child it might have grown up into something like the size of the impostor's brat—Now what would you advise me to do in such circumstances? I don't want such proofs as the old Humbugs and Vakeels in Edinburgh would require but before a man parts with one half of his property just now and makes up his mind to leave the other at his death it is reasonable that he should know what he's about and to whom he either gives the one, or leaves the other. My friend Dr Dewai came home with a large fortune, a writer's wife in Dundee palmed herself on him as his near relation, and got the old fool to leave her a legacy of ten thousand pounds; but when he died and her husband had got the money, it turned out that her mother had been his mother's chambermaid, and so got acquainted with the secrets and connections of the family—How d—d foolish I should look if it were discovered after my death that I had been as silly as Dewai! I never knew such a silly fellow as Dewai. When I was resident at Lucknow, he was surgeon to the Residency—"

Apprehensive that the Nabob was again digressing from the matter in hand, I brought him back to the point by asking if he had examined the Stranger as to any evidence in his possession of the facts he affected to state.

"O, to do the fellow justice," replied the Nabob, "his story is plausible enough and he says he has some letters of my own to Mrs Bayfield; but which, out of regard for the boy he calls Charles, he will only shew in the presence of witnesses—I like the fellow for his caution. I want, however, you and that very sensible lady Mrs Soorocks to come over in the morning, and tiff at Nawaubpore tomorrow, when we shall meet the fellow and will be able to say something more about it. 'Tis a d—d hard case, however, to be plucked so unexpectedly and that too by one whom the unconscionable sea has given up, as it would seem, for the express purpose. It puts me in mind of a story which once happened in Calcutta. An officer was going up the country, and somewhere above Cossembazar, his budgerow was upset, and the Doudies all drowned; he was himself ashore at the time, and so escaped.

When he found what had happened, his business being urgent, he got to the nearest village, where he procured some kind of conveyance to a station, and proceeded by Dawk. The vessel, however, was picked up and as he had not been heard of it was presumed he had perished with the rest. So his agents in Calcutta immediately mounted black waistcoats and entered a probat to his will. But lo and behold they received a letter from their late friend dated at Agra, stating that as he had lost all his *Shraub* by the upsetting of his budgerow, he'd thank them to send a fresh supply."

Here I found it necessary again to interrupt the Burrah Sahib, by saying that I would not fail to be with him at the time proposed—asking him at the same time if he would take something after his ride.

"Thank ye, my good Sir," said he, "I'll take a glass of Brandy Pawney, as the evening's hot."

I immediately ordered the brandy and some spring-water fresh from the well. While preparing the beverage, he resumed—

"The would-be genteel coxcombs of Calcutta scout Brandy Pawney as vulgar, but we old sportsmen of the Mafussil know better than that comes to.

"There's my worthy friend old Sir Thomas—When he came round to Calcutta he took up his quarters with old Frank at Barrackpore. Now the old peer always kept lots of the very best wines, chiefly French, and other thin potations that did not at all suit the tone of Sir Tom's stomach—still, by way of kindness, Frank used to press him to drink every wine on the table. The Knight was obliged to comply from politeness but often while swallowing the well-cooled stuff he would sigh for his old friend the brandy-bottle—One day he got to Calcutta, and slipping quietly on board of a Dinghy[2] he pushed off for the ship which had brought him round from Bombay and declared to the captain that he was apprehensive of a gangrene in his bowels from the gallons of sour trash he had swallowed and though it was only two o' clock P. M. the brace of them sat down, and finished their six tumblers apiece, which the gentleman declared was the saving of his life—O it's a famous thing Brandy Pawney. My worthy friend Dr Jock recommended it both by precept and example—By the bye, Jock sent me out some of the d—d black draught he's so fond of when some time ago I felt myself bilious and queesy; but as I was well before it arrived, I thought it a pity such good stuff should be thrown to the dogs so I

---

[2] *Dinghy*: Moir misread and printed the meaningless 'Drughy'.

ordered a dose of it for my best China pig for it was then slightly indisposed, as a Cockney would say, and do you know it poisoned her! She died within the hour—d—d lucky I did not take it myself."

Here the Nabob having finished his tumbler rose and requesting me not to forget my appointment, adding that he would send his carriage to fetch Mrs Soorocks, bade me good night.

CHAPTER XXVIII

I went by times next morning to the residence of Mrs Soorocks, but on approaching the house I discovered many signs which indicated that the Lady could not conveniently accompany me. It was washing-day and the little grass plat within the sweetbriar hedge between her house and the high road was covered with all manner of female and household drapery. Ropes fastened in various directions to the iron railing, the lilac-trees and the bolts and bars of the window shutters were fastooned with shifts, sheets, and night gowns, fixed on by split pieces of wood feruled with tin—napkins and towels were spread upon the rose and gooseberry bushes and the large tablecolth so admired at her New year's day festivals, for its damasked views of Amsterdam in Holland, and other foreign cities, hung upon a special cord, like a mainsail between the lime and the rowan tree across the path leading to the front door—Access at one entrance being thus shut out, I was obliged to go round to the back of the house, the great scene of the operations of the day.

In the front of the wash house with her petticoats kilted far above her knees,[1] in the midst of a washing tub, my friend Leezy like Tam o' Shanter's Nansy ravishingly "lap and flang" enveloped in a spray of soap suds, like a goddess amidst the spouting tritons of a Parisian fountain.

Deep within the steamy shade of the wash house, the full round physiognomy of the cook, like the moon in a mist, loomed through the rising vapours and in the darkness beyond, Jean Japples the hired washerwoman stood elevated on a tripod like another Medea over the cauldron renovating the contents of it with an ex-broomstick.

Not seeing Mrs Soorocks, I turned round to enquire at Leezy for her mistress; but at the same moment, the lady herself made her appearance, in dishevelled morning apparel, with a watering-pan in her hand—On seeing me she set it down and coming forward begged that I would walk into the house. I explained, however, on the spot, the object of

---

[1] *her petticoats kilted far above her knees*: Moir made suitable modifications to this paragraph.

my visit and the wish of the Nabob that she would accompany me "but I see," said I, "that it is a pleasure I cannot expect today."

"It's vera true," was the reply, "for we're thrang and in confusion wi' our summer washing; it's just extraordinar what a family files in the course o' half a year, forbye the filing o' sma' claes atweenhands—but it's a trouble you men are never fash'd wi'—some of ye even laugh at us drudging women—My dear Mr Soorocks used to say in his jocosity that twa washins were equal to one whitewashin, twa white-washins to one flitting, and twa flittins to one fire—Really, I'm fash'd that I canna go wi' you, and I wad fain stretch a point if it were possible, for the Nabob's cold collections are verra nice, and he himsel so much o' the gentleman—But, dear me, is na that his carriage coming alang the road—it's no in possibility to come up to the door, and I hae naebody to gang to the yett to speak to that gran fitman—Leezie, put down your coats[2] and step out o' the boyne and say I'm dressin, for I maun go noo, as nae doubt he has just sent the coach on purpose."

Accordingly while Leezy went round to the gate, taking time to adjust her own apparel which was no more in a state to receive visitors than that of her mistress, Mrs Soorocks went into the house and in less time than could reasonably have been expected, (she is a clever woman) returned prepared for the visit.

As soon as we were seated in the carriage I related with some degree of minuteness what the Nabob had told me of the state of his feelings towards the family of Colonel Bayfield.

"Weel," said the lady at the conclusion, "I aye said that Nawaubpore had a generous heart for a' his vanity and ostentation but it will be a dreadfu' thing if a man like him—so kind a neighbour and who may be a blessing to the country side—should he empoverished by an impostor. I'll no soon forget the genteel way he pardoned at my intercession that daized remnant Auldbiggings and maybe in requeesht-ing me to be present this day at the precognition it may be put in my poore to return his condesension."

"But surely, Mrs Soorocks, if the case is clearly made out that the boy is the son of Colonel Bayfield you would not think of intercepting the just intentions of Mr Rupees?"

" 'If's' a word o' poore—It's no in the course o' nature, Sir, for a ship burned at sea and all hands on board perished, should send forth a leevin witness to contradic the fac."

[2] *put down your coats*: put yourself right (Moir).

"True, but it would appear that all on board had not perished."

"Now that's what I'll no credit and I'll gie you the reason of my misdout. Wha's the testimony?—A land-louper that naebody kens onything about—Ah, Sir, if ye had sic experience of the devices of man that I hae had, ye wadna be sae credulous. A man comin out o' the deep, like a Robinson Crusoe, wi' a white Friday, to claim awa' the biggest half o' a gentleman's fortune—it's just a thing for playactors, and the likes o' Sir Walter,[3] to mak a clishmaclaver o'; but amang people o' understanding, it canna but be seen through as a contrivance begotten in sin, and brocht forth in eniquity."

"There are many circumstances in the story," said I, "singular and almost improbable, I admit. But Mr Coball, the Stranger, appeared to be a man of unaffected sincerity—warm in his feelings, and simple in his manners."

"Simple manners—that shews that ye're an author that may be skilled in books but scant o' skill in the wicked heart o' man—Did ye no hear o' the leesin makin that I was made the innocent victim o', nae farther gane than last year when the ne'erdoweel wi' a blackit face came through the kintra, makin a wally-waeing about how he was blawn up in a bombshell by the Algerines. I had my doots o' the story when he cam to my door though he made it be a very true-like tale, as your condesciple from the uttermost ends o' the earth tells his—but no to be thought a'thegether hard-hearted, I put doon a sixpence in his book o' beggerry wi' my name til't, and what do ye think the graceless Gehazi did? He gaed to Widow M'Plooky's public, and waur'd the sixpence on gills; so waurin the sixpence on gills he forged ten shillings before my sixpence, makin it look in the book like half-a-guinea. Then he gaed to Mrs Scuitles and she seeing my name doon for ten shillings and sixpence, and knowin me for a woman o' moderate means, and o' a sifting and discerning spirit, she put doon hersel for a whole guinea. Syne he gaed to auld Leddy Roughills and she, no to be behint hand, gied him another guinea and then he ventured to my lord's, wha wi' his dochters could do nae less than double the example. But as he was on his way to the Nabob, the drink—for of course he had been dry by the way—took his head, and he fell on the road at the toll, where he was kent, and was there brought to light, for in dighting his face, he dighted aff the cork coom, and stood before the tollkeeper a barefaced malefactor—Think what I was obliged to endure, wi' the wite o'

[3] *Sir Walter*: i.e. Scott. Galt first had Scott write a 'novelle' but he amended the line and had him write a 'clishmaclaver'.

being such a simpleton as to gie him such a lovegift largess; ye see what it is to believe stories o' folk blawn up in the air, and what ye're like to get for your pains."

"You have certainly assigned, Mrs Soorocks, very good and sufficient reasons for doing nothing rashly; I have, however, no apprehension that Mr Rupees will suffer himself to be easily deceived."

"He'll no be alloo'd were he e'er sae willing, if I hae ony voice—It would be even doon compos mentos to give ear to the tale o' a Jonah frae the whale's belly; but whisht, whisht, for here's the house, and there's ane o' the heathens leadin Mr Caption's whuskey to the stables. Weel, I'm glad o' that—deed it was na to be thocht that a man 'o judgement and sensibility like Nawaubpore would be content on sic an occasion wi' the like o' you, or even o' me, to bear witness."

CHAPTER XXIX

On being shown into the library, we found already before us Mr Coball with a small red leather brass-nailed trunk in his hand and the boy at his side seated on a sofa. The Nabob was at the writing-table opposite with Mr Caption at his right hand. The reception of Mrs Soorocks was particularly gracious nor had I cause to complain of any deficiency of heartiness in mine.

The proceedings were opened by a summary statement of the whole story from the Nabob, who on this occasion shewed both his shrewdness and good sense as a man of business; he made no digressions but concluded with requesting Mr Coball to produce his vouchers.

The red case was accordingly unclosed, and the letters laid on the table. The Nabob took them up one by one and having looked at them carefully was on the point, as I thought, of acknowledging at once their authenticity when Mr Caption said, who probably thought the same thing:—

"It is not enough to be certain as to the writing—look at the paper, the seals do not appear to me as if they were exact impressions of an original seal."

The Nabob knit his brows but made no answer.

Here Mrs Soorocks stepped forward and lifting one of the letters looked at the seal, and said—

"It's opinion this is no wax at a', but fidler's rosett, wi' gold foilzie in't, and oh it's waff paper—Nawaubpore, ye wad never write your letters on huxtry tea paper."

The Nabob smiled and shook his head and Mrs Soorocks looked to me with a triumphant countenance.

"Any dishonest servant," said Caption, "might become possessed of such papers, admitting—for the sake of argument—that they be genuine—"

"True," replied Mr Coball, "but such letters do not appear, from anything in their contents, to have been worth the stealing."

"Hoo can ye tell what a covetous minded servant wad think worth stealing?" cried Mrs Soorocks eagerly. "I had a servant lass that stole one o' Mr Soorocks' Greek books—What use could a Greek book be to her? But she confessed that she did steal it—There's no telling what dishonest servants will do."

The Nabob interposed.

"The letters are mine," said he and turning to the lady, added jocularly, "as to the wax, I know it well, I bought it at Hazaribang; and the paper is Chinese, I brought from India with me. Moreover on reference to my Dawkbook now before me I find that the dates agree."

"But," he added, addressing himself to Mr Coball, "it is strange that you should have obtained possession of these letters only—Have you nothing else—for they prove nothing as to the identity of the boy there."

"With these letters," replied Mr Coball, "were several valuable trinkets and two packets of pearls."

"And what have you done with them?" cried Caption eagerly.—"'Tis easy to say so—"

"He'll hae made awa' wi' them," said Mrs Soorocks in a half whisper to me.

"No, Madam," replied Mr Coball, who had overheard her, "they are here," and he laid the packets and trinkets on the table.

Caption was evidently confounded, while the Nabob's countenance brightened.

"But I canna see," resumed Mrs Soorocks, "hoo a wheen gew-gaws can prove that black's white or, ony mair than the letters, mak it a bit clearer that this bairn's no anither."

"Certainly not, madam," said Mr Caption firmly—"Certainly not, you are quite right."

"I thocht I wad be sae," said Mrs Soorocks and she looked significantly to me.

The Nabob in the mean time was examining the trinkets and I observed that he noticed a necklace with particular attention.

Mr Coball at this crisis took out of the trunk a small neat pocket memorandum book and presented it open to the Nabob, saying—

"I think this must have been a diary which Mrs Bayfield was keeping of our voyage—the last entry is the date of the very day preceding that night on which our calamity happened."

"I acknowledge," said the Nabob at the first glance, "that the writing appears to be Mrs Bayfield's."

"But what does that prove?" said Mr Caption.

"You will find," said the Stranger calmly, "that my name, James Coball, is mentioned in a list of the passengers at the beginning."

Here Mrs Soorocks begged to look at the list.

"To be sure," said she, "there is the name of a James Coball; but whaur's the proof that ye are that James Coball, or that ye are a James Coball at a'?"

The Stranger looked confused.

"Yes," cried Caption, "where is the evidence of that fact?"

No immediate answer was given but after a short pause, Mr Coball answered—

"I think sufficient evidence has been produced to convince any honest man that there is truth enough in my story to induce the executor of the late Colonel Bayfield to examine the whole circumstances although there is not enough to make the heir in possession of Colonel Bayfield's property surrender to this boy, but when I add that several of those who were saved with us in the boat, and particularly the officer to whom we were so much indebted, are alive, and I believe are at this time in England it would seem to me that beyond a decent investigation of the facts there would be little honour or honesty in resisting the claim."

The Nabob looked at me and said—

"He's an honest man, after all."

"Dinna be deceived, Nawaubpore," exclaimed Mrs Soorocks, "for there's mair depends upon this matter than being beguiled wi' a blackened ne'erdoweel as I was, ye ken, last year."

The Nabob turned to Caption—"Ought we not immediately to institute an enquiry to find those witnesses?"

"No, Sir," replied Caption, with a professional smirk—"No, Sir, the *onus probandi* lie with this gentleman, who hath spontaneously placed himself *in loco parentis* to the infant."

"Ye're a man o' discretion,[1] Mr Caption," cried Mrs Soorocks, her countenance brightening with satisfaction—"Ye're a man o' discretion. I aye thocht there was something in your head, whatever ill-natured folk might say o' the bossness o' your heart."

The lawyer took no notice of this remark which, like most of the good lady's compliments, cut both ways but resumed—

"It is not to be expected that the respondent is to furnish the pursuer with evidence; even the jury court would hardly require anything so unreasonable."

"But, Mr Caption," said the Nabob, "it may turn out in this case that I am both plaintiff and defendant and all I require is full and suffi-

---

[1] *man o' discretion*: man o' observation (Moir misreads the script).

124

cient proof; for another heir may make his appearance. I wish I had Craigdarroch with me to set us on a proper train; but, d—n him, he's doing patriot just now, and humbugging the nincompoops of the Stewardry. If we had him even fresh from one of his election dinners, I should be content, for I have known him after a hard drink, and before going to bed, give a clearer and sounder opinion than any of his bre-theren could after a light supper and a sober sleep—He once conducted a case for me—"

"Na," interrupted Mrs Soorocks, "if he's a man o' that discernment he'll do us some credit in the parliament house, and that's mair than can weel be said of a' 'the chosen five and forty.' "

The Nabob here rejoined,—

"This business, my dear lady, promises no good to your friend the Laird for, in duty to myself, it will be necessary to forclose his mortgage immediately—Caption, you will take no notice of my note of last night desiring you to stay the proceedings against Mr Mailings."

"Very well, sir," replied Caption—"misjudged levity, as I said—but as your order was in writing you will be pleased instruct me in writing to the contrary effect."

"Oh, Mr Roopy (Nawaubpore, as I should say)," exclaimed Mrs Soorocks, "haud your haun and be melted to tender mercies or what will become o' the puir auld man? Work he canna and want he maunna —he'll be a burden upon us all and little do you ken o' the woe ye may bring upon a most excellent woman, for he's on the point of marriage wi' Miss Shoosie Minnigaff, ane o' the amiable leddies o' Barenbraes—She'll dee o' a broken heart if she does na lay violent hauns on hersel."

This sad and gentle appeal, instead of producing the desired effect on the Nabob, only served to make him burst into an immoderate fit of laughter.

"Married! the old guddah! and to one of those cameleopards too! Who the devil contrived this hopeful union? It must have been yourself, Mrs Soorocks for it never could have entered into the heart of man—of any man—to marry a crane—an adjutant is corpulent compared to her —Why, my good lady, if the worst comes to the worst, he can only simply be starved; but if your benevolent scheme were accomplished, he would be starved and pecked to boot—But this long sederunt as you would call it, Mr Caption, will go well nigh to starve us all, so I shall order dinner, when I hope you will all honour me with your company —Mr Coball do you, as soon as possible, procure the necessary evidence.

You may rest assured, that there shall be no unnecessary or vexatious delay on my part—only make good your proves and I shall be delighted to do justice to the son of my old friend."

"Na," said Mrs Soorocks aside to me, "the man's demented—Did ye ever hear o' sic a distracted action? To give up a property—and sic a property—without being obligated according to law—I ken advocates in Enbro', Nawaubpore, that could keep the case in Court for a' your days. There's my frien W—."

Here dinner was announced, and we adjourned to the banquetting-room.

CHAPTER XXX

Next morning, agreeably to an appointment which I had made with Mrs Soorocks as we came home together in the Nabob's carriage, I went over to her house to carry her with me on an expiatory visit to the ladies of Barenbraes. We had agreed that the decision of the Nabob's character, notwithstanding his vanity and foibles, was such as left no hope he would again recede from his determination to foreclose the mortgage on the lands of Auldbiggings; I had therefore urged her with all my powers of persuasion to call with me on the venerable sisters in our way home; the cares, however, of her great washing pressed heavily on her mind, and she could not at the time think of consenting; but, to do her justice, she evinced no reluctance to make an ample apology to Miss Shoosie, and in consequence, it was agreed that the ceremony thereof should be deterred till the following day.

On the day following, accordingly, I went to her house and we walked leisurely on together.

"I'm thinkin," said she, as we got on the footpath of the high road— "I'm thinkin that the auld man, if we were to forsake him now, would be a perfec object but I feel that we are agents in the hands o' providence, raised up as it were like babes and sucklings, to bring him out o' the house o' bondage, the which in my opinion, is the debtor's-hole in the Talbooth, if waur than captivity were not to be his lot."

"I agree, Ma'am, in all you say; it is most consolatory to think that we are both afforded an opportunity to shew how mankind are capable of doing a disinterested action."

"I'll mak nae rouse o' mysel," replied the lady; "but I ken the secrets o' my own breast; and though I dinna wish to lightly your loving-kindness towards Auldbiggings, I hae a notion, it may be something like a bit spunk o' curiosity that has helped to heat the zeal o' your disinterestedness; for I have remarked—I mean no offence—that ye hae a particular pleasure in lookin into the catastrophes o' ither folks. For my part I am thankfu' to walk wi' a humble heart and a contrite spirit. For if good come o' my sma' endeavour sure am I that nane o' the merit thereof can be attributed to me."

Thus piously discoursing we plodded onward to the door of

Barenbraes and, as it was agreed between us, I entered first and thus opened the business:—

"Ladies, I have brought with me a person whom we have all great reason to esteem—ever since she had the misfortune to incur your displeasure she has been the most wretched of womankind—she comes to confess a fault, to acknowledge a sin, and if you require it, even on bended knees, to kiss the hems o' your garments—"

"In a figurative sense," interrupted Mrs Soorocks.

But I waved my hand to her to be quiet, and continued:—

"Miss Girzie, I have long respected your prudence, and valued your excellent sense; so I told our mutual friend here, that although her offence was of very great enormity—"

"Her impiddence was large," cried Miss Shoosie.

"Yes, Miss Shoosie, her impudence was large, indeed, but her repentance is without measure—"

"In a certain sense," said Mrs Soorocks.

"But," continued I, "it would be idle to waste words on ladies of your piety were I to attempt to urge that this was a case for the exercise of the Christian grace of forgiveness. If Mrs Soorocks be hasty in temper and rash in tongue, you know, Miss Girzie, that you have the failing of sometimes giving provocation, and Miss Shoosie, mild as ye are, which my friend Mr Mailings regards as the greatest grace of your gentle sex, yet you know that there are times when the best of us may err, and even when you yourself—"

"If," interrupted Miss Shoosie, "Mrs Soorocks has come to beg my pardon, she'll find that I'll no be insensible to the dishonour she has brought upon hersel."

"She comes to beg your pardon but you must not use such words as dishonour when we are treating of peace—Mrs Soorocks, do you ask pardon of the ladies?—Ladies, do you on your part acknowledge that faults were on both sides? For in the exercise of a sound discretion reciprocal concession is what I would recommend to all."

"Weel, leddies," said Mrs Soorocks, "since it maun be sae, what can we do but submit,—

I think, Miss Shoosie, ye give baith the sore stroke and the loud cry; howsever, since it's a' past, and we're friens again—"

"Friends!" cried Miss Girzie, with an English accent—"Friends! we may forgive what's past but I see no obligation for us to be friends."

"Come, come, ladies, neighbours should be neighbour-like," said I, "and, Miss Shoosie, if you knew the cause that has brought Mrs

Soorocks here today, instead of standing so far aloof from reconciliation, you would embrace her in your arms, and press her to your heart—She has been explaining to me the mournful situation of Mr Mailings ever since he has been told that the woman of his choice has set a price upon her love. Scarcely had you left my house the other night when the poor dejected gentleman came in, dressed from the bottom of his coffer, and told us—Mrs Soorocks was present—that he was so far on his way to visit the lady whom he was desirous of making his wife. But judge what his sorrow and disappointment were when we spoke of you, knowing as we did (alas! too truly) the mercenary motives by which even in charity we could not but acknowledge you were actuated."

"It's no my fault," interposed Miss Shoosie, "for if ye had waited to hear what me and my sister were going to say the other night you would never have thocht us such mercenary women as to have broken off with a gentleman like Mr Mailings for the lucre o' gain."

"Na," said Mrs Soorocks, "considering the jeopardy that you and your sister are in, o' a sudden retribution frae your sister, Leddy Chandos like a thief in the night, ye wud hae been waur than mad had ye made a hesitation and swuthering, for oh it rins before me,[1] Miss Shoosie, that the time is at hand when the cry o' the bridegroom coming will be raised, and—as I often tell you-see that ye be not found a foolish virgin with no oil in your lamp—I canna imagine, leddies, what maks you swither."

"We dinna swither; but we would act prudently."

"Ca'ye't acting prudently, in your situations to risque the loss of a most estimable man's affections for what canna be modesty, Miss Shoosie—you sure hae lived ower lang in the world to ken what modesty means between fifty and threescore—Leddies, leddies, I maun use the freedom o' an auld frien wi' you—ye're tyning your time. Just come ower the night, and tak your tea wi' me, and I'll send for Mr Mailings and as Nawaubpore's a Justice o' the Peace I dinna misdout his coming, and we'll get the marriage put out o' haun—"

Miss Shoosie cast down her eyes as she replied—

"I could never think of such a rash step."

"Oh! Mrs Soorocks," exclaimed Miss Girzie, "it's what I never could alloo—twa clandestine marriages in my father's family—oh no!"

"You are quite right, Miss Girzie, it would make folk expect a third."

"Deed," said Mrs Soorocks, "noo, when I think o't, it might

[1] *it rins before me*: Moir altered to the end of the paragraph, changing the sense and deleting all references to virgins and bridegrooms.

occasion malicious insinuations to the great damage and detriment of Miss Shoosie's fair fame, considering the well-known and long-tried affection subsisting between her and the Laird; so I'll no resist, but come to your tea and I'll hae Mr Mailings o' the party, when we can arrange a' about the booking and the buying o' your bridal braws, since ye will hae a regular marriage."

Having thus established peace and arranged as I had supposed the business of the evening and being regaled with the ladies' home-made wine, Mrs Soorocks and I bade them adieu and bent our steps towards Auldbiggings. Before we had, however, reached the bottom of the avenue, we discerned Jock coming from the house like an ostrich at full speed, his arms swinging in the air, and his skirts streaming behind. As he drew near, horror and consternation were legible in his countenance, and in one hand he held a letter, which he gave to me, before he could collect breath to explain the burden of his haste wherefore he did so. As the shortest means of discovering the motive of his speed, I opened the letter and read as follows:—

To Malachi Mailings, Esquire of Auldbiggings

Sir,

I am instructed by my client Mr Walter Rupees of Nawaubpore to beg your attention to my last dated 3d current and further to state that if satisfaction is not rendered thereto *quam primam*[2] diligence will immediately issue.

I am further instructed with respect to the matter of the interest due last month, and *toties quoties* called for to request an answer *quam primam*.

I am Sir,
Your obedient Servant

Hugh Caption

By this time Jock had recovered his breath, and said,—

"Weel, ye see the last trumpet's noo blawn,—what's to be done?— is't no possible to get a respite till the lottery be drawn?—The Laird's just gane by hinsel—he's toddlin bot and toddlin ben the house, whiles wringin his hauns and whiles makin murgeons as if he was speakin, puir auld man—It was a better world when gentlemen were na fash'd wi' law—I'm sure the ten commandments are worth a' the King's statutes, and ye'll no fin' a word in them about payin' o' debts, e'en an

---

[2] *quam primam: quam primum* (Moir). But Galt *intended* his lawyer to make a mistake in the Latin.

ye were able—I'm just wud to think o' the mischief that this law—law—law has brocht upon poor Scotland—But oh! I'm glad to see you and Mrs Soorocks—ye'll be a great cordial to him under his calamity and oh, Mem, dinna mak your charity on the present occasion a bit and a buffet wi't; but speak him kindly, for oh, he's helpless, and far past the power o' Jenny Clatterpans and me to gie him ony comfort even though we baith fleeched him and clapped him on the showthers, yin at every side, to tak anither tumbler o' toddy; for hath not Solomon said in the words of Robin Burns,—[3]

> 'Gie him strong drink until he wink,
> That's sinkin in despair?'

Blyth was I when I saw you comin but when ye gang to the house, dinna let wit that ye hae seen me or ken ony thing about what's gaun to happen, for our Laird was aye proud and this misfortune has made him a power for pride—he storm'd at Jenny Clatterpans and me for our kindness and push'd us awa and wonder'd hoo we daured to be sae familiar wi' our master, cryin out—a wee deleerit as I thocht—that had it no been for the poortith come upon him we would never hae been sae upsetting and he wited it a' on the liberty and equality spirit o' the times and the taxes and the high wages that were grindin the rightfu' gentry frae aff the face o' the earth.—Noo, dear Sir and Mem, I beg and beseech that ye'll speak him kindly and mak much o' him, for oh he's grown thin-skinned—Mrs Soorocks, he canna thole a taunt noo."

This sad account of the Laird's condition had the effect of embarrassing us both and on leaving the simple and faithful creature, we proceeding towards "the Place," without exchanging a word or making a single comment on what we had heard.

---

[3] *Solomon . . . in the words of . . . Burns*: The verse is from Burns' epigraph (from 'Solomon's Proverbs') to his 'Scotch Drink'.

CHAPTER XXXI

On approaching the door, Jenny Clatterpans was standing there, and from time to time she looked towards the garden—the other maid was also visible behind her and every now and then took a peep in the same direction. The aspect of Jenny was visibly troubled, nor did her companion's wear a more tranquil expression, but still the countenances of both betokened something which commanded deference to their feelings.

Whether Mrs Soorocks felt exactly as I did, it were impossible to determine by any thing in her voice or gestures, but she abruptly left me and went towards the maids. At the same moment I happened to turn round and discovered the Laird walking to and fro in the garden, with his hands behind, his eyes perusing the grass of the walks, and his whole figure by the bend and by the solemnity of his air indicating the perplexity of his spirit.

I went immediately towards him, none displeased at that moment to be relieved from the presence of Mrs Soorocks. I put on the blithest face I could assume, and tuned my voice to cheerfulness as I drew near to the dejected old man. But although he saw me coming, and nodded in his wonted familiar manner as I approached the walk which he was pacing, he soon relapsed into his reverie, and moved along unconscious of being so observed.

I stopped, some ten or fifteen yards from him, I looked forward, and the distress of his mind though visibly mingled with a strong ingredient of absurdity, was yet such as could not be seen without sympathy.

As he walked along the dank unmowed grass,[1] he paused suddenly, and stooping forward, he pulled a rose.

"It's my ain yet," said he with a smile, as he turned round and smelling it, held it out towards me.

"It has grown in my forefathers' land," he added, "I got the slip frae Castlesemple[2] garden—I set it mysel—I made the hole for't wi'

---

[1] *dank unmowed grass*: dark unmowed grass (Moir's misreading of the script results in nonsense).

[2] *Castlesemple*: estate, 5 miles west of Paisley, Galt's topography is, as always, accurate and 'real'.

my ain very finger—I watered it wi' the china jug that was my father's punch porringer, as I hae heard my kind mother say—and what can be a man's ain, if that bush and bud be na mine?"

Then he moved some four or five paces, and tearing the flower into pieces he scattered the petals around, and knitting his brows and clenching his hands he rushed with his left hand extended as if he entreated and deprecated some afflicting power, revealed in form only to himself. It is the particular characteristic of all grieful emotions to move and gesticulate with the left arm as in like manner it is for those of power and exertion to indicate their predominance by the energy and emphasis of the right.

When that brief paroxysm had subsided, he returned leisurely and sedately towards the spot where I was standing.

"Is there no a possible o' ony kind, by the which this may be eschewed?"

He seemed to think by the expression that I must of course be acquainted with the cause and sources of his trouble, and had his perturbation been less obviously painful, perhaps I might have played a little with his perplexities, but his look was so vacant and infantine that it was impossible to regard him with any other sentiment than pity.

"I understand," said I, "that the Nabob has resolved to follow out his determination. I am sorry for't but his own condition half pleads in extenuation of his rigour."

"It was a luckless day," was the answer, "when the thread of my life was ravelled wi' his knotty thrums—my lot and station, though lanerly, was lown—I had nae law fashin me, but only an uncertainty about a bit heritable bond, that in sense was na worth the speaking about—Noo, I'm driven to desperation— There's that limb o' Satan, Caption, greetin in the King's name—there's John Angle, the surveyor, demanding a compensation for detriment—and there's that goolden image o' Nebuchadnedzor, Rupees—Oh, oh, and alas! if I was na preserved I wud droon mysel—My book I canna write—to work I'm no able—the curse o' Gilbert, when he was a beggar man, has overtaken me for when the three pound in the desk head is spent and gone I'll no hae a penny left for a morsel—I'm a destitute creatur—I'm a forlorn auld man—I'm a vera object—Oh, I'm an object!"

I endeavoured to console him as well as I could but the sense of desolation was so strong upon him that the endeavour was ineffectual.

"It's a terrible thing," cried he, "for a man to be miserable—O, Adam and Eve, ye hae muckle to answer for—If I was young, I would be a sodger—If I was composed, I could write an instructin book—Had I been bred a tailor I could have made claes but I canna even sing ballats; for the Lord in his displeasure[3] made me wi' a timmer tune. I can do naething but beg. I'll no can lang even gang frae door to door—for I'm auld, and I hae an income in my leg—I'll hae to sit on a stane on the road side wi' a ragged hat on my knee and my bare grey head in the shower—Heaven preserve me, will I be sittin beggin at my ain yett!"—

The last sentence was uttered with a tone of horror that made me shudder, and I said,—

"Mr Mailings, do not give way to such frightful presentiments; I beseech you to be more composed."

"I'll be put in a prison," cried he—"I'll be fastened doon wi' an airn chain in the debtor's hole—but what will they mak by that? for I hae naething—the Dyvor's bill[4] can do nae gude to a failed and broken hearted auld beggar man—To be sure, I might steal cocks and hens and be sent to Botany Bay but what could I do there—O dear, I wish I was in another world, for my use and part in this world is done now."

He then walked away from me, and continued for several minutes pacing another part of the garden—Sometimes he halted and raised his hand as if he were arguing with himself, anon he quickened his pace and at last he turned briskly round and came rushing towards me with exultation in his countenance.

"I hae found a redemption," he exclaimed. "I'll marry Miss Shoosie Minnigaff. She has goold in goupens. I hae heard my mither say there wasna sic a plenished napery chest as the yin at Barenbraes in a' the west o' Scotland and if I dinna like her, ye ken she'll hae the means of providing hersel wi' a separate maintenance."

So intense had been the distress of the old man that I really felt as it were relieved when he proposed to adopt this sinister and sordid expedient and in consequence—it may be not in a spirit of the purest morality—I applauded his resolution, and began to commend the merits and qualities of the lady with many a magnifying augmentative.

At this juncture, Mrs Soorocks joined us; it was evident by her manner as she approached that the servants had very sensibly affected

---

[3] *the Lord in his displeasure*: Heaven in its displeasure (Moir). Some of Moir's changes are curiously reminiscent of those that legislation made necessary in the First Folio text of Shakespeare.

[4] *the Dyvor's bill*: bankruptcy.

her compassion and her exhileration was at least equal to mine when I told her that the Laird had resolved to marry Miss Shoosie.

"It's a wark" said he, however with a sigh.

"And of mercy to yoursel, Laird, that ye'll alloo—But no to mak mair clishmaclaver about it—I expect my friend Bailie Waft frae Paisley in the afternoon, so ye'll come ouer and tak your tea and a crack wi' him and I'll send for the leddies and we'll soon get a' settled."

"It's a soor drogue, Mem," replied the Laird; "but the ill and the ail need the dose—I canna but say that it's a most extraordinar thing that a man has na a choice o' his ain in choosin the wife of his bosom. That weddings are made in heaven I'll ne'er believe—or the angels are as yet but prentices[5] in the craft and calling o' match making—to think that ever I should hae been brocht to marry such a grey gull as Shoosie Minnigaff—it's an iniquity—it's a cryin sin—it's a sellin o' me to the Ismaelites—D—l tak baith law and gospel, I'll no marry her yet—"

"But consider," cried Mrs Soorocks, "there's Mr Caption—"

"Whare?" cried the Laird, starting and looking round.

"And Mr Angle," resumed the lady, "demanding, as I am told, twenty golden guineas for his curiosity."

"He may thank the government," replied the Laird, "that it's an impossibility to get them; was na the guineas put doon and hidden frae the light o' day, and the sight and reach o' man, in the bottomless dungeons o' the Bank o' England, like prisoners doomed to everlasting captivity, a' to let the King raise money by a stamp act on bank notes, by the which—"

Here the old man was getting on his hobby when Mrs Soorocks interfered with—

"Hoot toot, Laird, we dinna want to hear o' your standard unit the noo when we're speakin' o' marriage—so ye'll just come to your tea and meet your bloomin bride and leave a' the lave o' the trouble to folk that understand thae matters better than yoursel."

[5] *angels . . . prentices*: Moir eliminated this 'irreligious' reference.

CHAPTER XXXII

At the time appointed, and punctual to the hour, I was at the door of Mrs Soorocks. My friend Leezy admitted me with a pleasant and significant smile—I was desirous of saying something to her on the occasion but, the parlour door being open, I could only smile in return and walk forward.

On entering the room, I was delighted to see the Laird in full dress and the two ladies of Barenbraes, all there before me. Miss Shoosie was sitting far aloof, with downcast eyes, and looking interestingly bridal, to the best of her ability. The air of Miss Girzie was more disengaged and she was seated beside the Laird seemingly on terms of easy conversation. Mrs Soorocks herself was busy spreading and cutting down the greater part of a large loaf.

As the entertainment[1] was of a pre-nuptial character, it was of course of more than wonted ceremony and, accordingly, the custom prevalent not only among the higher circles of the "canny town" but generally among the country gentry of Renfrewshire, "clumsy tea," was dispensed with—by clumsy tea I should explain for the benefit of the ruder world is meant a very substantial meal is served at which, in addition to the delicacies of jellies, marmalades, shortbread, puffs, cookies, seedcakes and carraways, the cheese and the ham always appear and at the time of the killing of the mart cowheel with tripe and onions are sometimes superadded and not infrequently that inscrutable luxury, whose ingredients must not to genteel ears be described— *videlicet* white pudding.

A little behind Mrs Soorocks and not observable on first entering the room, her cousin, Bailie Waft, was seated refreshing himself after his walk with a glass of whisky and water sweetened with Muscovado sugar.

"Dear me, Bailie," exclaimed Mrs Soorocks, looking around after I was seated, "what have I been about—no to gie you a lime when

[1] *the entertainment*: Moir deleted entirely this description of a Renfrew 'clumsy tea' (or 'towsie tea', the more usual term). But Galt clearly intended this list of 'vulgar' delicacies, cowheel, tripe and onions, and white pudding, to set the tone of the whole chapter.

I hae got five left o' the half a dizzen that was sent to me by the carrier frae our frien Mrs Puncheons. What dainties thae West India folk in Glasgow enjoy! They weel ken hoo to mak turtle soup wi' Madeira wine, and no like the lady o' their port that boiled a whole turtle fish wi' barley and kail and was feared to eat it, thinkin it was na wholesom because it didna turn red in the shell like a partan."

So saying she rose and opening her cupboard door took out a lime from five lying in a small china plate, shrivelled on the skin and as brown as walnuts.

By the bye, Mrs Soorocks' cupboard was what in Renfrewshire was called a dining room press, being one of those exhibitions of domestic Museums peculiar to the royal county and as hers was an example of the kind it well deserves to be particularly described.

The folding doors disclosed an arched niche, with pilasters on each side. The shelves were scolloped in the edges, the whole painted of a bright green and the edges of the shelves and the capitals of the pilasters were gaudily tricked and gilded.

On the bulging centre of the first shelf lay inverted a large punch bowl, on the bottom of which stood one of lesser dimensions out of which rose a curious cordial bottle with two necks. The bowl was flanked with a row of long shanked wine glasses, with white spiral ornaments in the stalks, and at the extremity of each wing stood a tall urn like china pot with a lid. In the obscurity behind the glasses you might discover a row of china plates on their edges; and above each on a brass nail, hung as many custard glasses by their handles.

On the second floor the curiosities were somewhat reversed. The shelf receded in the middle and sweeping forward on both sides projected over the trays, below which each projection was adorned with the tall spiral stalked glasses already described. On each of these projections, two middle sized punch bowls were inverted—the bottom of each surmounted with a china teapot of an antic and fantastical form; in the centre was a vacant place generally occupied by the silver teapot then upon the tea table—at each side of it usually stood a lofty porcelain tower of tea cups and saucers but one of them was at this time demolished and placed on the tray for the use of the company—a variety of minor *bejeuterie* and wine glasses filled up the interstices.

The centre of the third shelf again projected and on it stood a stately chrystalline structure, consisting of several stories of syllybub glasses, crowned with a large and lofty shallow goblet which at the new year's festival of Mrs Soorocks, when the whole power and splendour of her cupboard were made effective, was usually occupied with a venerable preserved orange—a gift of some years antiquity from one of her nieces, confected *a priori* to her own wedding. On each side of this glittering and fragile pile, stood a miscellaneous assemblage of marrow-less cups, cracked poory's[2] and ale glasses flanked by two enormous goblets with the initials of the late Mr Soorocks engraved thereon. Like many of the other things, they were never used, save on the great annual banquet so often referred to; on which occasion, the one was filled with ale and the other with porter after dinner.

The tea urn having been brought in, Mrs Soorocks said—

"As ye're the young Leddy, Miss Girzie, ye'll mak the tea," and so saying, she rose from her chair at the tea table and then came and seated herself beside the Laird while I drew my chair close to the left of Miss Girzie; her sister also moved in *echelon* upon her right.

Miss Girzie having lifted one of the little silver tea cannisters, began to take out the orthodox quantity with a spoon by one spoonful for the teapot and one for each guest. During this process I heard the intended bride whisperingly say—"Girzie, dinna be wastefu', shake the spoon and no heap every yin as if it were a cart o' hay."

Tea being made, the task of handing it round was imposed upon the Laird, he being, as Mrs Soorocks observed, the young man of the company, though this chronologically was not exactly the fact.

During the time the entertainment was being served our conversation was of a general and ordinary description. Bailie Waft talked political economy and argued with the Laird against the corn laws; Mrs Soorocks expatiated on the felicity of the married state; while I said agreeable things to Miss Girzie, interspersed with exhilerative allusions in parenthesis to her sister.

So passed the time till tea was finished; and when the equipage was removed by Leezy, and the door shut, Mrs Soorocks thus began the prologue to the matrimonial theme:—

"I have long wished to see such a meeting as the present. Time wears out all things and lairds and leddies are like the flowers that bloom, and plants that perish—creatures of a day and butterflys o' the sunshine. It has often been a wonder to me how year after year should have passed away and the affection so long nourished in secret atween—I'll no say wha—should never hae come to an issue."

The Laird hemmed sceptically, and Miss Shoosie looked for her

---

[2] *poory's*: Moir altered this Scots form to 'cream-pots'.

pocket hole that she might no doubt be ready with her handkerchief.

"But," continued Mrs Soorocks, "whatever is ordained will sooner or later come to pass; and seldom hae I ever had in my life a pleasanter reflection than in seeing here twa young persons made for one another."

The Laird looked with the tail of his eye towards Miss Shoosie, and seemed as if he smelt Sinna or mandragora, while she drew her hand over her face, and perhaps pressed her cheek to make it blush.[3]

The Bailie interposed—

"There's nae need, cousin, to mak thrown up wark o' the web we hae in haun—the young couple understand one another and if the hesp has been reveled for a time it's weel redde noo—The only thing that I would object to is the delay and for twa sound and substantial reasons—first, it's an auld byeword and a true, that delays are dangerous and under the second head, I would speak o' oconomy, and anent the expense o' what extravagant wasterfu' women ca' bridal braws."

"In that," said I, interrupting him, "I agree with you, Mr Waft; on this occasion, such expenditure is quite unnecessary."

"But," rejoined Miss Girzie, "would na my sister, Mrs Soorocks, don't you think, require a riding habit for the wedding jaunt?"

"It's vera true," was the answer, "that mony a young leddy that ne'er was on a horse's back nor expects to be gets a riding habit at her marriage, the which is put to nae ither use after, then to be made up into the first breeks o' her auld son, and in that respect, there might be something to be said for your sister getting ane; but all things considered—"

Here the Laird groaned from the depths of his spirit and the Bailie quietly interposed—

"But if there is no marriage jaunt, and I see no need of such a thing, where is the need to mak an outlay for a riding habit at all?—Deed, my friens, if you'll be ruled by me, you'll mak up for your lost time and declare a marriage at once without farther summering or wintering about the matter."

"Oh," cried Miss Girzie, lifting her hands, and spreading her fingers, "Is't a possibility?"

Miss Shoosie sighed. The Laird rose from his seat and walked with his hands behind his back to one of the windows; and Mrs Soorocks,

[3] *pressed her cheek to make it blush*: Moir deleted this revealing action.

winking slyly to me, rung the bell and ordered in wine and "the things for punch."[4]

"Laird," said she, "I'm no ane that's for hurrying on a solemn business in a rash manner. Before we come to speak o' the wedding seriously—for we're only jocose yet—"

The Laird looked round and said tartly—

"I houp ye'll be lang sae."

"Weel, weel, Laird," replied the lady, "you know it's all your ain doing—it depends on yoursel."

"What a lee," muttered the Laird.

"Every joke's a lee o' its kind," cried Mrs Soorocks, "but come and help yoursel to a glass o' my old wine or, an ye like it better, mak a tumbler o' punch to keep the Bailie in countenance—no that he requires either precept or example when the mercy's before him."

For some time after this there was a visible embarassment in the manner of all present. Mrs Soorocks alone was the providence of the hour and she ruled with undismayed equanimity. She persuaded the Laird to take one glass of wine, which for good luck she made a brimmer, and then to mix a tumbler of punch, of which when he had drunk about the half, she exclaimed—

"Sweet pity me, Laird, but that's sma' drink, I'm thinkin—let me pree't."

Having accordingly tasted it with a tea spoon, she shook her head and made a face of exaggerated aversion, crying—

"It's no wholesome; it's as wersh as water; it's eneugh to breed puddocks—no no, Laird, I man help to mend it."

And she dashed in a large quantity of rum which having been procured from Col. Archy of Greenock was of a suavity as mild as its vendor and calculated to steal upon the senses without alarming the palate.

This put courage into the Laird's heart and Mrs Soorocks continued, from time to time, to pree his mixture, in order to determine whether or not he was doing justice to himself and something for the good of

[4] *Mrs Soorocks, winking slyly at me . . . ordered . . . "the things for punch"*: Moir eliminated both the sly wink and the order for rum, and then wrote an entire new chapter on six sheets of paper, suppressing the drunken scene that ensues in Galt's chapter, padding out his material with a sentimental parable put in the mouth of Mrs Soorocks. The alteration of this chapter is his most radical change. Elsewhere he softened and amended. Here he altered virtually everything that Galt had written and intended.

her house—sometimes she helped him to sugar, sometimes squeezed the lime, and sometimes added rum—the complection of the punch rubyfying more and more in a congenial sympathy with his countenance.

The general jocularity in the meanwhile was on the increase—the Bailie became garrulous and talked to Miss Shoosie in rich hints of connubial bliss—Miss Girzie argued with Mrs Soorocks against clandestine and irregular marriages but in a tone of concession gradually softening into reconciliation. The Laird continued to wax still more cheerful and bold—boasted of the sprees of his youthful vigour, and in one instance made a valiant sally to embrace Mrs Soorocks.

"Na," cried she, "if it's come to that wi' ye, Laird, it's time to bring ye afore a magistrate, and let your bride hae her dues. Bailie Waft, I tell you to put him to the question."

Here the Bailie rose and, looking as grave as the occasion and the punch he had drunk would let him, he said, "Mr Mailings, is this lady" —pointing to Miss Shoosie—"your wife?"

"Ony lady's my wife," said the Laird, "that will condesend to tak me."

The Bailie then turned to Miss Shoosie—"Do you, Madam, acknowledge this gentleman for your husband?"

"Confess, confess," cried Mrs Soorocks, "and dinna spoil our ploy."

Miss Shoosie simpered and said, "Sister, I canna refuse ony langer."

Here there was a general clapping of hands and the health of Mr and Mrs Mailings was drank in bumpers by all but themselves. The bride acknowledged the courtesy with a solemn propriety and the Laird answered with a loud laugh—but there was a ring in its sound wild and sardonic, but another tumbler, however, soon restored his hilarity; and in a few minutes after, supper, which Mrs Soorocks had prospectively prepared for the occasion, was announced, and as it was agreed that the young couple should spend the Bridal night in her house, we separated at an early hour—the Bailie and myself, talking of matrimonial felicities, conveyed Miss Girzie weeping to her now solitary home.

CHAPTER XXXIII

Early next morning I went over to Mrs Soorocks to assist her in the *revellie* of the young couple but, on approaching the door, she chanced to observe me from the parlour window and let me in herself.

"O," said she in a voice of serious alarm, "what have I no got to tell you?"

I was thunderstruck at the earnestness of her exclamation, and cried,—

"My Gracious! has the bridegroom run away?"

"Waur than that, waur than that—meikle hae ye to answer for—Nawaubpore yestreen, when we were at our daffin—blind mortals we are and little ken the perils o' our situation—Nawaubpore, as I was saying, sent ower his London newspaper to read—but I was so taen up that I neglecket it till this morning, and what do ye think was the first thing that met my consternated eye—the marriage o' Dr Lounlans, and to whom?—Guess."

"I hope your suspicions have not been verified."

"Verified! they have been dumbfoundered. He is married—and married to Miss Clawrissy Chandos, the great heiress, and failing her mother, the rightfu' leddy o' Barenbraes—Now, think o' that and weep."

"This is indeed extraordinary news!"

"It's a thunderclap," said Mrs Soorocks, "it's an earthquake—I think I fin' the world shooglin beneath my vera feet. We thocht the Nabob wad be an oppressor, but what has the puir Laird to expect frae the hauns o' Dr Lounlans, on his mother's account—Na—I canna think at a' about Mrs Mailings. Na, it was never ordained that she should hae been married!—O, Sir, what have ye no to answer for?"

"Upon my word, Mrs Soorocks," replied I gravely, "it has been all your own work; I have been but an innocent spectator. I took no particular part in the business. You first suggested it to me; I remember very well the time and the place. It was in the avenue of Auldbiggings. Me, Mrs Soorocks! no one can impute any blame to me."

"Weel! after that," cried the lady," I'll be surprised at nothing that man may say. But, hoosever, let us get them quietly out of my house, and you and them settle it as ye may—for I hae lang promised Mrs

Puncheons a visit and I'll be aff to Blythswood place this blessed day—I declare I dinna ken whether I'm standin on my head or my heels; surely it's all a dream and a vision o' the night season: Shoosie Minnigaff married! the thing's no possible, though it has taen place in my ain house."

"But, my dear Ma'am, let us be calm—let us consider what is the next best to be done."

"Consider yoursel—what have I to consider?" exclaimed the lady, "I wash my hands—I have had nothing to do with it from the beginning to the end. I deny't. They'll be a cess upon us baith—They'll be on the parish—Oh, oh, oh!"

At this moment a knock was heard at the door, and Mrs Soorocks, giving a hasty glance out, cried—

"Whaur shall I hide mysel?—here's puir misfortunate Girzie."

And she immediately began to compose herself so that by the time that dejected maiden was admitted she had mustered fortitude enough to break the doleful tidings to her thus with gravity, composure, and decorum.

"Have you had any letters by the post, Miss Girzie, for I have gotten the newspapers?"

"No," said Miss Girzie, "not *this* morning;" dwelling, as I thought, rather emphatically on *this*, which excited my attention.

"Your sister is a lucky woman," rejoined Mrs Soorocks—"a most lucky woman indeed—she has just been married in the vera nick o' time."

"I hope she'll be happy," replied Miss Girzie, composedly.

"But do ye ken what has happen'd? Dr Lounlans is married."

"We expected that some time ago, you ken."

"But wha has he married?" cried Mrs Soorocks. "No less than—your niece and deedly enemy, Miss Clawrissy."

"So we have been informed."

"Informed!" exclaimed Mrs Soorocks, "and whan were ye informed?"

"Yesterday morning by the post, in a most kind letter from Dr Lounlans himself."

"And did you know of that last night?—Girzie Minnigaff, you and your sister have long been known as twa sordid wretches but such deception, ye deceevers, to practise on a worthy gentleman! I think it's reason enough for a divorce—at ony rate, it canna fail to bring a judgment upon you—and what's to become o' you, Miss Girzie?"

"It was agreed between my sister and me that I should live with her."

"What did ye say, Girzie Minnigaff?"

"It was agreed between me and my sister that I should bide wi' her at Auldbiggings."

"It's a confessed plot," cried Mrs Soorocks, turning to me, adding, "So, Sir, a bonny haun ye hae made o't; the Laird's to be burthened wi' the twa."

At this juncture the young couple came into the room,[1] seemingly on much better terms with one another than I had ventured to expect. The lady had herself informed him of the event, at which, instead of expressing any feeling of apprehension for the consequences, he was only confirmed in stronger feelings of dislike against the reverend doctor, vituperating the whole body of the clergy and considering the ambition of his adversary as dictated by insolence to mortify himself.

Mrs Soorocks, who had neither anticipated the felicity of the new pair nor the complacency with which the Laird appeared to regard his lot, said "But, Mr Mailings, tak thocht, remember ye're a ruined man—ye hadna left yoursel the means to maintean you alone, how do ye think that ye can maintean other two?"

"I have made my calculations," said he, "I'm going to Edinburgh. I'll publish my book in numbers and mak a monthly income by that. Miss Girzie's to bide wi' us, for, as my dawty here says, (chucking Mrs Mailings under the chin) the house that can haud twa, can haud three; the fire that can warm four legs can warm six; the same pot that boils for twa can boil for three, so that, you see, no to be entering into particulars, Miss Girzie can leeve wi' us at no expense, and she'll be company to her sister, when I'm in my study concerned wi' my works."

Mrs Soorocks clapt her hands together and turning up her eyes, said, with an ejaculatory accent, "Who could have thocht o' this!"

Breakfast was then announced which, considering the calibre of the respective parties, passed off with so much propriety that my conscience began to be a little appeased. It really appeared to me that the part which I had taken in the business (for I no longer now affected to deny, even to myself, that I had been instrumental to the completion of the marriage) was rather commendable; so much are we prone to judge of

---

[1] *the young couple came into the room*: To conceal his tampering with the previous chapter, Moir inserted a passage (between this 'entry' and the previous paragraph), in which Mrs Soorocks and the narrator leave her house and walk over to Auldbiggings.

the rectitude and propriety of even our own actions by their results. The same sentiment seemed to strike Mrs Soorocks, for when the party left us for Auldbiggings[2] after breakfast, she whispered to me—

"Weel, sir, I think we haena made sae vera bad a job o't after a', only what's to become o' them?—we maun try what can be done by working on the tender mercies o' Dr Lounlans and I hope Mrs Lounlans will be found to hae bowels o' compassion and, if she has, I'm sure she'll be the first o' her kin, by the mother's side o' the house, that ever had ony. As for her aunties, the state o' hunger and starvation that they hae aye lived in is next to a proof that they hae nae bowels at a'.[3] Could ye hae ever imagined that the twa deceitfu' creatures would hae had the sense to do as they did yestreen! I'll ne'er put trust in the countenance o' womankind again."

Much more of the same sort on both sides passed between us till we separated, having previously arranged that we should watch the return of the Doctor and endeavour to complete our good work by soliciting him to allow the three Graces, as Mrs Soorocks called the Laird, the bride, and bride's sister, to enjoy the remainder of their days at Barenbraes.

[2] *the party left us for Auldbiggings*: we were returning from Auldbiggings (Moir). A further piece of concealment.
[3] *As for her aunties . . . nae bowels at a'*: deleted by Moir.

CHAPTER XXXIV

On returning to my own house, I was somewhat surprised to find that during my short absence Mr Loopy, of the respectable house of Loopy and Hypothec, writers in Glasgow, had been calling, very urgent to see me, and had mentioned to my housekeeper he had several places in the neighbourhood to visit—among others Auldbiggings.

As there had been for some time a rumour through the country of an expected dissolution of parliament, I was at no loss to guess, from the connections of my old friend Loopy the probable motive of his civility in calling upon me, with whom he had no particular ostensible business; but I could not account for the circumstance of his intended visit to the Laird who in his political predilections had ever been opposed to those of the present ministry.

Having given up the day to idleness, it occurred to me that perhaps I might be able to intercept the worthy man of business either on his way to or from the Place and induce him to take a quiet dinner with me, for I have ever found his shrewd conversation particularly racy and relishing. Accordingly, after giving orders for the leg of my last killed five year old to be dressed, I sauntered along the high way towards Auldbiggings but seeing nothing of the lawyer till I was at the bottom of the avenue, where his post chaise was waiting—the approach to the house being in such a state with ruts and stones, that the postilion did not venture to take his carriage and horses to the door.

I went up to the house but long before I reached the entrance everything indicated that there was indeed a change of administration within.

Jenny Clatterpans, bare footed and bare legged, with her pettycoats kilted and her hair falling in masses from under her cap, was standing on a stool whitewashing the lintels of the lower windows with an old hearth-brush; her whitening pot was a handless and cripple tureen. The cook, ghastly and piebald with soot and whitening, was rattling with the remnant of an old blanket in her hand, in the midst of a numerous assemblage of all manner of kitchen utensils, brazen sconces, pewter trenchers, that might for magnitude have been shields of Ajax, copper lids of departed fish kettles, a warming-pan, damasked with holes in the lid, and the handle of which had been lost beyond the memory of man, a brass basting ladle, a superannuated tormentor, a bright copper teakettle, the spout of which had long become loose by many scourings but still it was the pride and glory of the shelf on which it was wont to stand, flanking a long array of various sorts of brass candlesticks which were lying on the grass around it. Beyond her lay a mound of featherbeds, pillows, and bolsters, which Jock, without his coat, was manfully thrashing with a flail, raising such a dust that he could only be seen at intervals like a demon in the clouds of a whirlwind.

As it was impossible to think of interrupting so many indications of a radical reform I walked into the house, intending to go up to the old gentleman's study, but the lobby was so crowded with old casks, tubs, and firkins, empty bottles and boxes, that I with great difficulty made my way to the foot of the stair, on which the bride and her sister were endeavouring to bring down a large worsted wheel which, from the death of the first Mrs Mailings, had been removed from the kitchen, and placed upon the great napery ark that stood at the stairhead being the first stage on its way to the lumber garret.

Having assisted the ladies to bring it round the turn of the stair, I at last reached the room where the Laird and the Lawyer were seated, engaged so earnestly in conversation, that neither of them hardly observed me enter. Their topic was the impending general election, and it soon appeared that Mr Loopy was not canvassing for the vote, but for the purchase of the superiority of Auldbiggings.[1]

"Three hundred pounds," Mr Loopy was saying as I came in, "and of money down too, no trouble but to count it—it is a very large sum for my client to give."

"But your client, Mr Loopy, is a capitalist and kens hoo to mak his outlay productive," rejoined the Laird, "when he bad you offer me three hundred pounds he was thinking o' my agricultural distress but this is no sic a rainy day as to cause me to sell my hen below her marketable value. It's but the second, ye maun ken, o' my honey moon, and when will a man be croose if he's no then? and is nae my wife yin o' the heirs portioners, as ye wad ca't, in law, o' the estate o' Barenbraes? But noo when I think o't, Mr Loopy, I'll no sell at a', for it may be a mean hereafter to help me to get a post in the government, or a Cadetcy to Indy for one of our younger sons—Three hunder poun, Mr Loopy! I wud na tak three thousan: the superiority o' Auldbiggings is 720 pun

[1] In Scotland, the lordship (or 'superiority') of a landed estate conferred parliamentary franchise. It could be sold off, detached from the land, as a separate asset.

147

scots, auld valuation, and it wud na be kittle to mak a piecing, as ye weel ken hoo, that wud gie ye the poore and capacity o' twa votes instead o' yin."

"But, Laird, how could I be aware of that circumstance?" replied Mr Loopy; "however, although it does make a difference, I admit, yet you should consider that votes are falling in value for *you* know"—and the lawyer appealed to me in verification of the fact—"that the great landholders in this country are splitting their superiorities to the utmost extremity and actually giving them away for nothing; they are a drag in the market, that is to say in manner."

I now began to see the drift of Mr Loopy's visit to the Laird and with the more satisfaction, as it never had occurred to any of the helpless man's friends to think of the value of his vote for the county as a means to lighten, if not to avert, the misfortune with which he was immediately threatened, nor probably had it ever before occurred to himself, for such was the improvidence and slackness in all his affairs that nothing was ever done in them until it became absolutely necessary or inevitable.

The Laird was touched on his weak side by referrence to the multiplication of votes tending to reduce their value and being evidently at a loss for an answer, I thought it my duty to interpose saying, "that the making of so many new votes was only a proof that the ensuing contest was expected to be a hot one and that those who kept aloof from either party till the proper time could not fail to realize the full value of their influence."

"Oh!" exclaimed Mr Loopy, "it would be most abominable and what no honest man like Mr Mailings could think of doing, to sell himself to the highest bidder—and besides, the general election is not expected before the fall and a vote made at this time will, in that case, be of no use, for the infeftment must run a year and day. But, Laird, to mak short work o't, notwithstanding all these disadvantages, I think I could almost promise—for my client is a liberal as well as a wealthy man—I could almost promise that he might be brought to go the length of five hundred pounds."

"I can say nae mair about it," replied the old man, "without consulting my amiable spouse, Mrs Mailings," and he vociferated, "Dawty, come ben the house, dawty, and help me to mak a bargain wi' Mr Loopy."

The lady, however, did not immediately answer to the summons— her labours had dishevelled her dress and discomposed her temperature, but when she had somewhat arranged the former and cooled herself with a towel or handkerchief, after being again called, she came into the room, followed by Miss Girzie, whose complexion was equally heightened by her share in the toil and her dress even still more discomposed.

The Laird briefly stated that Mr Loopy had come to buy, if he would sell, the superiority of Auldbiggings and had offered five hundred pounds.

"If he would speak about fifteen, it would be mair wise like," said the leddy, looking askance at the lawyer, who pushed his chair back, and regarded her with the utmost astonishment of features, gradually relaxing into a smile expressive of incredulous wonder.

"Mr Mailings," he exclaimed, "Oh, ye are a happy man to have such a wife, and when you come to have your children round your table like olive plants she will indeed be a fruitful vine!"

"Dawty," said the Laird, quite delighted to hear such commendations bestowed on the lady of his love, "Dawty, let us be reasonable, and not rigorous."

"Be just before you're generous," cried his spouse.

"Think o' wha's to come after you," rejoined Miss Girzie.

"Consider your small family," cried I, "and your young son, that you intend to send to India."

"Mony a Laird's daughter has been waur tochered than wi' her father's vote at a contested election, Mr Loopy," interposed the Laird firmly, "your client may tak his five hunder pound and mak a playock o't wi' a whistle in its tail or he'll either get heft or blade o' my vote for sic a triffle. Five hundred pound! talk o' a thoosan and I'll maybe hearken wi' the hearing side o' my head."

"A thousand," exclaimed Mr Loopy, starting up and affecting to move towards the door, "I never heard anything so unreasonable."

"Weel, weel," cried the Laird, "will ye split the—"

"Hold your tongue, Auldbiggings," exclaimed Mrs Mailings, "and dinna mak yoursel a prodigal son; an ye wad pairt wi' your patrimony in that gate, ye wud weel deserve to eat draff wi' the swine; na, na, a thousan pounds is ower little!"

"I wonder," said Mr Loopy, still standing on the floor, "I wonder, Mrs Mailings, that ye wadna say guineas, when ye think there is such fools in the world as wud gie a thousand pound and for what?—"

"For a vote" said Miss Girzie, sedately, "and ye ken the full value o't, Mr Loopy."

The Leddy shook her head significantly. "I thank you for your gentle hint, Mr Loopy," cried she, "and we'll no take ae farthing less than a thoosan guineas."

The lawyer turned round, with a well-affected huff, and at that moment Mrs Soorocks made her appearance, puffing and blowing, crying out,—

"I hope I'm in time—I hope ye hae na concluded the bargain—I hope, Mrs Mailings, ye'll protect your gudeman—Mr Loopy, Mr Loopy, hoo could ye think after wheedling, as I hae heard this morning, auld Peter Kethcart out o' his bit laun for little mair than the half o' its value, to say naething o' the superiority, to come fleeching here to beguile Auldbiggings; knowing, as ye do, Mr Loopy, that it's a the' residue left o' his patrimony—but, leddies, when I heard he was here, I cam running like a maukin to snatch you as brands out o' the burning for he has a tongue that wad wile the bird aff the tree!"

"I'm no safe here," rejoined Mr Loopy, with a smile, and turning to the Laird, he added, "As I was instructed by my client to go a certain length, if you are willing to treat with me I shall be liberal. You shall have a thousand pounds for the superiority down, if you choose to take it, and further I am not empowered to go."

The Laird was evidently on the point of accepting the offer when Mrs Soorocks exclaimed,—

"The superiority o' Auldbiggings sellt for a thoosan pounds, that is sae weel worth double the money! Oh, Miss Shoosie, Mrs Mailings, as I should ca' ye, tak that man o' yours into your bedroom and gie him admonition—it's no for a sma' profit that my friend Mr Loopy's scamperin frae Dan to Beersheba.—"

"I certainly think," rejoined I, "that Mr Mailings ought to have some time to consider of the marketable value of his only remaining property."

Here Mrs Mailings cried,—

"It would be cheatry to bargain awa' a right and property that Mr Loopy's sae ready to gie a thoosan and fifty pounds for—na, a thoosan guineas!"

With that she turned round to the Lawyer, and said, with a mim mouth and a dulcet accent,—

"If ye'll call the morn, Mr Loopy, maybe ye'll hae an answer."

"Deed," rejoined the Laird, "it's my solid opinion, that if the qualification o' Auldbiggings be worth a thoosan guineas at this time, it ought, wi' discreet management, to be soon worth a great deal more because you see all trade is in a state o' panic and calamity and folk will have nae other way o' leevin[2] but by gettin posts in the government so that if a vote noo be worth sae mickle, what will it no be worth when mair customers for posts come to deal in the market? For you know, Mr Loopy, that there's a standard o' value by which the price of every thing may be measured and all we want to know is what this natural standard is?"

"I doot, Mr Mailings," replied the lawyer, "that, like the other political economists, ye run some risque o' mistaking the ellwand for the cloth, but I observe you are not in a humour to deal with me today so I will take Mrs Mailings's hint and revisit you in the morning."

Accordingly, he left the room, and I followed, to beg his company at dinner which, however, he declined at first, but seeing the confusion in which the house of Auldbiggings was at that time, he said, "Perhaps the Laird might be induced to join me"—and he would look in upon us in the afternoon on his return to Glasgow.

[2] *way o' leevin*: way o' making their bread (Moir).

CHAPTER XXXV

On returning into the room, I found the Laird alone. The ladies had retired to an inner apartment to determine, as he informed me, in what manner he should deal with Mr Loopy.

"Is na my wife," said he, "a clever wife? Weel does she ken how many blue beans it taks to mak five. Had I marriet her twenty years ago, I wouldna hae needed this day to stand in awe o' lawyers and naubobs and sic like o' the clanjamphry—and she's sic a pleasant young creature that she blithens my vera blood—I could na hae thought it possible for matrimony to mak a man sae happy. It's true, I had an experience o' the conjugal yoke before, but then my first was a forced marriage, whereas this, my second, has been a free-will offering—a' o' my ain instigation, the which maks an unco difference—I did na think, when I tellt you in the garden that I would fain marry Miss Shoosie Minnigaff, that I had sic a sincerity o' sound affection for her, as a' my friens had sae lang discovered; but you know, it is written in the word that we do not know ourselves—and behold, I am a living illustration of the text—Hoosever anent the thoosan pounds for the superiority, what's your opinion?"

I told him that I considered it a great Godsend but remarked that, as it was not sufficient to procure for him any effectual relief from his mortgage, it would be much better to give up the estate at once to the Nabob and buy an annuity with the money on the joint lives of himself and Mrs Mailings.

"Had we no a prospect of a family, what ye counsel would be worth hearkening to."

"I doubt, Laird, that's but a barren prospect and, besides, you ought to consider the great wickedness of augmenting our national distress, by increasing the population of the country already so redundant. I beseech you, Mr Mailings, to respect the admonitions of economical philosophy."

"Hoots, Hoots—dinna talk sic Malthusian havers to me. The cause o' our national decay and agricultural distress, broken merchants, ravelled manufacturers, and brittle bankers come a'thegither frae another well e'e—Were sic calamities ever heard o' in this reawlm before the turnip farming cam into vogue? Answer me that? Weel do I mind that it was in the hairst o' that vera year, when the first park o' turnips was sawn in the shire, that the sough came through the kintra o' the Ayr bank gaun to pigs and whistles—My auntie, wha was then in the laun o' the livin and has since been sleeping in Abraham's bosom wi' Sarah his wife and the rest[1] o' the patriarchs, said, on that melancholious occasion—and she was a judicious woman—that to gar sheep and kye crunch turnips was contrary to nature, their teeth being made for garss[2] and kailblades, and that it would be seen that the making o' turnips pastures would prove a sign o' something—Never did I forget her words o' warning, though I was then but a bairn, a very babe and suckling, in a sense, and I hae noted, year by year, that her prophecy has been mair and mair coming to pass for, with the ingrowth o' turnip farming, there has aye been a corresponding smasherie amang the looms and sugar hoggits. Last year, I was in a terror for what was to happen when I saw sae mony braw parks that used to be ploughed for vittle to man, saun for fodder to beasts."

"Your theory, Laird," said I, "well deserves the attention of his Majesty's Ministers, for some of them, in my opinion, have been finding similar effects, as legitimately descended from causes equally proximate. But if turnip fields were sown with corn, would the distress be abated?"

"How can ye misdoot it?—and the redundant population would be abated too—for, as they baith came in wi' the turnips, would na they gang out wi' them?—Is na that a truth o' political economy?"

At this crisis the ladies returned into the room, and the Laird addressing himself to his bridal wife,[3] said,—

"Weel, dawty, hoo hae ye settled the government anent the price o' the superiority?"

"We hae disposed o' it a' to the best advantage," interposed Mrs Soorocks; "and ye need na trouble your head about it—We'll get Mr Loopy to lay out the money—for he's a clever man in his line—on a life rent for you and Mrs Mailings; and ye'll gang intil Enbro' and live comfortable, like tua patriarchs, begetting sons and dochters, if ye can[4]—There, Laird, ye may spend the evening o' your days in lown feleecity and hammergaw frae morning to night wi' the advocates

---

[1] *Sarah his wife and the rest o'*: deleted by Moir as 'vulgar'.
[2] *garss*: grass (Moir) An example of Moir's modification of dialect forms.
[3] *bridal wife*: Moir deleted 'bridal'.
[4] *begetting sons and dochters, if ye can*: deleted by Moir.

about corn laws and circulating middims, and my friend Bailie Blackwood—he has a great respec for me—he'll, on my account, let you write in the Magazine,[1] which has noo got a character for a' kinds o' national distress and the ruination o' trade and the shipping interest."

"Deevil's in that woman," muttered the Laird aside—"She's a torment to me and to every other body—But, dawty," he subjoined aloud to his lady, "I hae a plan far better than the veesions o' life-rents that Mrs Soorocks would beglammer us a' wi'—this Godsend o' the thousan pounds—"

"Thousan pounds!" exclaimed all the ladies with one voice—"Ye'll surely never tak a farding less than the twa thousan?"

"For which," continued Mrs Mailings sola, "Mrs Soorocks tells me we may get mair than two hun'er and fifty pounds a year-paid down in Bank notes without ony stress o' law, and would na that be a grand thing?"

"But if the banks break," cried the Laird.

"If the lift fa's, it'll smoor the laverocks," retorted Mrs Soorocks—at which the Laird bounced from his seat and giving a stamp with his foot, exclaimed,—

"I'll be master in my own house—I'll be ruled by nobody—I'll hae a will o' my own and I will—The Deevil's in't, if a man o' my substance is to be snuled in this gait."

He then turned round to his wife and said, in a softened accent,—

"Dinna be frightened, dawty—I'm no in a pawshon wi' you, but ye'll let me hae my ain way."

"And what's that way?" inquired dawty, in a tone which did not indicate an entire acquiescence in the doctrine of passive obedience.

"I've had a notion," said the Laird, addressing himself to me, "that there's a mine o' copper ore aneath the whinny knowes, and don't you think it would be very advisable for me to work it and pay off the wadsets wi' the profits—"

I participated in the alarm and consternation of the ladies at the propounding of such a scheme—Miss Girzie clasped her hands in agony and sat in a supplicating posture. Her sister stood erect, many inches taller than her wont, with her arms extended and her fingers spread out like the leaves of the palmetos, while Mrs Soorocks burst into an immoderate fit of laughing, exclaiming, "Did ye ever hear sic a

[5] *the Magazine*: Moir deleted the rest of the sentence, which gives an ironical list of contents of *Blackwood's Magazine*.

goose wi' a golden egg—a copper mine—I wonder when ye were at it, that ye didna dream o' a potosi."[6]

"Weel, weel," said the Laird, nettled at the effect he had produced, "mak a kirk and a mill o't—but my plans will get justice some day."

At this juncture, a rattling voice on the stair drew off our attention from the matter in debate and Jock, with his flail over his shoulder, and covered with feathers, as if he had been in a snow-storm, rushed into the room, crying,—

"Odsake, odsake, here's ane o' the Minister's lasses, wi' news that'll freeze your vera marrow. The minister's come hame wi' his bridal wife and they're awa in a cotch o' their ain—set a minister up wi' his ain cotch!—to ha'd the infare at Barenbraes—Leddies—leddies—oh, my leddy madam mistress, he'll tak possession o' the house and heritage—and what's far waur—here's likewise the Nawbob in a' his glory, comin nae doot to drive you and the Laird, like Adam and Eve, out o' this pleasant paradise and garden o' Eden, that it might be, for the sma' cost o' a little reparation."

Mrs Soorocks was the first who broke silence after this portentous announcement—addressing herself to the ladies, she said,—

"Weel, cousins, have na ye found at last the true prophecy o' my words?"

"Cousins!" said I to Mrs Soorocks "you told me they were only distant connexions?"

"But near eneugh," replied she calmly "to hae been a cess upon me, had I no got them otherwise provided for, and I thank you, Sir, for the helping hand ye hae been to me in the wark."

I felt much inclined to exclaim with the Laird, "the Deevil's in that woman, she's a torment to me and to every other body" but the sound of the Nabob's voice, as he forced his way up through the chaos of chattels with which the staircase was encumbered, arrested the imprecation.

[6] *a potosi*: a silver mine (from Potosi, Bolivia).

CHAPTER XXXVI

The Nabob came in with well-acted jocularity and, totally regardless of his sulky reception, began to rally the Laird on his spirit in choosing so young and so blooming a bride. Nor was he less lavish of his compliments on the leddy. On Mrs Soorocks, to whom he justly ascribed the entire merit of having designed and accomplished the match, his commendations were without end. Nevertheless, in all this bustle of boisterous gesticulation it was soon evident, that he had come for some other purpose than to felicitate the happy pair.

After the first rush and froth of his merriment had subsided—or run to waste—he began with his characteristic straight-forwardness, seemingly unconscious of the abruptness of the transition,[1] to state he had been informed that Mr Loopy was buying up the superiorities of sundry small parcels of land with the design, as it was conjectured, of uniting them together so as to enable him to dispose of qualifications for the county election. "And I hear, Mr Mailings," said he, "that the snaky vakeel has been with you—Have you sold yours?—if you have, recollect the purchase money is mine."

"We'll hae twa words about that," replied the Laird dryly.

"Is not my security over all the estate?"

"Deed is't—it's o'er the whole tot o' the lan'—but I may say, in the words of a reform in Parliament—'the whole land-and nothing but the land.' "

"If that be the case," cried the Nabob, piqued, " and that the superiority may be sold by itself, I think you ought to have given me the first offer—a man has but the half of his estate when he has not all the rights belonging to it."

"And for what should we hae gien you the first offer?" exclaimed Jock with indignation, as he still stood in the middle of the room, feathered, cap-a-pie, and with his flail shouldered.

The Nabob looked with a tygerlike scowl and going sedately towards him, seized him calmly by the collar and walking him to the door, pushed him headlong out, tartly applying his foot, at the same moment,

[1] *transition*: transaction (Moir's misreading). Moir makes 'sense' of Galt's handwriting, but not what Galt meant.

to the seat of Jock's honour. But Jock was not to be so touched with impunity. In the instant of his expulsion, he ran after Mr Loopy, and watching him just as he was stepping into the chaise, which was waiting at the avenue gate, he worked upon him to return.

"I tak you a' to witness, leddies and gentlemen," cried Jock, as he returned with his man of business "I tak every ane o' you to witness anent my bottomrie. There's the panel that did the deed, Mr Loopy—deal with him, as he has written on the brod at the corner o' his planting—'according to the utmost rigour o' law.' I'll be even wi' you noo, Nawaubpore, for a' the dule and sorrow that you and cleeky Caption would sigh and wallywae about, for the bit clink I gied wi' a harmless fishing rod to John Angle's brazen whirligig."

Whether Jock had informed Mr Loopy of the immediate cause of quarrel, as he brought him back to the house, did not appear by anything in the manner of the lawyer, but after some altercation, partly in good humour, and partly sparringly, the assault which poor Jock had suffered was forgotten and the man of business, with an equivocal deviation from the fact, reminded the Laird that he promised to sell the superiority to him, warning him to beware of dealing with any other.

"Hooly, hooly," cried the Laird, "ye ken, Mr Loopy, that if, for ceeveelity, I maunna in my ain house ca' that a lee, it would be the next thing till't, to say it was na like ane. But since we hae gotten twa candidates on the leet, I'll play even down justice wi' you baith—a thoosan pounds sterling for the superiority o' Auldbiggings—wha bids mair?"

"Eleven hundred," cried Mrs Soorocks.

Mr Loopy looked at her, and raising his outspread hands in mirthful amazement, said, however, with more sincerity than he intended should be discovered, "And what would Mrs Soorocks do with a superiority?"

"Sell't to you for an advantage," replied the lady with a significant nod, and a smile to me.

"Eleven hundred pounds sterling for the superiority of Auldbiggings," resumed the Laird—"wha bids mair?"

"Twelve hundred," said the Nabob with a perplexed and embarrassed look, as if he was not quite aware of the consequences of the bidding.

"Mr Rupees—are ye really in earnest?" said the lawyer, with a slight inflexion of the voice almost in the key of alarm.

"I'll bid thirteen hundred," said Miss Girzie, with a giggle, "for I hae heard o' ae vote sell't for more than seventeen hundred pounds."

"Thirteen hundred pounds for the superiority of Auldbiggings—going for thirteen hundred pounds"—resumed the Laird, drawing his chair towards the table and striking it with his snuff box for a hammer.

"Nay, if ye're making a diversion o't," said the lawyer, "I may as well give a bod too—so I say fourteen hundred, Mr Mailings—but mind I have no intention of standing to the bargain."

"The devil!" exclaimed the Nabob—"then I say fifteen hundred, Mr Mailings, and I intend to stand by the offer."

"Do as you like, Nawaubpore," interposed Mrs Soorocks, "but, Laird, if ye get a better, ye're free to tak it; so I say sixteen hundred, Mr Mailings, and I intend to stand to the offer."

Mr Loopy was every moment plainly becoming more and more excited; he endeavoured to appear calm and to smile, but his eyes were eager and restless, and his nether lip quivered "This," said he, "is the most extraordinary proceeding I ever witnessed—Surely, Mrs Soorocks, you can have no intention of buying, and, Mr Rupees, you could never think of giving any such money?"

"Sixteen hundred pounds sterling for the superiority of Auldbiggings! once"—shouted the Laird, chuckling with delight.

"I beg, Mr Mailings," cried the lawyer, "that you would allow me to say one word."

"Sixteen hundred pounds sterling for the superiority of Auldbiggings—mind, Mr Loopy, it's pounds sterling" was, however, all the answer he got.

"Seventeen hundred, and be damned to it—" roared the Nabob.

"Remember, Mr Mailings," interposed the lawyer, in professional expostulation, "remember, you have no licence to sell by public roup or auction."

"Seventeen hundred pounds sterling, Mr Loopy, for the superiority o' Auldbiggings—will ye gie me another bod?" was the Laird's reply—and rubbing his hands in ecstasy, he added, "Seventeen hundred pounds, ance—seventeen hundred pounds, twice—going, Mr Loopy—going."

"I know all this is but a joke," rejoined the lawyer, " and so humour you. I'll go the length of eighteen hundred."

"And just for the joke too," said Mrs Soorocks, "I'll bid nineteen hundred, Mr Loopy."

"I think," cried Jock with a guffaw like a cataract, "that it's cheap at twa thoosan."

"I'll give the money for't, Laird," growled the Nabob, "and end this foolish competition."

"Many a droll sight and sale have I seen," said Mr Loopy, "but never one like this—Mr Rupees, are you serious?"

"If you are," was the emphatic answer.

The lawyer made no farther observations, but turning to the Laird, said, in an accent which could not be misunderstood—"Then I bid another hundred."

From that moment the contest lay between him and the Nabob, till their respective offers reached six and twenty hundred pounds.

"Going, ance—going, twice!"—shouted the Laird.

"Another fifty," said Mrs Soorocks quietly, but slyly.

"We're all mad," said the lawyer.

"Twa thoosan sax hun'er and fifty pounds sterling," said the Laird— "Mak it guineas, Mr Loopy, and bargain's yours."

"Guineas be't," exclaimed the lawyer—and in the same moment, the Laird struck the table and roared out, "thrice." The ladies all screamed and rushed upon him, while the Nabob made the house quake with his stamp,[2] but Jock, flourishing the flail in triumph, smashed a looking glass into a hundred pieces, and fled.

[2] *stamp*: stump (Moir's misreading).

CHAPTER XXXVII

When order was restored, the lawyer took out his pocket book, and drew from it a ready prepared minute of an agreement for the purchase, with a blank in it for the money—He then went to the mantelpiece, where an ink stand with pens stood, and taking one of the pens, looked at it between him and the light, and afterwards touched it with the tip of his tongue.

"You are a noble hand at auctioneering, Laird," said he, as he spread the paper on the table. When he had filled up the blank, he laid it before the Laird who, in taking the pen turned and addressed his wife, "Is this, dawty, a gran hansel to our marriage?"

"Nawaubpore," said Mrs Soorocks, "ye hae lost a gude bargain."

The great man made her, however, no answer but inquired, with more energy than the question required, if I thought the sale valid.

I excused myself from giving any opinion by reminding him that I was no lawyer, upon which he wheeled abruptly, and without the courtesy of leave-taking quitted the room—and the lawyer soon after, having finished his contract, also retired, and although I had come on purpose, I neglected to ask him to dinner as I had intended. Indeed, the sudden change which had thus taken place in the condition of the Laird was so extraordinary, that it engrossed my whole mind, nor was the good fortune which so crowned his marriage confined that day to the successful sale of the barren superiority. Before the lawyer had left us many minutes, and while Mrs Soorocks was with indisputable justice lauding herself for the part she had played in the biddings, the arrival of Dr and Mrs Lounlans was announced.

The Laird's complexion changed at the name to the ashy paleness of fear and aversion.

"What's brought them here," cried he, "the cheatrie dominie! Is't no eneugh that he has rookit my wife and my gude-sister out o' her father's heritage, but he maun come in triumphing chariots to trample us in the mire—It's a bonny pass the warld's come to—the heiress of a house like Barenbraes and the dochter o' a bauronet to marry a dominie! No wonder that our aunciate gentry are sae fast weedit awa like cumberers o' the ground."

"Wheesht, wheesht, Laird," said Mrs Soorocks—"Harken—they're on the stair."

"I'll gar ding the door in their faces," exclaimed the indignant Malachi, but before he had time to put his threat in force the Doctor entered, with his lady leaning on his arm.

The effect of this apparition—for, by its immediate impression, it may as such be described—was instantaneous. Miss Girzie sat with her hands elevated and her elbows pressing against her sides. Mrs Mailings, with more self-possession, went forward to receive the strangers; Mrs Soorocks, who was seated beyond Miss Girzie, stretched forth her neck and inspected the young lady with sharp and jealous eyes, her most peculiar and characteristic features, and the Laird sat twirling his thumbs, as if resolved to take no heed whatever of his visitors— every moment, however, he stole a glance at them; and in so doing slackened his twirling, and then as often resumed it with redoubled vigour—But the appearance of Mrs Lounlans was calculated to con- ciliate a kinder reception.

She was one of those unaffected and prepossessing young ladies who, without any particular personal endowment, wear an air of so much good sense and natural gracefulness about them as to attract confidence and esteem at the first sight. When she withdrew her arm from her husband's and came forward to meet her aunt, Miss Girzie rose, and Mrs Soorocks put on a countenance of ineffable benignity.

Doctor Lounlans having introduced the ladies to one another, turned to the Laird and said, "Our next friend here is Mr Mailings."

"They're a' friens that are na faes," was the answer, the sullen res- pondent endeavouring to sit erectly dignified, twirling his thumbs with accelerated velocity. Mrs Lounlans had evidently, however, been prepared for an uncouth reception and being none dismayed by his ungracious mood and repulsive manner lifted one of his hands and with much conciliation of accent felicitated herself on being numbered among relations—"My mother too," she added, "whom we have set down at my aunt's—for we expected to have found them at home— was happy to hear of what has taken place, for she recollects you as one of her early friends."

The Laird was subdued by the gentleness of this address, and looked up with a smile, half indicative of pleasure and of incredulity, while Mrs Soorocks said to the Doctor—

"And is't possible that Leddy Chandos has ta'en actual possession?"— and she added with a significant sigh, "Oh, Miss Girzie—"

The Doctor replied, with more archness than belonged to his grave and habitual equanimity, "You know, Mrs Soorocks, that the estate is entailed and that Lady Chandos is the elder sister"—but observing that the sisters misunderstood him, he addressed himself to them, saying,—

"Her ladyship waits impatiently to see you—tired with her journey, and deeply affected with the many tender reminiscences of youth and childhood, which every object in the scene of the early pleasures has revived, she found herself unable to come with us."

By this time, Mrs Lounlans had so far ingratiated herself with the Laird that he drew a chair towards his own and requested her to sit down beside him.

"Dawty," said he to his wife, "I think she has a cast o' thee, but it will be late in the day before she'll can compare."

Mrs Soorocks here again addressed the Doctor, inquiring if Lady Chandos was come "to spend her auld days among her forefathers?"—adding, "but I need na be surprised at it, for she was aye a sweet sentimental lassie, a perfect Clarissy Harlowe, though I maun say it's no vera like a heroine in a novel to come and take possession—deed, Miss Girzie, I feel for you. It's just like the cuckoo dabbing a wallydraigle out o' the nest—but I'll reason wi' her."

"Give yourself no uneasiness on that head," replied the Doctor, "for to remove all anxiety from her sisters, she has settled the house and property on them during her life—she could do no more."

"But when she dies?" said the anxious and apprehensive lady. The Doctor smiled and then told her that Mrs Lounlans had, before their marriage, confirmed and extended the settlement for her life also.

"Noo, that's Christianity, Doctor"—and she justly commended the delicacy with which the settlement had been made, ascribing it all to his influence and advice.

———————

Little remains to be added to this brief domestic tale.[3] The Nabob prosecuted with ardour excited by disappointment, under the pretext of doing justice to his ward, the claim which he had on the Laird of

[3] *Little remains to be added* . . . . . *End*: Galt in the manuscript drew a double line after the previous paragraph, and then concluded the novel as printed here. Apart from a few salvaged lines, Moir suppressed Galt's conclusion, and wrote three concluding chapters, on extra sheets, with a variety of 'new' material—a 'conclusion' of the Nabob's affairs; a conversation between the narrator and the Laird;

Auldbiggings till the old Laird, fairly worrited and driven to his wits' end, abandoned the home of his ancestors and removed with his leddy and her sister to Edinburgh where by the purchase money of the superiority and the gathering and income of the two ladies he is enabled to live in great comparative respectability.

Regularly whenever "the season" is over they revisit Barenbraes to hain for the winter, and like the other Athenian gentry they return to town when the courts open. The Laird still talks of publishing his Memoirs, but since he has ceased to be interested in the fluctuations of agriculture he has become a strenuous advocate for a free trade in corn. When the weather is calm and fair he is sometimes met with in Princes Street with one of the ladies on each arm, but in general he prefers to sit at home watching the mutations of the clouds from the window or the shapes of Saracens or Salamanders in the fire. In this solitary occupation he is allowed to spend many an unmolested hour, for the ladies are great forenoon visitors, talking much of their sister Lady Chandos, rarely, however, alluding to their niece Mrs Lowlans, of whom when they do chance to speak, one of them makes a point of sighing to indicate how much they feel for her imprudence in having married so far below her own degree.

When Mr Tansie the schoolmaster during his last vacation visited the metropolis he called as in duty bound on the Laird and the leddies, and I was much pleased with his description of their habitation and the remarks to which it gave rise.

"They dwell," said he, "in a fine double house with two entrances. One opens to a common stair that leads to the upper flat and attics which certain of the lower orders inhabit. The other is a genteel door with pillars and architraves such as befit the porch of a house for a family of rank and pedigree. You cannot go amiss in looking for the house, for it has a brass plate on the door with *Malachi Mailings Esqr of Auldbiggings* on't at full length. The which to observe caused me much perplexity, for I could not divine what the Laird had to do with a sign. That advocates and writers to the signet should like other tradesmen have recourse to such brazen devices to make themselves notorious and to bring custom seems not unreasonable, but for landless Lairds and freeholders of parchment to set themselves up as a titular

a description of the Laird's personal hat-peg; a comic story of the Laird's pocket watch (provided by Blackwood!); and the wooing and wedding of Jock and Jenny. This expansion and tidying-up of what Moir regarded as loose ends ruined Galt's tightly written and sensitive conclusion.

nobility, and expect fame and renown by inscribing their names— 'teetles', as they call them—on brass is to say the least o't not the way that Horace took to raise himself a monument, but I dare say it is done by the poor Laird in a spirit of bravery—for I was told that he still refuses to sign or assent to any legal surrender of Auldbiggings to the Nabob—and may be brought to trouble for his contumacity."[4]

[4] Mr Tansie, in this final speech, has abandoned his astrological style. It is, in fact, John Galt, making his own comment. See *Introduction*, p. xviii.

END

GLOSSARY

A. Indian terms used by Nabob

aubdaar, servant
bahaddar, hero; **Bahádur Jáh** (as title) 'very gallant'. *See note* p. 74
budgerow, river craft
burrah, big
coolie, labourer
dawk, relay of transport for mails (between 'dak bungalows')
dawk book, mail book
decoit, bandit
dhoolie, palanquin
doudie, boatman
ghuddah, ass
ghur, house
kilhdar, vassal
kidmutgar, servant
lack, lac, million rupees (lakh)
lattee, wooden stave

mafussil, 'up-country'; 'off station' area
paugul, mad
pawney, water (brandy pawney: brandy and water)
sahib, 'Sir', master
seer, measure (kilogram)
shraub, drink (alcoholic)
sirdar, military chief
soors, pigs
suttee, suicide by fire
tatties, window-screens
vakeel, 'pleader', lawyer
Vishnu, Hindu god
wallah, person employed (orig. 'owner') usually in combination e.g. Jungle Wallah: worker in jungle
Zemendary, feudal estate

B. Scots

a', all
aboon, above
ae, one, a
aff, off
ahint, behind
aiblins, perhaps
ain, own
airn, iron
airt, direction
alloo, allow
almous, alms
an, if
ance, once
ane, one
anent, concerning

aneugh, enough
art and part, (Sc. Law) party (to)
aught, eight
auld, old
auld days, old age
aye, always

baith, both
bawbie, small coin
beglammer, bewitch
begrutten, tear-stained
behaudin, beholden
belyve, soon
ben, inner room
ben the hoose, inside, 'further in'

bide, dwell, remain
big, build
bike, nest
bizzin, buzzing
blains, weals
blate, shy
bod, bid (at auction)
bodie, person
bodle, small coin
booking, entering names in kirk session book (for 'regular' wedding)
boss, hollow
bossness, hollowness
bot, 'but' (outer room) 'but and ben'
breeks, trousers
brod, board

canny, pleasant, easy
cast, likeness
cess, tax, charge
chaummer, chamber
cheatrie, cheating
claes, clothes
clanjamphry, rabble
claw, 'clause'; section
clash-clecking, scandal-hatching
cleck, hatch
cleeky, cunning
clishmaclaver, garrulous story
clype, tell tales, sneak
collops, slices of meat
compos mentos, crazy
coom, dirt; dirty
corruption, anger
cotch, coach
crack, chat
craig, crag
crined, shrivelled
croose, spirited; proud
cutty, 'cutty stool' (stool of repentance in church)
daffin, frolic (esp. between the sexes)

dang, struck
dauner, stroll
daunert, stupid
daur, dare
dawty, darling
deacon, head of trade guild
deacon, good (at something)
decreet, decree
dee, die
deed, indeed
deedly, deadly
deil-be-licket, 'devil a thing'; nothing
denty lion, dandelion
dight, wipe
ding, strike; slam (a door)
dinle, tremble
dirgie, funeral feast
dirl, shake
div, do (interog.)
divaul, cease
dizzen, dozen
doited, crazy
dominie, schoolmaster
doot, doubt
dorty, choosy; supercilious
draff, refuse of brewing malt (pig food)
drogue, drug
drookit, drenched
drowthy, thirsty
dub, dirt
duddy, ragged
dunkle, dent
dwine, fade away
dyke, wall

ee, e'e, eye
een, eyes
eikrie, 'eking out', supplementation
ettercap, spider
even (vb), equate, compare
even-doun, plain, obvious

fa', fall
faring, gift bought at a fair
fash, trouble
file, dirty
fin', find
fleech, coax
flitting, moving house
forgie, forgive
fou, 'full' (drunk)
frae, from
fraising, 'making a phrase of'
frichts, frights
frien, frien', friend

gaed, went
gairner, gardener
gaizent, dried-up
gambollan, gambolling
gang, go
gar, cause; compel
gardevin, whisky-jar
garss, grass
gart, compelled
gash, pale; ashen
gaumeril, fool
gaun, going
gawpe, 'gulp'; gape
gett, offspring
gie, give
gied, gave
gied, geen, given
girn, snarl; complain; complaint
goupens, handfulls
graduwa, 'graduate', doctor
gran, grand
greet, weep
grue, shudder; sick
grumphy, pig
gude, good; god
gude-brother, brother-in-law
gudeman, husband
gude-sister, sister-in-law
gurl, growl

hae, have
hain, save
hairst, harvest
hamewart, hame 'art, living at home; untravelled
hammergaw, talk volubly
hansel, give the first gift; initiate; an 'earnest'
harl, drag
harns, brains
haud, hold
haun, hand
haver, talk foolishly
haverel, idiot
hempies, rogues
heritable bond, *See note* p. 26
heritor, landowner (with liability for upkeep of parish church)
herry, harry
hesp, skein of yarn
hirple, limp
hizzie, hussy
hoo, how
hooly, slowly!
hoosever, however
host, cough
houp, hope
howk, dig
howf, howff, snug place for meeting and drinking
huff, indignation; hasty movement
hunder, hun'er, hundred

idleset, idleness
ill faur'd, ill-favoured
income, abscess
infare, wedding reception
inns, inn
in-taed, in-toed
intil, in; to
I'se, I'll

jocose, jolly; jocular

jocosity, cheerfulness

jougs, juggs, metal neckband for punishing offenders; 'bonds'

kale, borecole ('simple fare')
keckle, cackle
keek, peek
ken, know
kennawhat, 'I don't know what'
kent, known
kintra, country
kipple, couple
kirk, mak a kirk or a mill o': make the best of (something)
kithing, showing forth
kittle, tickle; (of words) obscure, difficult
kitty langlegs, daddy longlegs
knowe, hill
knule kneed, knock-kneed
kye, cattle

laborous, labouring
land-louper, traveller
lanerly, lonely
langsyne, long ago
laun, land
lave, remainder
laverocks, lark
lee, lie, falsehood
leesin, lying (telling lies)
leet, list (of candidates)
leeven, living
lift, sky
link, conduct by the arm
lippy, glass filled to the 'lip'
loan, lane; narrow street
loup, leap
louping-on stane, stone for mounting horse
lown, pleasant

mair, more

maukin, hare
maun, must
meal-pock, meal-bag
meikle, muckle, mickle, much
mented, intended
mercy, drink, 'dram'
mess and mell (wi'), have dealings (with), lit. 'dine and mingle with'
midden, dung-heap
middims, mediums
mim, demure
minched, minced
misliken, miscall
morn, the morn, 'tomorrow'
mortification, charitable bequest
mudge, stir
multiple-pointing, *See note* p. 49
murgeons, grimaces

na, nae, no
neb, beak, nose
needcessity, necessity
nieves, fists
nicht, night; **the nicht,** tonight

o', of
overly, very much
ower, over
oxter, armpit

pannel, panel, (Sc. law) accused person
partan, crab
pawkie, sly
pawmie, stroke of schoolmaster's 'tawse' (q.v.) on pupil's palm
pawshon, passion
piecing, division into pieces
placing, appointment of new minister by presbytery
plack, small coin
playock, toy, plaything
plook, *See note* p. 77

ploy, sport, frolic
pock, bag
pocky-aurr'd, scarred (by smallpox)
poopit, pulpit
poore, power
poory, small jug
potato bogle, hollowed potato carved with face
pouket, plucked
poun, pun, pound (money)
powl, walk with help of 'pole' (i.e. crutch or 'stilt')
precognition (Sc. law) trial
preses, (Latin) president
prig, haggle, bargain
prin, pin
puddock, frog
puir, poor
pushon, poison

quean, girl
queesht, quest

rampler, rowdy
rax, reach, stretch out for
redde (1), advise
redde (2), disentangle (of yarn)
reisted, withered
requeesht, request
reveled, ravelled
rookit, stripped, emptied
rosett, resin
roup, aution

sae, so
sair, sore
sappy, convivial ('sodden')
saul, soul
saumon, salmon
saun, sown
saut, salt
saw, sow
shaloon, a woollen material

shooglin, shaking
sib, relation
sic, such
siller, money, 'silver'
sine, then, thereafter
skail, empty out
smiddy, smithy
smoor, smother
sneck, door-catch; to 'lock' a door
sned, cut
snule, snool, humble, snub
sonsy, jolly
soogh, noise, rumour
sooh, ?convivial. pos. a misreading for 'sosh' (friendly) cf. 'sosherie' elsewhere in Galt
soor, sour
sowther, solder
speed, success
speer, enquire; **speer her price,** propose (marriage)
spunk, spirit
stabs, wooden planks
'stated, 'estated' (land-owning)
steek, fasten close (door)
stedt, imprint
stighy, (usually **stechie**) slow, corpulent, stiff-jointed
stilt, crutch
stinchers, bars or grating on window
stoup, jug
straemash, fight, riot
straik, stroke
superiority, *See note* p. 147
sugar-hoggets, sugar-barrels ('hogsheads')
swither, swuther, hesitate, in indecision

taen, taken
taigle, delay
talbooth, tolbooth, *See note* p. 98
tangs, tongs

tappit hen, large container (stoup or bottle) for claret, orig. with tap, and figure of hen on lid

tawse, schoolmaster's leather strap for punishment

tent, care

thae, those

thole, endure

thoosan, thousand

thrang, busy; crowded together (with secondary sense of 'sexually intimate', as in next entry

thranger wi', more intimate with

threep, argue

thrums, warp-threads (in loom)

tig, touch

til't, to it

timmer, timber, wooden

tochered, doweried

toom, empty

toosie, shaggy

tormentor, implement for toasting bannocks

trowth, truth

true, believe

twa, tua, two

tyke, dog; **tyke auld:** worn out (like an old dog)

tyne, tine, lose

unco, strange; (as modifier) considerable

vera, very

wad, wud, would

wadset, mortgage

waff, inferior

wally draig, weakest bird in nest

wally-waeing, lamentation

want, (mental) deficiency

wanter, suitor

wark, work

warsle, wrestle

warst, worst

wasterfu', wastefull

wastrie, waste

waur (1), worse

waur (2) spend

wean, child

weel, well

wersh, insipid, tasteless

wha, who

whaur, where

wheen, few

whiles, sometimes

whilk, which

whist, quiet!

whuskey, light carriage

wi', with

writer, lawyer, 'Writer to the 'Signet'

wud (1), **wad,** would

wud (2), mad

wull, will

wyte, wite, blame

yeleranes, yellowhammers (birds)

yett, gate

yin, one

yince, once

Note: The Laird's occasional 'illiteracies' and Mrs Soorocks' frequent 'malapropisms' (not glossed above) are best understood in the context of the text.